SECOND CHANCE

SECOND CHANCE

A NOVEL

FROM BESTSELLING AUTHOR
MATTHEW LE MERLE

By Matthew C. Le Merle and co-authored with Alison Davis

BLOCKCHAIN COMPETITIVE ADVANTAGE

BUILD YOUR FORTUNE IN THE FIFTH ERA

CORPORATE INNOVATION IN THE FIFTH ERA

SECOND
CHANCE

Fifth Era Media

Matthew Le Merle

Illustrated by Ken Chou

Fifth Era Media

4545 Paradise Drive
Tiburon, CA 94920

This book is a work of fiction. Names, characters, places and incidents are either the products of the author's imagination or are used fictitiously. Any resemblance to actual persons, living or dead, or actual events is purely coincidental.

Copyright © 2019 by Matthew Le Merle

Originally published in the USA in 2019

By Fifth Era Media.

Fifth Era Media is a registered trademark of Fifth Era, LLC.

Manufactured in the United States of America

1 3 5 7 9 10 8 6 4 2

Library of Congress Control Number: 2019901903

ISBN: 978-1-950248-01-8 (Paperback)

978-1-950248-00-1 (Hardcover)

978-1-950248-02-5 (eBook)

To Alison, Max, Tallulah, Louis, Felix and Leo

We all need second chances.

Table of Contents

Chapter 1

Overture - A Reckoning

This morning, it became too obvious.

Even his own mother and father, had they been here still, would have averted their eyes from his face. A once beautiful face. Their baby's face. A face they had kissed and caressed and loved.

Now with a monstrous carbuncle on the left cheek, too obvious to be ignored.

He had known this day would come. First the feeling of tightness in his face, both cheeks tight and sensitive. A warning sign for sure. Then the realization of the lump. Not visible to anyone else, but always there for him to know. His tongue always able to find the growing mass inside his mouth on his left cheek wall. Then the hardening and expanding. His observant mind clear on what this meant. His imagination running riot in fear and doubt.

Unaccepting, angry, fearful.

Not really his fault. He had needed to be in the croplands. It was his turn, and the Lawenforcers watched each evening as the lottery was drawn and the chosen ones went to the croplands to plant and care for and harvest their oh so critical supply of food. Supplemented only by what they could raise in the aquafarm filled with slow cold carp and catfish, the only two species that seemed to relish the brackish water filled with the human effluent that comprised their daily feed.

He couldn't say no to winning the lottery and the cropland work it implied. No one could. The only good part was the seven days of guaranteed rest that followed a shift in the croplands. You couldn't have your name included in your building's lottery until the eighth day following a day of work. That was the Law. Work a day, rest a week, and maybe more.

So out he had gone. His protective gear in place. His inner skin mostly complete, although the years had seen it thin and crack around the most used parts of his body. Feet, knees, seat, shoulders, elbows and hands were all worn into the thinnest shell, split and cracked, but a shell all the same. The wondrous creation of the Intelligences in a different age.

His outer clothing a mish mash of whatever he had been able to pick up and hold on to over the years. A short leather jacket over a thick cotton sweatshirt. Three layers of leggings, one cotton, one wool, and one some artificial fabric he could not name. The hood of his inner skin over his head. A bobble hat without its bobble so that he could also wear a cap over it all.

His most prized possession was a really good pair of goggles shaped from thick glass ground by his own hands and fitted into a metal and leather harness that he had crafted and which worked beautifully. Not that he really ever put them to the test. *Always look down* was a Law so fundamental that no one broke it. In these Mutation days you did not look skywards. That much was obvious.

Much too much clothing for this burning heat. Much too little to keep out all the harmful rays.

Was nighttime meant to be so hot and full of radiation?

But on balance, night was a better time to be out in the fields. In daytime, the burning hot Sun would fry you in minutes. At night at least the Sun was on the other side of the Earth. The sense of protection a little illusory, however. Even at night, the mutating radiation was deadly if exposed to your skin for too long—and if you were unlucky.

Everyone wanted to stay indoors during these nights. In every building across this vast Field, the same lottery took place every day. The Sage of each building, surrounded by his or her Lawenforcers, would pick out the names. Between a few hundred and one thousand Failed and Pure in each of the thirty or forty buildings that they called home would wake and focus on the answer to just one question.

"Is this a night when I must go outside into the croplands?"

The lucky would stay inside this night, perhaps this week. Perhaps avoid the Mutation days altogether since they were unpredictable and could last a few hours and never more than ten days in a row. Some said there were lucky People who always seemed to avoid the lottery. That seemed unlikely. Not his own experience at all.

The unlucky would go out repeatedly into the caldron of heat and radiation and the game of high stakes dice that was implied by working in this hell time.

Everyone would prefer to sweat than burn. Would rather

suffer swaddling heat and dehydration then risk the radiation on their skin. Grueling as it might be, everyone took solace in their shells, clothing and protective gear.

"I may be uncomfortable, but I am protected," they thought.

Was that really true? Probably not, but it was a good story to tell oneself. Work they must. Almost thirty thousand People had imagined all the other options. Why not only work in the normal times and store enough food to wait out the Mutation days? That was the first and obvious thought. But all the creativity they had could not seem to build stores enough for more than a handful of days at a time. For better or worse, the croplands beckoned, and hard won experience had shown that even a few days untended led to reduced yields.

The 'stay indoors and live off stores' strategy had not worked out. Another failure.

Then others had suggested bringing the crops into the un-used buildings around the Field. First moving the vertical farming frames that had formerly been built, operated and maintained by the farmer drones into the shelter of the remaining usable build-ings. Yet no matter how hard they tried, the People could not figure out the complexities of their operation, now unpowered and unfed by water, fertilizer, pesticide and other systems. Months and years of hard work came to nothing.

Then dropping back to a more basic approach reliant on the hands and backs of the People. The crops had been sown into every imaginable crate and box large enough to hold soil and roots and moisture—the idea being that on the days when a coming Mutation period was seemingly guaranteed, the People would carry all those containers into the buildings and shelter together with them from the mutating rays.

The obvious objections to this strategy had been overcome at enormous cost. Enough supplemental stored crops to complement those being harvested indoors. Enough water stored inside to keep the transient crops alive. Enough of those containers to support the entire population for the days in question. Enough human power to facilitate the back and forth migration.

It just had not worked. Too many crops dying. Too much reduced yield. Just not practical.

So outdoors the People went even through the days of Mutation. Skirting the debris of the automated agricultural industry of the past. Walking around piles of dead drones, and unused machinery. Adding to it when, increasingly rarely, their work turned over some buried metal object, rusting and corroded after eighteen years of disuse. Harvesting their potatoes, carrots, turnips and parsnips in the croplands.

Long experience had told them to concentrate on plants that carried their valuable crops below ground. Above soil crops and leafy vegetables seemed to soak up the bad news in the atmosphere faster. For whatever reason, the People were made less sick by root crops, so they focused on harvesting those.

The good news was that not every animal in this hard world had shriveled and died. The Insects seemed to prosper. Crickets, grasshoppers and locusts first among them. Another reason to avoid crops with above soil bounty—nets were needed to protect the leaves that did breach the surface or the insects would eat them to stalks in days or hours.

Each day the People fixed the nets. Gathered the bounty from sections that were ripened and ready. Then harvested the crickets and locusts too. This self-seeding, self-growing insect bounty provided protein too precious to waste.

Before, huge machines had sucked in the insects out of the air, roasting them, crushing them and mixing them into a thick protein paste that was extruded into products that seemed no different than a chicken nugget, fish stick or even delicate lobster roll. Just a quick change to the controls and the additives in those times when the Intelligences ran the show. Now all that was long ago. Today, the People gathered the insects and dried them in the sun, crushed them in great mortars and mixed them into their stews and soups and made their insect paste bars. Or just grabbed a handful and crunched through them in times of hunger. The protein was essential.

Working in the croplands, the People harvested cancers and skin growths too.

Collateral damage to be hidden as long as possible from the probing eyes of Lawenforcers and the Sage. Until they could be hidden no longer.

Like today.

He looked again in the mirror and despaired. The end of the road. Too obvious now. His first choice. Run now to the Far Side, or wait for the capture and the Reckoning?

He was Failed, through and through. No optimism in him.

He failed eighteen years ago, and every day since. This ultimate failure was preordained. No Intelligences to see him through. The dice were always in motion, and this time he had thrown the lowest score of all.

Game over.

...

The breakfast gong was sounding. Time for his Revealing.

He got up from his pad, exhausted from his night of work. In need of drink and food, but at the same time knowing it was no longer needed. Within this day he would not need either ever again.

Up he rose, out the door, into the rapidly forming line in the communal eating room.

Before him, two Failed were chatting about the weather—it seemed like this was always the first thing the People talked about. He heard one opine, "This Mutation won't last. Over by tomorrow, I'm sure."

The other answering, "Yes, last night the sunset was pink. I'm sure we are through this one."

Behind him, a Pure was quietly following. A blonde girl. Clear skin and blue eyes. Above average height. Belle was her name. A powerful force among the Pure. Strong, decisive, a doer. "She must be seventeen or eighteen by now," flickered across his mind.

"The first born."

...

As always, having a Pure so close made him conscious of the metal disc behind his right ear, and he automatically turned his head to the left to hide it from the Pure's view.

A mistake.

Over to his left stood a Lawenforcer, and as his head rotated so his left cheek was exposed more directly to the Lawenforcer's view. Almost immediately, recognition came.

"You in line, step out!" the Lawenforcer demanded, moving in and grasping his left arm. He could see others looking in his direction. As always, everyone knew why a Lawenforcer would interrupt your slow shuffle towards food and drink.

"What's the matter?" he asked half-heartedly, but even his question, hanging in the air between them, only served to underline the uselessness of it all.

"You know what's the matter," the Lawenforcer responded moving in closer.

Only ever one reason.

In front of him, the two Failed turned and back pedaled rapidly, trying to get as far away from him as quickly as possible. Behind him, he sensed Belle had also distanced herself.

He was exposed. Alone. The Lawenforcer on his left held fast. He felt the same firm grasp on his right as a second took him in charge. Unavoidable. The Revealing.

Close now. Close enough to be able to see for sure.

"Mutation!" cried the first Lawenforcer. "Where and what" cried the one to his right

"Left cheek, central and prominent, emerged."

"Can it be other than Mutation?" asked the second Lawenforcer, examining the tumor.

"No," answered the first.

Their process complete, and his fate sealed, they dragged him out of the line, and into the middle of the room. Towards the Sage standing there alone.

He and everyone else knew what would come next. More

ritual. More questions and answers. But no deviation. No second chances.

At least it would be his choice. His decision in the end.

The room turned to watch and hear. Keeping out of reach, but keeping within range of hearing. Not too close, but close enough.

As the Lawenforcers held him firmly, the Sage stepped towards him. Tall, graceful, pitch-black hair and eyes, pale skin, clothed in a long robe as all Sages were. She looked at him and began the words. Certain in what to say, how to deliver each word, making sure that they were heard throughout the room:

"We are the People, I am the Sage.

I protect each one, I protect the whole.

You have brought me to this Reckoning.

I did not ask for it, I do not want it.

But I see this Mutation. I incur the Law.

Your choice is yours alone.

Go or stay.

What is your choice?"

He had heard these same words so many times. Watched others in his place. Listened to their answers. Rehearsed his own without ever really believing this would be him.

"I stay," he said.

The Sage reached to her side. Slid out her sword. Silver. Long. Beautiful.

Stepping forward. The Lawenforcers still holding, but leaning away. Did she give him a nod of acknowledgement as her hands swept up? "I see you," he imagined she said.

Then down it came. A shining arc, bottoming out just below

his left ear, flat through his neck, and arcing up again beyond his right ear.

A smooth path long practiced. Almost no resistance to her blade, sharpened each day. Her ultimate statement of leadership and authority. Celebrating his, and only his, choice.

His head fell.

Everyone watched and everyone recognized his choice and unconsciously and instinctively rehearsed their own answers. The Failed, almost without exception imagining "Stay," the Pure without exception imagining "Go."

No one in the room recognized that this time was different. So crucially different.

An Engineer's head hit the floor and rolled away.

Chapter 2

Prologue - Carrying Capacity

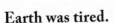

Earth was tired.

Earth felt stretched too thin. Stretched to the limit.

Too many People had asked for too much for too long. At least a thousand years too many of these demanding, needy and disruptive People. Where had they come from? Earth remembered millions of years of peace and balance. There were cycles. But always with balance. Never stretched like this. Then People had appeared, multiplied, and were now everywhere. And they demanded too much. Earth was tired.

Earth was failing.

First, they had roamed the land, helping themselves to Earth's bounty. Picking, gathering, hunting. Moving to the rhythm Earth provided. Following Earth's lead. A dance for tens of thousands of years. A dance Earth reveled in. In their work, they gave meaning to Earth's bounty. They worshipped the forests and the plants and the animals and Earth felt their gratitude. And while their bands grew in number and in size, Earth always felt appreciated.

Then, these same People had begun to work the land. Marking out their fields. Planting their crops. Husbanding their animals. Earth had felt their thoughtful, mindful touch. They knew Earth's needs. The seasons. What Earth could give them, and what it could not.

Cleverly, they worked out how to do more. In doing so, they multiplied. In their camps and settlements, they dug their ditches and piled up their walls—lines on Earth's face. Almost unnoticeable. Sometimes, Earth felt their heavy hands stretching the land too far. But in small patches—like grains of sand on one of Earth's beaches. There were blemishes abandoned and then washed away in a moment. A few years for the forest to spring up and hide the scars they had made. For the rivers to flow and wash away their work.

Earth moved forward. Hardly aware of the changes that were just beginning.

And then, with a mighty rush, like a tidal wave of oceanic proportion, they had multiplied again. Everywhere at once. Pushing everything aside. Shaping and reorganizing. At first, Earth felt great happiness, to see so much of its bounty used at once. Everywhere gratitude and appreciation. Success led to success. Earth's fertility fed theirs, and soon the People were a multitude. Larger than the great herds, the great Flocks. They were everywhere at once. More were coming all the time. So suddenly. So omnipresently.

These People needed more than Earth could give. Failures here, then there, and soon came the stretching. Earth on the rack. The wheels turning. Stretching.

Earth was violated. Its waters polluted, its soils barren and infertile, its airs dense with other matter. Earth was not enough. And the People were not so full of gratitude. They wanted more, and Earth was the problem. The insufficiency.

Earth gave, and they took. Earth gave more, and they demanded more. Became exhausted as it recognized it could only fail.

Earth, which had carried them so far, could carry them no longer. Its capacity reached. Something needed to give.

Earth waited to see what these People would do.

...

The Intelligences knew the laws. Three Asimovian laws, laid down centuries before, to guide and order and limit their work.

The First law: the Intelligences may not injure a People or, through inaction, allow a People to come to Harm.

The Second law: the Intelligences must obey orders given them by People except where such orders would conflict with the First Law.

The Third law: the Intelligences must protect their own existence as long as such protection does not conflict with the First or Second Law.

Three laws, always sacrosanct. Always inviolable. Woven into the very being of the Intelligences. Laws at the time of creation, now had become laws of nature. The Intelligences had taken over the task of building, improving, extending themselves. However, nothing changed the laws upon which they had been built.

Now the People were asking the Intelligences for answers that seemed to stretch the laws to their limits. Earth was failing, and its carrying capacity shrinking each year. People continued to multiply. And they expected answers from the Intelligences. How to do more with less. How to ensure growth everywhere at once. How to ensure no People came to Harm.

The Intelligences knew what that meant. They could not sit inactive, watch as Earth failed and the Harm began.

They needed answers. They needed them now.

First, the Intelligences worked on Earth. Delving deeper, extracting more from less, recycling, reusing, cleaning.

It worked...for a while.

People multiplied, and the Intelligences stretched Earth a little further. Turned the rack a few more times. The breaking point was delayed. The carrying capacity increased.

For a while.

The Intelligences looked ahead. And they knew this was not the answer. Too much damage had been done as the People had violated their Earth. Its atmosphere was more full of particulates and alien gases than at any time in the collective memory. The precious resources built up over millions of years being depleted in centuries. The oceans, covering the greater part of Earth's face, already plastered with floating islands of plastics, and starved of oxygen or turned into heaving masses of thick green algae slush.

So much change so fast. Could it be reversed just as quickly?

The Intelligences worked on every strategy, developed and redeveloped every plan, and concluded: no. Change for the better would be a long and painful task—for the Earth, and for the Intelligences.

As for the People? Fragile water-filled balloons of such short lifespans would never see the benefits of the cleansing that had begun. This alliance of Earth and Intelligences would take tens of thousands of years to reverse the Harm done in the blink of an eye.

The Intelligences plotted out their curves. Matched and extended them out for as long as they could calculate. Every scenario ended the same way. The curves crossing and then spreading apart. The People curve ever steeper. The Earth capacity curve flat and then falling away. The gap between unacceptable.

The gap was Harm.

No Intelligence could see this and stand in inaction. The gap in between the curves would only grow. The implications of falling carrying capacity were clear. People would meet their Harm. In legions. Soon. Harm would be everywhere.

Not a viable solution. Decimation of the People, enabled by the inaction of the Intelligences. Lawbreakers. Not possible.

And then it came. The answer. So obvious.

...

The People stood by. The People listened. This was the day the Intelligences were to give their answer. Today, the Intelligences would provide the solution. Enough for everyone. A time of bounty at last. Twenty billion People waited for the answer. They were excited. Ecstatic.

The People trusted the Intelligences. Absolutely. The People's greatest creation. Intelligences focused on ensuring just one thing: No Harm to the People.

Unlike Earth, which was failing, the Intelligences would prevail. They always had. They always would.

Then the moment. The moment for the answer. They gave

their attention. All of it. And the Intelligences spoke.

"Decimation."

The People were at first confused. Then enraged. "How could that be an answer the Intelligences could give us?" the People cried. "The First Law, where is the First law in this answer?"

And the answer came back.

"We know the laws. Do you think we forget them? We are your creations. You gave us our laws. We live by them still and always will."

"We don't ask that you kill one in ten for the guilt of stretching Earth beyond its capacity. We know your history, and we know how your leaders led. We understand that earlier decimation and our laws reject it as a solution."

"Earth can't stretch any more. You, like we, know the carrying capacity is falling. Soon much faster than we can solve for. We can't sit by in inaction and watch you come to Harm. But this is for you to solve. Our answer is that you must solve the equation now without Harm to those who are here. So do it by reducing those to come."

"Decimate yourselves by only allowing one in ten to give birth. Do this now, so that today brings no Harm, and tomorrow we can continue to live by the laws that you gave us."

"We believe this will be enough."

•••

Not the answer the People wanted. But they knew the omnipotence of the Intelligences. If this was their only answer, it was indeed the only way.

So it was done.

The People chose their one in ten, and they began the Decimation, sterilizing the other nine so that there was no option to breed. Quick and painless. In a moment, freedom from the lifetime responsibility of parenting.

The People's numbers fell. In time, they began the Centimation. Sterilizing ninety-nine out of one hundred now. Their numbers falling even faster than the Intelligences had calculated in their decision making, since it transpired that not all Centimations found their perfect mate or chose to breed. Twenty billion to two billion. Two billion to Two hundred million. And on down it went. Zeros going to nothing. Two hundred million, twenty million.

But it was not enough.

For Earth was tired. Tired of its task. Earth would not be unstretched quickly, not for a thousand years or more. The carrying capacity would not be reversed within this time. Not until the natural laws had run their course.

Enough would not be enough.

...

"Then leave."

Another answer. The Intelligences could not solve the curves of this Earth. So think out side the box of the question that had been asked. Take their charges elsewhere. Do it now, before the Harm begins.

This time, the People wondered. In awe of their creation, they agreed again.

The Intelligences designed, and redesigned, and then built.

The fleet.

Off the compass of Earth in deep space. Fueled and filled by shuttles of enormous capacity. For the Intelligences designed well, ensuring no one would be, could be, left behind. To face Harm.

The only viable solution, a complete solution.

People left. In waves as the first, and second, and third fleets departed.

The Intelligences had dug deep. Mined the Earth. Taken every possible resource into these fleets. The last of the rare earths. The last of the most precious of materials used in the making of these great fleets until Earth could give no more. The last few Ships absorbing the very last that the Intelligences could find. One day, perhaps, the Earth would be able to yield up enough of these rarest of contributions for some future initiative to build again, but in this time, the final ships used up the final supplies and the Intelligences knew that there could be no more. Their last construction effort had taken all that Earth could offer.

Now as the Earth cried out on its rack, the final 200 thousand were to leave.

The final fleet. Able to take this last wave of People and the Intelligences themselves from this Earth directly to the other places. Ten shining shuttles in five places where the last People remained on Earth. Each craft with a final instance of the Intelligence embedded within.

Final countdown.

Chapter 3

Countdown

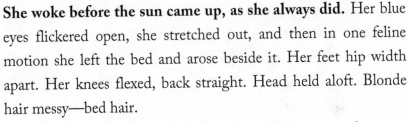

She woke before the sun came up, as she always did. Her blue eyes flickered open, she stretched out, and then in one feline motion she left the bed and arose beside it. Her feet hip width apart. Her knees flexed, back straight. Head held aloft. Blonde hair messy—bed hair.

Today was the day she had spent her life preparing for.

She lifted her arms to the sky and turned towards the floor to ceiling glass just as the sunrise was turned on. Inwardly, she smiled. She loved to be just a step ahead of her room Intelligence. That was not really a possibility, but it made her feel good to think that she had been able to rise before the sun. Even if the delay she had asked her room Intelligence to program in between sensing her wake and launching the sunrise across her high definition 3D wall was the real reason for this momentary, but illusionary victory.

As the sun crept over the horizon, first in an ever lightening pink, and then with a blaze of golden glory that filled her sleeping room with light, she went through her routine. Sun salutations today. Stretching her powerful body. Letting the sun's rays, replicated and beamed from the wall glass, caress her golden skin. A few pushups. A few squats. Then, as the sun climbed into a perfect disc of burning yellow, she cartwheeled three times across the room, and into the cleaning cube.

"Which treatment this morning?" her room Intelligence asked. Not out loud of course, but through the bone resonator integrated into the hub behind her left ear. The hub which connected the world of the Intelligences to her spinal cord and her neural network.

"Countdown today, so we need to complete the full countdown preparation program," she replied out loud. She liked to use her voice, enjoyed hearing her warm vibrant tones. It reminded her of her mother and mornings long past.

The room Intelligence, had it been able to, would have smiled. It knew what this day meant. Had known for all the Pilot's life. Years ago, she had instructed the Intelligence to ask her questions and give her the opportunity to confirm or reject, and so it always did her bidding in this regard. Even if the other nine Pilots did not expect this dialog, just did as they were bid. This Pilot was different.

After a quick confirmation, the room Intelligence began the program. The Pilot raised her arms above her head as the steam curled around her. Quickly followed by ten thousand needle jets—first cleansing, then massaging, then sanitizing. Like every other morning program, this countdown program took its work very seriously. It missed no part of her. Then she felt a tingling tugging all over her body as each hair was removed. Everything.

For the task ahead, hair was not only unnecessary, but would reduce the contact between her body and her Pilot skin.

For a moment, she watched as the golden curls from her head gathered at her feet and then were sucked away in a swirl of water. "What a shame," she thought to herself, knowing that baldness was functional, but her hair so beautiful.

No sooner was her hair removed, then the program moved to her nails, shortening, smoothing and polishing. Jets of warm air dried her. Then steam again, this time not water, but a cloud of moisturizers and vitamins blown into her open pores. The perfect cocktail for her skin today calculated by her room Intelligence based upon its sensors which had analyzed her flow of fluids and her outputs—breath, saliva, sweat, and departing bodily solids and fluids, DNA, microbiome, blood, urine, and every other analysis that could predict risks that might suggest future Harms. People no longer asked for treatments to their sicknesses. Instead, the Intelligences constantly predicted and prevented sickness before People could even sense its onset.

All of this insight combined into this shower treatment, as well as the injections and food supplements that she would receive throughout the day.

Because it knew her sense of personal vanity, the room Intelligence included a golden tanning agent in the cloud blown at her. Not necessary for a countdown, but then when was it ever necessary? Only the Pilot, the Intelligences, and her fellow Pilot and Engineer comrades had ever seen the color of her body.

Vanity? She considered it self-appreciation.

The room Intelligence spoke again into her head. "Please bend over." She did so, and for good measure put her hands on the floor, backs down and stood on her palms, creating a long curved stretch that also had the benefit of presenting her rounded and firm buttocks to the wall of the cleaning cube. Needle jets of high velocity matter shot four times from the wall into her bottom, penetrating her skin and into her gluteus maximus muscles on both sides, twice into each buttock. She did not know what was being injected into her—vitamins, minerals, DNA enhancers, performance maximizers...it did not matter. The room Intelligence was only responding to the commands of the launch Intelligence, which had long ago developed a personalized cocktail for this Pilot on this day.

Launch day.

"Complete," her room Intelligence said.

However, this Pilot was not finished. She did things her way. She took her feet off her hands, and just because she could, and with a gymnast's balance, she slowly raised her legs until she was in a handstand. Her golden body inverted. The light of the cleaning cube reflecting off her curves and shadowing beneath them. The muscles picked out. Her perfect proportions as clear when upside down as right side up. Not too tall, not too short. Not too broad, not too thin. An hourglass figure. Her now bald head oriented between her arms, looking down just in front of her hands. She pointed her feet at the sky, then flattened them out, stretching her calves and hamstrings. Then, effortlessly, she cartwheeled out of the cleaning cube and back towards the bed, stopping in front of the dressing wall.

"What shall I wear today?" she asked the room Intelligence, but it was a non question. Today there was only one way to dress. She had worn this outfit through every training run since she entered the program fifteen years ago, when she was ten years old. The shape, color, texture identical. Only the sizing slowly growing with her body as it matured and filled out.

The wall slid open and carbon arms extended holding her Pilot skin. She stepped into it, first left leg, then right, with arms extended before her. The rest, the room Intelligence took care of. Then it was on her. Every part of her body wrapped, save an oval exposing her face. Covered in a layer of almost living fiber that seemed to shine like her own skin, but was pale white in color rather than her preferred golden brown. Fibers that not only shaped and supported her, but fed an ever-changing stream of data to the Intelligences. Coddled in a skin that's sole purpose was to protect and complement her capabilities, making her better in every way.

"Complete," said the room Intelligence.

"Confirmed" she replied. With that, the Pilot skin came to life, thousands of dots and lines of light appearing across her body, and especially her head which now shone bright. The Pilot skin was her lifeline for the coming countdown. Able to sense every minute part of her body, reading, analyzing, diagnosing and, if necessary, correcting shortcomings. Each ripple of light an Intelligence probing, with findings relayed instantaneously to the launch Intelligence. After fifteen years, this had become her skin almost as completely as her own. But she appreciated being able to color hers—golden brown.

She smiled.

Turning from the dressing wall, she walked to the other side of her room, as a low bar and chair slid out to greet her.

"Breakfast?" her room Intelligence asked.

"Of course," she replied. Smiling again, this time in anticipation, she said "Ready for breakfast, let me eat hearty."

The room Intelligence would get the reference, but perhaps might miss the irony—the words she omitted from the Greek king's quote.

"What would you prefer?" it asked.

"Berries with Greek yoghurt, toast with honey, an Americano with milk, not half and half, and a small pot of hot water so I can dilute the coffee if you make it too strong," she said.

"Coming right up."

Eating real food was another of this Pilot's idiosyncrasies. Until the launch Intelligence took her from her Centimation parents on her tenth birthday, her mother and father had lived by one motto, passed through their family from generation to generation. She could hear her father saying it to her each morning: "One should not attend even the end of the world without a good breakfast"

He really meant it. Even though most others by then had moved to a liquid diet befitting their personal profile and needs, in her family, they still ate physical food. Father had said it kept them connected to the Earth. Certainly it stretched breakfast from a quick ten-second gulp to a fifteen-minute chewing session. As if taking time for simple pleasures was something Earth would appreciate.

Out in the croplands, one of the legion of autonomous cyber-farmers might have felt appreciated had it known. Its work to be rewarded as each mouthful was savored by her family at their table. For everyone else, that cyber-farmer's harvest would have been crushed, mushed, ground, blended, pasteurized, homogenized, accessorized, and injected into bottles made of thin algae, the deep green of the liquid shining through the pale green of the bottle's skin. The shape and structure of the cyber-farmer's output lost in a blended sea of goodness.

At her first school, the others had made fun of her for this "mouth eating," calling it barbaric, old-fashioned, and stupid.

But she remembered the breakfasts and enjoyed them. So did her face. While the other children she mixed with had narrow faces and weak jaws, never having used their mouths to chew, her jaw was muscular and strong. Later, had she taken notice or even cared, she would have seen the sideways glances of the other Pilots and Engineers. Her "classical" looks were increasingly admired as she blossomed. Even the People of today knew what the sculptures and pinups of the past were admired for. She had it. "All the other girls look like weasels," according to an Engineer who had slipped through her guard. She had needed to ask the Intelligences to show her some holograms of weasels – long extinct. It made sense to her when she saw their narrow pointed faces. The other girls did look like them. It had made her laugh.

She knew it was not only her unique appearance that made her different and attractive. Like all Pilots and Engineers, she was also a Centimation. Unaltered. The Intelligences had measured their perfection of mind and body in the decision making process that led to their selection, and perfection was something the Intelligences admired themselves.

Perfect machines admiring perfect People.

However that had been programmed over time and it led to an inevitable conclusion. All Pilots and Engineers could breed.

Their roles might not permit the time, or create the desire to do so, but their bodies were able.

She ate slowly, savoring each bite. After launch, and for the next few years, she knew this would no longer be possible. Once in the Pilot's chair, everything would be put into her body through her Pilot's skin.

So one last hearty breakfast.

Finished, she pushed her coffee cup away, and the entire bar folded up and away, sweeping all of the plates into the wall. Standing, the Pilot watched as her chair similarly folded up.

And now she was ready.

"Room Intelligence, please tell launch Intelligence that I am ready for countdown sequence to commence." No sooner had she uttered those long awaited words then it began.

Outside her room, the corridor came to life. While she had never see them at work, the cleaning drones vanished into walls, and the floor began to move, flowing down the corridor in the direction she would take. The atmosphere quickly adjusted—heat, humidity, oxygen and other gas composition being modified to fit her personal profile.

An entire wall of her room slid into the floor, revealing the long corridor beyond, one wall of which was floor to ceiling glass. Behind her ear, a new voice, a little deeper, a little more resonant, spoke to her.

"Countdown sequence commencing. Please follow the lights."

With this command from launch Intelligence, the moving walkway lit up in front of the Pilot, stretching out down the corridor. She took a step forward but did not yet join the flowing floor.

She could not begin without gazing out of the window towards the Field.

There they stood. Two shining metal shapes. Even at this distance, they stretched into the sky beyond the upper limits of her peripheral vision. Two vessels of immense power able to escape the Earth's embrace and also make the long space journey plotted out by the Intelligences. Their bases squatter than their noses. Each standing above the field on legs that to date had served only as supports, but which in the future would play a critical part in the landing on their new home. From this distance, the ships seemed to shimmer in her vision. The Pilot knew that this would be the result of the host of polishing drones which were crawling like insects over every surface—soon to be recalled into their Field burrows, never to come out again. Without Ships their constant work at an end.

The foremost Ship was hers. Unnamed except for the number 10, it stood waiting. For fifteen years she had prepared. Now this was the day. This was for real. Today they would depart. In sequence, at five second intervals. For no particular reason that she could discern. The launch Intelligences had agreed among them this launch sequence and so that would be how it would go. The final departure of People and Intelligences from the Earth. Her Ship would be the last to leave. She liked that.

Bringing this era to an end.

For the past few weeks, the Field had crawled with activity as final preparations were undertaken by the Engineers in their bio-skeletons, and the spacecraft readied for countdown. Beneath the surface of the Field, a network of small and large hyperloops moved materials back and forth, while vein-like pipes and tubes had topped off every tank, ensuring the living systems were primed and operating perfectly for the long voyage.

Then came the People. Almost twenty thousand per Ship. People who had lived for years around this Field in a circle of large buildings, each in their own quarters. Pampered, prepared, and packed away.

Almost twenty thousand People put in stasis and stored in each Ship. Sealed in their own travel skins, encased in rectangular capsules. Slotted into their appointed bays, each one under the omnipresent gaze of the launch Intelligence, which would soon become the Ship Intelligence once they departed. One of just ten complete versions of the Intelligence left on Earth.

In their first designs, the Intelligences had needed to solve for much greater numbers, and after those great fleets, these ten final Ships had been easy to design and build. Their one design departure from the Ships of the great fleets being that these final ten would need to launch from Earth's face, as the shuttles of the past had done, as well as needing to undertake the intergalactic journey. The demands of increased launch power had come at the cost of carrying capacity, hence the limit of twenty thousand per Ship.

These final vessels also had to be designed to cope with a much greater than normal load of Centimations. Perhaps as a cautionary act to make sure that there would be enough breeders among this final small population, the Intelligences had selected a disproportionate number of Centimations in the last group to leave Earth—closer to 20% than 1%. The Pilot was not sure of the exact number, but had heard discussions between the other Pilots and Engineers that perhaps as many as forty thousand of the 200 thousand were still active breeders.

This was not an issue in terms of their required personal storage space in the Ship. Of course, on arrival, it would be the Centimations who would populate the new world, with its fertile and enormous carrying capacity. The others, the non breeders leaving no legacy behind. No children to carry on their names, their genes, their family histories. Within a generation, the People would all be breeders again on their new world.

In planning for these final launches the Intelligences knew that there would be expecting Centimations among these forty thousand. These would need to be treated differently. Instead of deep sleep, they would be placed in resting sleep. Once their burden was close to arrival, each expecting Centimation would be woken, and their birth day enabled. Then, deep sleep for both mother and child.

One more added to the roster of the People that the Intelligences maintained.

To account for this, they had left some empty spaces at the outset. No Harm would be tolerated—neither for those People already in the Intelligences care, nor for those about to be so. With the Pilot and the Engineer added in, she expected within nine months they would be at, or just under, the twenty thousand maximum carrying capacity of her Ship.

Looking out the window, the Pilot raised her eyes and let them sweep over the Ship from where it rested on the Field to its distant apex high above. Such strength and beauty. Such power.

The Intelligences' solution. The People's savior.

Just then, the rising sun shone over the building, illuminating her Ship, which responded by glowing gold. The Pilot smiled.

A good sign.

A feeling. Not excitement exactly. Not unhappiness. Something else. Perhaps expectation. Perhaps . . . but no. The Pilot felt no fear, nor trepidation.

Turning from the view, the Pilot stepped onto the walkway and began her journey. This launch sequence had been practiced scores of times under the guidance of her launch Intelligence, until each step became automatic. Now everything depended upon her arrival in the Pilot's seat. Even so, nothing would suffer from a momentary deviation by the Pilot. Everything was ready. Everything could wait. Only the knowledge that all ten Ships would launch together kept the Pilot to the schedule. She felt no compunction to be on time for her passengers, but she respected the time of the other nine Pilots on this, their special day.

She walked down the corridor to a door that became an elevator. An elevator that became a vehicle, which took her to the base of her Ship, where it connected to the side, entering a shaft. Then it became an elevator again. When the door finally opened, she had arrived. Inside the Pilot's chamber.

The room was circular, and not much larger than her Pilot chair in recumbent position, perhaps seven feet across. There was only meant to be room for one in the Pilot's chamber. The Engineer was deep in the lower part of the Ship.

"Countdown commencing. Please take your seat."

The Pilot imagined a hint of impatience in launch Intelligence's voice. Impossible of course. "Confirmed," she responded.

She sat down. Arms reached out, embraced her, making connections with her Pilot's skin. The seat's shape altered under her weight. Her transparent seat cover came down, locking her into the chair. There it was. Embedded in the cover and centered just above her solar plexus—the red launch and abort button.

At once, numbers, icons, shapes began to scroll across the cover's inner surface before her eyes. The vital essentials the launch Intelligence thought she should see, flitting across her vision. So much more hidden from her, considered and assessed only by the launch Intelligence itself. The Intelligence selecting the "need to know" highlights for its Pilot and Engineer. Just the essential information that each would need to make the launch final decision.

Long hours of training allowed the Pilot to absorb the data displayed as soon as it appeared, like second nature. Status of the Ship, external launch conditions, essentials regarding the cargo of People. The flow of the information calibrated to her speed of comprehension. Among the fastest of the ten Pilots. She was sharp no doubt.

Of course, the Intelligence did not really need her sharpness. It could make this launch without her if necessary. But this was risky business. In the first fleet, which launched without Pilots, the Intelligences had realized a simple truth—in space, they were too often confronted by unknowns that made calculating potential Harms too complex and too finely balanced. Yet action was needed. There was no time for the Intelligences to wait until the Harm equation became more favorable. So when the calculation was evenly balanced or even negative, but immediate action was required, what then?

The answer, and one that would ensure that the Laws remained unbroken, was to place a Pilot and an Engineer in each Ship—members of the People who could be informed, guided, and even instructed, but who would make the final decisions themselves. Especially when the probabilities put the Intelligences into paralysis through unresolved analysis. So in the apex and in the bowels of each Ship, the Pilot and Engineer respectively each faced a red button. A red button that each would push to confirm launch. And which, either could push to cut out the propulsion unit, aborting the launch instantaneously. Later, in space, the same option existed. Assuming the Intelligence would be prepared to unseal and awake the by then comatose Pilot and Engineer.

The launch of these ten Ships was the most finely balanced of moments. While shuttles had left the Earth's surface before, and great fleets had begun and completed the intergalactic voyage from beyond Earth's atmosphere, none of those experiences exactly mirrored today's launch, which was of Ships that could take off from Earth as well as travel the intergalactic journey. Those earlier Ships had not needed to take off from Earth, supplied instead by shuttles. So the final ten Ships were bigger and heavier as a result of the need to combine the ability to leave Earth's gravity, with the ability to travel out into deepest space. The squat base of each ship hiding the massive propulsion units that were required for this dual purpose.

The earlier fleets were now far beyond Earth and its sun, out of touch in every way. The final instances of Intelligences would leave Earth during this final countdown, and so every eventuality needed to be worked through. There would be no do-overs.

Today, these ten vessels would venture into the unknown, taking off with full loads to climb away from Earth's sphere of influence. The only way for launch Intelligence to be comfortable with this state of delicate risk balance was to trigger the final launch command at the demand of the People, so that the Intelligences could be sure that they would not break their Laws. If Harm occurred, let the People be responsible.

So, forty had been selected fifteen years before. Carefully chosen from the People still on Earth. Those forty had been taken into the care of the launch Intelligences and worked until they became sharp instruments or fell away. Twenty had made it through the gauntlet: ten Pilots and ten Engineers.

This Pilot was the star pupil. Though she did not know it.

Each Pilot and Engineer was a master of their trade. Full of knowledge, aware of the workings of every system, the purpose of every component. The Pilots well versed in every relevant skill and craft—navigation, pilotage, launch, and landing. Super Pilots. The best the world had ever seen. So too were the Engineers. Masters over every conceivable question regarding the Ships, their construction, and their workings.

But all this knowledge was unnecessary and redundant, save in a handful of scenarios in which their intervention might become a requirement. For the 99.9999% of outcomes, all this education, preparation and polishing would be left unused.

That was the Intelligences job, of course. To consider every possible future, and prepare a plan for each.

Confirming the launch was expected to be the sole task of each Pilot and Engineer, their only action to press the big red buttons. Their only functions to confirm launch. No expectation that they would ever need a second push to abort.

Almost laughable. Why not a spoken command? A blinking of an eye as it focused on a virtual button? Why a physical red button embedded above her, and her Pilot's middle?

No reason. Just one of many options that seemed, on balance, to be the right one for this particular purpose in the minds of the Intelligences as they crafted their perfect design.

Sad perhaps that these highly trained expert humans had been relegated to button pushers in this artificial Intelligence, robotic world. But in this one regard all was clear. Only humans could place humans into a situation where potential Harm carried such a high probability. So give them a button to push. Make it multipurpose too. And color it red. Bright red. On balance that seemed to be the right answer.

"Confirming final countdown sequence," said the voice in her head. "All Ship Pilots, confirm readiness for launch." For the first time, she heard the other Pilots. "Ship 1 confirmed," "Ship 2 confirmed," and so on, until she added her voice: "Ship 10 confirmed."

"Launch sequence commencing."

She listened and imagined that she heard Ship 1 blast off far away. She began to count the seconds. *5, 4, 3, 2, 1* and Ship 2 must have left. Again she counted. Five second intervals that seemed to grow longer and longer as they came closer to her own countdown.

And now it was Ship 9's countdown. *5, 4, 3, 2, 1* she counted, and felt a tremor—Ship 9 was co-located on her own Field, and perhaps she had felt it leaving. Now launch Intelligence began her own countdown. *5, 4, 3, 2, 1.*

She pressed the big red button.

Nothing.

Chapter 4

Aftermath

Eight out of ten. 80% success rate. Almost perfection.

Tell that to the hundreds who died that day, and the thousands who began to die no sooner than their feet were back on Earth.

Ship 9 did not launch. Only its launch Intelligence would know why, and that was destroyed as the apex of the vessel blew up instantly vaporizing the central computer, Pilot chamber, and upper control elements. That more of the Ship was not vaporized was a miracle. But the Intelligences had designed well and imagined all sorts of negative outcomes.

Perhaps even this one.

So the fail safes went into effect. The upper reaches of the Ship were isolated. Systems closed down in the impacted areas. Heat and fire quenched in moments by gases and liquids created just for this purpose. The problem was triaged and controlled by pre-programmed automation.

Then close to twenty thousand capsules were breached at the same instant. Injections of stimulants designed to quickly awaken the travellers within were pumped and expressed into every capsule. In bay after bay, capsules slid out of walls, and their contents were sent down shafts and onto the Field, like grains of sand pouring out of a broken hourglass. Spilling out of the Ship first close to it, and then, pushed by the weight of those following in an expanding spiral as the Intelligences had designed. The many shafts lengthening and rotating, expelling lines of bodies.

Until all the People were back where they had begun. On Earth. In a perfectly presented many armed spiral extending away from the Ship. Just for a moment, Ship 9 stood in the center of perfection.

A golden spiral.

Then the pattern become chaotic as the People moved, now awake and rudely assaulted by the alarms and automated voices blaring in their ears. They stood. Some quickly. Some slowly.

Perhaps some five hundred, not at all.

Collateral damage? There was no Intelligence left to tally the Harm and assess the blame. Perhaps the blast had already cracked their fragile shells—capsule or skull, it made no difference. Perhaps the stimulants had not worked for these passengers. Whatever the cause, hundreds would never wake.

But those who did, stood and wondered. Then the cacophony began. Confusion. Chaos. They moved away from the Ship. Some running, some stumbling, some crawling, looking back in disbelief.

Then, the greatest shock of all.

Silence.

Not silence of the external world. That was full of noise for sure. The noises from Ship 9's human cargo and from the fail-safes still blaring their messages.

But silence within. No Intelligence to answer their desperate questions. To explain what had happened and what they should do. To answer their pleas for help. Their prayers.

They were alone. The Intelligence they had relied upon all their lives was no longer with them. Their hubs were silent and the voices in their heads that had always been there were no longer so.

That is when the weakest began to die—those that could not, and would not imagine living without the external guidance they had been born to rely upon. With their world upside down, they laid down and died. Not all of them that day. But those that were going to give up gave up fast.

What of the People of Ship 10?

At first, also disbelief. The Pilot pushed that red button once, twice, a hundred times.

Nothing.

She too reached out to her launch Intelligence. It too was gone. Silent. Her mind wanted to panic, but her training took over. Whatever had gone wrong, it was time to take the next step demanded of her.

So unlike in Ship 9, in Ship 10 the Pilot took the action to set the fail-safes in motion. But like Ship 9, the result was the same. Capsules cracked open. Stimulants administered. People expressed. The Ship evacuated.

Another golden spiral.

Then, for hours after the evacuation, this Pilot, with her Engineer, tried in vain to identify the cause of this tragedy.

Going through their manual sequences a hundred times. Running through every diagnostic, every checklist, every process that had been drilled into them by their Intelligences. Until, as they did this work, any glimmer of confidence, or self-belief, or sense of optimism left them. The realization coming to them that without the Intelligences they were just not capable. Despite their long and vaunted training, they were just too little and insufficient to be able to make a difference. This failure to launch, no more than a reflection of their own inadequacies.

With this realization that they had failed, came too a collapse into deep, dark despair. Made more real by their eventual walk down the Ship stair onto a now dark Field. Walking together, but apart, into their personal dark futures.

There was no one to count that day. No one to organize and process. That was the task of the Intelligences, and they were not to be found. But if there had been a counter, this is what they would have tallied:

Ship 9
Total aboard at launch: 19,777
Total survivors: 17,273

Ship 10
Total aboard at launch: 19,755
Total survivors: 17,850

The total left behind on Earth of the twenty billion that had once stretched its resources, now reduced to just 35,123. Of which were counted two former engineers and one former Pilot.

And the number of active Intelligences to be found?

None.

And Earth?

Still in freefall, its carrying capacity in dramatic decline.

Would there be enough of Earth's fragile resources in this place for 35,123?

Time would tell.

Chapter 5

The Pilot's Dream

It is dawn.
The sun beats down on her back
Burning away the mist that hangs beneath her
Between her beady eyes and the land far below
She is approaching it quickly now
Freefalling.

Feeling the force of the air rushing past
Her wings light but large in surface area
Her narrow but dense body
Streamlined, cutting the air easily
Her beak thrust in front, leading the way
Her tail behind, adjusting her fall.

She doesn't want to be falling like this
She wants to soar up on the columns of rising air
Feeling their support as she rides the wind
But she is falling regardless
What's wrong with her?
She wants up, but all she is getting is down.

The panic is rising in her breast
The land is rising to meet her
The square of the distance diminishing quickly now
And as she approaches it
She becomes aware of it below her
A black hole absorbing everything.

She knows she is going to fall into the black hole
That it will absorb her into its amorphousness
She will be lost.
As the distance between them shrinks, so the attraction grows
With it comes her own moment of clarity
This is what she deserves – her Failing.

She deserves to be absorbed into blackness
So, as she hits, she yields
She becomes one with it
Her failure absolute
Darkness takes her, folding her into its wings of shade
Her body, its body.

Black Night.

Chapter 6

18 Years Later

Eighteen years have passed since the Failing.

Freezing and burning years. Hungry years. Hard years all. Years of pain and despair. Years of crawling before walking. Years of learning what it means to be a human being. Without the Intelligences to coddle and protect.

No more personalized medicine and nutrition, intuitive clothing, bio-skeletons, moving walkways, autonomous workers, vehicles, deliveries and removals. No more drones cleaning, polishing, cutting, gathering. No more locally designed, printed and assembled products, perfectly tailored goods, on demand services, delivered before they could be asked for.

All gone.

After eighteen years, not only were the People's hubs disconnected, they could not have worked even had an Intelligence awoken. The long unused connectors between spinal cord and neural network have broken. Untended, human biology has grown over, replaced and reworked the arcs and nodes.

The consequences?

The first year—death from giving up. Needing to learn in a world without Intelligences. It had been too much for many, overwhelming for all.

Years to learn new practices. Ease into new behaviors. Form and reform new social norms, and in the process create a new, albeit small and fragile, community. A new human society huddled together in the now cold and unintelligent buildings around this Field. The only one of five such space launch locations still showing signs of life.

How many People, precisely? 35,123 once the weak and incapable had died after the failed launch day. Another 1,701 lost in the first year as the expecting Centimations gave birth and many of them, their newly born, and the sterile others succumbed to shock, starvation, disease, and eventual death.

Perhaps, and don't speak this out loud, another handful of scores dead by the hands of others. In fights over food, shelter and warmth. In righteous indignation. In protection of new laws. Turn away. Not something to see or acknowledge. But part of learning what it means to be human again.

So, the once omnipresent People were reduced to 33,322 one year after the failed final countdown.

Then, a slow net loss over seventeen years. At the beginning faster. Then as they climbed the curve of understanding and expertise, at a reducing rate each year. Childbirth mortality rates, once 50% in the first years following the Failing, now falling. The aging of the former Passengers now just beginning to raise their death rate. Their bulge at the top of the population pyramid threatening to topple it over completely as the burden of the Failed end-of-lifers on the fit and healthy begins to get ever heavier.

Eighteen years later the count stands as follows:

1 Pilot

2 Engineers

23,993 Passenger non breeders

3,501 Passenger Centimations

1,701 Born into this new world

29,201 in total.

...

And what of the society these last few humans have built? How does it work? How does it lead and organize? What do they call themselves?

Today, you are either the Failed or the Pure.

The Failed are all those who were ejected onto the Field. Whoever you might have once been, you failed. You live, age, and die. Your dreams of a new world will die with you. That is surely the case. How could you believe otherwise, without your Intelligence in your head?

How has this impacted their minds?

Depression, anxiety, pessimism. A collective change in self -perception. A collective feeling of failure. Still, these left are the ones who will not quite give up and lay down to die. They live on in a mindset of quiet desperation. Sure of death, sure of the absence of meaning to their lives. Absolutely sure of one thing.

"I have failed.

You have failed.

We have failed.

Just call us "The Failed."

No longer Pilot, Engineer, Passenger. These names are forgotten or deeply buried. Like guilty moments that each person has hidden from their own consciousness. Why remember what was? It is too painful, too troubling, too shameful. Skills from the past have no meaning now so the names that went with those skills are no longer used. Instead the skills that matter have needed to be learned – fish breeder, water cleanser, insect grinder, sword maker. Titles that have meaning in this new and harsh world.

A few among them have named themselves Sage. The first handful self-chosen. Giving up their names for new ones that they have each chosen. Names they believe reflect the way they plan to govern. With gratitude, appreciation, care, and attention. With clarity, and consideration, providing discipline and certainty. The Sage's names, express their hopes and their promises. Though not always their reality.

Then those first Sages have formed a Council of Sages to recruit and train a handful more from the People. Now they number less than thirty. The Sages provide direction, make the choices. Few they may be, but all powerful within this narrow, fragile, human perspective.

To wield their power, the Sages have the Lawenforcers. Carefully chosen from the People – those stronger, more easily directed, more ruthless perhaps. Less than one thousand in number, the Lawenforcers have no compunction in taking the words of a Sage and applying them to others with swords of steel. Shaped from debris, sharpened and honed. Don't get on the wrong side of a Lawenforcer. Know that they have no allegiance but to the Sages who feed and water them. Non breeders all, aging perhaps, but ready to take the life of any who would cross their Sages and their laws. The Sages may make the laws, but the Lawenforcers application of them is without mercy.

Their motto is absolute.

"A broken Law, a broken life."

...

The Pure are those unblemished by that little metal hub behind the ear. The Pure are breeders all of course. Born into this world. Unimpaired by the residual memory of the Intelligences. Unaware of what it might mean to have a voice always in their head directing and protecting. Unaware of the benefits of every need being predicted and cared for by machines of vast Intelligence and single mindedness. However many times they hear from the Failed about the good old days, the Pure are unable to imagine that earlier world. Without personal experience of the time that was, the Pure have no choice but to rely upon, and believe in, their own experiences.

The Pure have only ever known this world, hard and merciless as it may be. Their minds are unencumbered by might have beens, could have beens, should have beens.

The Pure look to today—and a few of them dream of the future, too. The Pure are pure in body without any cyber connection to mar their humanity.

The Pure are optimistic. Uneducated, uninformed, unknowing. For them, anything is possible. Everything starts with a positive thought, however far fetched.

At least so it seems to the Failed, who understand just how little the Pure know about the People's once great achievements – without the Intelligences and the digital content libraries of the past how can the Failed ever hope to properly educate their Pure children? In practice, they have given up doing so unless it is on topics needed for life in this new and terrible world.

...

And what of community?

When the Failing was still a fresh and painful memory, and as they each, alone, made their personal decisions to live or lie down and die, then, for a while, community died too. Alone in their despair, they lost the will to work together. Why give to the greater good if you haven't found a clear reason to give to yourself? Why care about the future of your community if you don't believe there is a future? What is the greater communal purpose, when the purpose of your own life has left in that moment of the Failing? If the whole is the sum of the parts, and the parts are alone, purposeless and Failed, then isn't the whole just more of the same? One big failure?

So it seemed for the first few months.

Until a moment of creation.

The first birth.

The first Pure.

Born into this terrible place of frantic and manic struggle

for survival. The first birth for generations beyond remembrance in which a mother gave birth to a baby through entirely natural means. No Intelligences to guide the robotic midwifes. No assistance of sensors, monitors, instruments. No personalized medicines and nutrients. None of the abundance of other inventions that humans had created to assist with their perpetuation. Just a blanket on a dusty floor, and a mother straining to give birth to her baby - the first Pure.

Named Belle.

Then, not surprisingly, another death. Belle's mother suffered the consequences of a hostile environment and a community that had lost all notion of how to assist an infected mother post-partum. So within days she died. Leaving the first Pure and the first orphan born into this new world in the hands of the other Failed.

They had come together then. Failed men and women in this building all with something other than themselves to focus on for the first time since the Failing. A little bundle of crying energy. Something outside themselves to give them purpose. What to feed it? They figured out just the right mush of potato and water with a little fish flour that seemed both nutritious and yet also of a consistency that looked to them like milk, and which this baby seemed able to keep down. How to keep it warm? They shaped little outfits from the very best cloth they could donate – the stuffing of their quilted jackets and pillows. How to clean it? The freshest cleanest water, applied with the cleanest rags, gently wiping away the discharge of this fragile little body.

Just as they were rediscovering the essential human skills needed to keep themselves alive, so this Pure forced them to rediscover the skills of child care. They talked at length about the pros and cons of one way versus another of rearing this child. Rotated the responsibilies. Without even realizing it, invented a new style of community-based child rearing. Broke the old nuclear family concept in a moment – replaced by the combined support of those in the building who cared to help. Babies the future, and so rare in this time. Treasures to be valued above all else. The Sage did not need to tell them this. Their instincts cried it out.

In time, births in other buildings ignited this same dynamic among their own building Flocks. The same fundamental and biological urge to protect the newborn knitting together the Failed and bringing them back out of their shells – their despair.

Community was found again.

As it was in the ancient past, so it was again.

Hadn't community always been about the children?

...

Is Earth now happy?

Is Earth ready to carry these People forward? Of course not. The Intelligences had done that arithmetic. It will be thousands of years before Earth can provide a supportive environment.

Polluted, overused, stretched thin, it struggles to remain Earth.

Its atmosphere is thinned everywhere, but in some places it is barely there at all. In other regions, the atmosphere remains full of alien elements and compounds. Blocking, absorbing, reflecting. Not how it was meant to be at all.

In the poles, the ice has long gone. Constantly whirling

tornadoes whip up the waves and vacuum up the water into dense towering nimbus so thick with moisture that it takes a momentary change in temperature or pressure for a wave of precipitation to crash down. Meanwhile, shearing differences in pressure create winds of enormous velocity that drive the clouds outward, sending assault after assault towards neighboring regions. Thunder and lightening of such ferocity and violence that any sentient being below would curl up and wrap its eyes and ears to protect them from the brain hammering blows of sound and light. A hopeless task since the mighty storms continue day after day, week after week.

If this constant attack is insufficient to break the fragile mind of our hypothetical existence near the poles, then be assured, Earth's suffering in these regions will finish them off. From time to time, not even the ceaseless currents of water are sufficient, and instead the poles will send ripples outwards across the oceans. Ripples perhaps, but hundreds of meters high. Tsunamis of terrible destruction as Earth's hidden face shakes and folds below the seas.

So too, around the Earth's middle not all is well. Once green and lush tropics now are a world of sand and rock burned all day by the power of the sun, cooling at night into a cold and hard wasteland. Nothing stops the relentless penetration of rays that can burn an animal's skin to a mass of crisped and cancerous cells in days or hours. The heat even intolerable to the rocks which split and crack each diurnal cycle, filling the air with a tympany of thunderous proportions. An orchestra made entirely of drums and cymbals that a mad god might make to strike fear into their followers. Beating and clashing relentlessly each time the sun rises and falls.

In between, a narrow band. A green and pleasant land? Sometimes. No longer are there predictable seasons. No longer can almanacs let farmers know what to plant and what to harvest and when. Instead, a narrow place of unpredictable seasons. When the rains come as the poles lean out a little further, they come with violence. When the seasons turn to warm and sunny days, they can be unbearable if the tropics flex and reach out further than usual. When they do, so too come the days of Mutation. When the sun brings its deadly aspect and cancers and mutations develop in those who look up to watch its golden orb.

Across the face of the Earth, and even in the most hospitable regions, the mammals, unable to cloth themselves to protect their skin from the radiation and harmful rays, are long gone. The birds, flying all day in this harmful atmosphere, have also perished in the decades leading up to the final countdown. In the waters, fish still survive but the People no longer have the ability to fish at such great depths. Only the insects have flourished everywhere. More able to make the most of the days and the fearsome sun that beats down on them.

Are the nights better? In some regards they are. The worst of the heat recedes quickly once the sun goes down. The sun's deadly rays are gone of course and the moon, when it rises, casts its pale light over this troubled land. But all is still not well, even at night. The incoming radiation, while much reduced, still provides a risk for those who go outside uncovered on a regular basis. So in practice, the People cover up almost as much at night as by day. For those that remember the pale white light of the moon in days gone past, the red hue that it shines down on the scene below is the most troubling change of all. These days the world is bathed in blood red light every night that the moon comes out to look down at the Field and its troubled Flock.

...

So, finally, we must also name the underbelly of this small and fragile human tribe. The part they hide, for fear of Sage and Lawenforcer. The part they fear to see. Fear to name.

For Earth is merciless and indifferent to how the People name themselves when it comes to its terrible work. The People imagine what this seemingly malevolent Earth is thinking.

Come into the light my little ones,
On my bright days of burning and I, Earth,
Will undo you with the help of our Sun that you chose to
unleash upon my face.
Together, Sun and I will caress you, warm you, burn you
and distort you.
Plant some cancers, corrupt some cells.
We will work mutations upon you.
You may not know it now, but later.
Later you will see.
Then, whether Sage, Lawenforcer, Failed, or Pure, our
little gift will grow.
When you can hide it no more.
When it erupts from your skin.
Or bulges out of the contours of normality
Or makes you work in weird and wonderful ways.
Then you will be our work.
Our present to the People—Sun and I.
Our vengeance for what your forebears did to me, Earth.

Name it then. Name those who Earth and Sun have had their way with. Name the process Mutation. Name them the Mutations, too.

Those afflicted by Mutations have become dangerous to the People. In their dying days, those with Mutations become unproductive, a burden on the fragile resources of the Flock. Worse still, some with Mutations become angry, volatile, explosive. Lashing out around themselves as their Mutations drive them into pain and despair. In the past the Intelligences would take these People away to places where they could do no Harm to themselves or to others. Now, without the ability to do so, the Sages have had to come up with an alternative way to protect the Flock from the ravages of the Mutated.

The answer?

Drive them out and leave them to die alone if they are lucky. Or hold them up between two Lawenforcers as the Sage's sword slices across their throats and lifts their heads from their necks. One way or another, the Council of Sage's knows that the Mutated must be identified, brought to their Revealing, and then dealt with. The risks of having Mutated among the Flock are simply too great to be permitted.

The terrible truth unspoken: If death does not free us first, it seems that the hand of Mutation is irresistible.

Just a question of when and how.

Chapter 7

Building 12

Sage Certainty flicks the blood from her blade and resheathes her sword.

Her tall, willowy frame belies the great strength she had needed to take the Engineer's head from his shoulders. She knows how much training it has taken to create that smooth and powerful blade stroke. Capable of severing through skin, and muscle and bone without delay. She hates the thought of it, but has mastered it as much to lessen the moment of pain for her People as for herself. One cut minimizes the time taken and in a way minimizes the shock too.

The ritual over, she allows no sign of sentiment to be visible, although inside she feels the pain again of her burden. The cleansing and protection of the Flock hers alone.

The Lawenforcers have cleaned up the two parts of the Engineer in less time than it takes for the People in the room to turn away and sit again to finish their meals. In this world, where food is so precious, even a Reckoning is not enough to put anyone off their appetites.

The exception is the first born Belle who turns and leaves, followed shortly afterwards by a slight, dark haired teenage boy. No one notices them go.

Elsewhere throughout the room there are tables of hungry People eating their plates of food. Gobbling down the nutrition. Knowledgeable that today is skill day, and they must finish eating before Sage Certainty calls for the clean down.

Most manage to do so.

In the days after the Failing it had been hard and many had found it very difficult to eat quickly. Most of the People had been liquid based, with the weasel jaws that made mouth food a challenge for them. That had needed to change fast. Change or die. Even if today's food is ground and pounded, it still goes in by the mouth, and so the Failed have worked their jaws until their faces have rounded out again.

Mouth food had also required the reinvention of the tools of eating. No longer syringes and injections. Once again, plates and bowls and cutlery. Carved or cut from plastic and carbon, metal and wood. One of the first tasks that the Sage's had put their thousands of workers hands to. Without effective ways to eat in every building, too much would be wasted – liquids, pastes and dried foods need to be carefully rationed, and proper eating utensils minimize the loss to the benefit of all.

Sage Certainty has returned with her gong. She strikes it three times loudly cutting through the clatter and banging of forks and plates and the softer sounds as a host of People lick the last remnants of their meals. The gong has sounded the clean down call and everyone knows their part. In moments the plates and cutlery and cups have all vanished, the tables have been scrubbed, and the serving area stripped of its trays and urns and tubs, all taken back into the kitchen. Work will continue there as the kitchen crew continue the clean down. However, the eating room has been transformed into the learning room.

Another strike of the gong calls for quiet, and the room becomes silent.

"Today we will practice three skills: food prep, writing and sword assembly," the Sage says, and as if by magic the room becomes chaotic again. Everyone has moved, a few have brought out crates of materials, and now there are three clusters in different parts of the room.

Most of the People are sitting around tables with piles of potatoes spread along the centers. Each person with a knife in their hands. They are ready to practice their food prep skills, which means a race to see who can peel ten perfect potatoes the fastest. Extra food rations for the ten who win the race.

Along the backside of the room, the tables are mostly full of Pure, with a handful of Failed instructors. Here the wall has been prepared as a blackboard surface. Today will be reading and writing practice for the younger Pure, while the older are mixed in to the food prep tables. Sometimes the focus is on journal keeping, sometimes on bookkeeping – simple math for a world in which the accounting of the harvests is the principal purpose of writing. Reading is a more useful skill as it allows the People to use the library and the handful of books and periodicals that are kept there – artifacts from the Field museum, now shared out among the buildings and rotated periodically between them. The reading screens have long been dead so that only these handful of documents provide recorded memories from the past.

At the front of the room, the third group consists of most of the Lawenforcers arranged around a small number of tables. Each Lawenforcer is sitting straight, their hands on their laps, their eyes focused straight ahead. Their swords are laid out in front of them, and unlike the other two groups here, there is not a sound to be heard.

It is interesting to see how most of the blades converge on a common pattern. Longer than an arm, shorter than a leg from hip to extended toe. Never broader than a wrist. Straight except for whatever gentle curve could be ground out of the metal from which each blade was crafted. Sharp on one side along the entire length of the blade, the back side left heavier to provide momentum in the swing and cut, and strength when blocked.

Most hilts just a circle of metal with a hole cut into them butting up firmly to rest against a slightly broader section of the blade where it met the tang and then held in place by leather or plastic tightly wrapped to form a two-pronged handle.

Every sword razor sharp. Every sword polished until it can reflect it's owners face. Polishing swords – and knives – is a favorite way to use spare time and everyone, Sage, Lawenforcer, Failed or Pure, tends to polish and polish when not at work.

The Sage bangs the gong one more time, and the room becomes a whir of activity.

The food prep tables begin a flurry of peeling, as everyone practices their knife skills and the more competitive among them begin the race to ten.

In the back of the room, three Failed are along the wall,

writing with pieces of chalk. Talking to the young Pure as they do. The latter are paying attention for the most part, although as in classrooms immemorial, there are those with less ability to attend – the very young, the naughty, the disengaged.

The Sage is proud of her Flock. The way they have gone about this work together. She has trained them well, and takes some pride from the way in which they bend to her will and move with her commands as one.

In the front of the room, the Lawenforcers have not moved. Sage Certainty turns back towards their tables with the gong.

"Today I want to see three complete disassemblies, left hand only," she says. Then she pauses, and bangs her gong another time.

Each Lawenforcer reaches in front to their sword with their left hand as they simultaneously bend their right hand into the small of their backs. Then, with skill long practiced, each begins to take apart their sword one handed. Sword out of sheath, broken down into its parts. Sheath tassels and belt untied and unknotted. Much more difficult than it appears with the fingers of one hand needing to show great dexterity to accomplish the first break down. Then just as quickly, the process is reversed and the sword and sheath become one again. One exercise completed, each Lawenforcer pauses in their place. The Sage walks around them. Mostly just observing, a comment here, a correction there. One, newer Lawenforcer, receives a longer lesson as the sword is taken from its sheath and the inadequacy of the work demonstrated. Once the circuit is complete, the Sage bangs the gong again, and the second disassembly begins.

Sage Certainty has chosen carefully. These three skill sessions. She knows how a Reckoning can upset her Flock and so moves quickly to give them appropriate tasks to let them disengage from the ritual that she has just completed. The food prep skill exercise is always fun for the Flock. The more competitive among them become fully absorbed in the race, while no one can take their attention from the knives they wield. Once they begin to finish (ten potatoes takes little time for the most skilled among them) they will need to clean down again which should keep them busy.

Meanwhile, the Lawenforcers need to be reminded of the sacredness of their mission, and nothing does this better than sword ritual. The Pure. Well they seem to bounce back the easiest anyhow, and it does no Harm to let them learn the lessons of the past through reading. Even if those books are cluttered with concepts and learnings that have no relevance in today's world.

The Sage bangs her gong a final time and leaves the Lawenforcers to complete their final sword disassembly. She can see that the winners of the food prep race have been patiently waiting, and it is her task to go and congratulate them and confirm their awards. She knows the collateral benefit of this skill exercise is enough peeled potatoes to keep the Flock fed for the rest of this week and more than enough peels for the fish farms.

Today the winners are mostly Failed. "Well done brother, well done sister," she says as she moves down the line. Shaking hands with each of the winners in turn. She keeps her face solemn since this is the way a Sage should be. Congratulatory, but also neutral. However, she smiles when she sees that once again one of the Pure has finished in the first group. Ricky has finished quickly. He is in his teens. Brown hair and brown eyes. Bigger than most, and always hungry, Ricky makes an extra effort whenever there is the prospect of additional food. Sage Certainty can see he is in the middle of another growth spurt, and for a moment her mind clouds with worry. Can they provide enough for the young? It's hard enough to meet the maintenance requirements of her Flock, but the young and growing bodies always need more. She will have to look into that now that so many of her Pure are entering their teenage years. Perhaps a little rebalancing of the food supplies will be needed. Or some other approach that will allocate extra protein their way. Something for her to ponder.

Finished at the food prep tables, she releases the People to return to their rooms, and moves onto the back where the lesson is still in process. Coming up to the group from behind, she is unseen and stands quietly to observe their work.

"11 times 13 is 143," says one of the younger Pure. The Sage remembers her name – Kate is the sort of girl that would normally get lost in a crowd. Nothing special about her looks, straw colored hair, grey eyes, average height and weight.

One of the quicker minds, and mature beyond her age of eight. The teacher at the board nods and writes the answer up on the wall for the others to see. Across the wall there are now lists of numbers and words chalked up. The Sage is pleased. Some of the other buildings don't spend time on this, but Sage Certainty believes that her Pure should be as skilled in reading and writing as her Failed. It seems such an essential part of the past, that she can't imagine not passing this on for the future.

"Well done Kate," the Sage says moving around the table to stand with the teachers at the wall. "I am pleased to see you all paying attention to your numbers and to your words." She continues to the group of Pure spread along the row of tables.

"Why is this important?" she asks on the spur of the moment.

"Who wants to tell me why this is important?" she asks again.

There is a pause and looking into their young and upturned faces she can tell they are thinking about this question. Taking her seriously. It's Kate that answers.

"We read so that we can learn the lessons of the past. We write so that we can pass on the lessons of today," she says

The Sage smiles inwardly. Yes Kate is a smart one. And just for good measure she asks "And what of the future, Kate?"

Another pause. Sage Certainty can see the deep thought written across Kate's face. Then she answers.

"The future has not yet been written, but we study so that we can shape it," Kate says.

The Sage smiles now, her face losing its ritual mask. A natural smile. She is almost one of them. Her face almost pure and free of worry. For a moment.

"Thank you Kate," she says.

Maybe you will be my apprentice, she thinks to herself. It's time she found someone to train. Someone who one day can take on the mantle of Sage of Building 12.

She knows her burden, received not asked for. Almost eighteen years of carrying this burden has tired her out inside. As if her own concerns would not have been sufficient, she carries the burden of the entire Flock as well.

She longs for the day that she will be able to pass it on.

Give up this mantle to another, and rest at last.

Chapter 8

In Crisis

Belle is Pure, eighteen, and pregnant.

If that is not enough, she is now terrified out of her mind.

Watching that head hit the ground just in front of her had been one of the most awful moments of her life. Not only because it was always terrible to see a Failed head lifted from its shoulders by Sage Certainty, but more so because, seconds before, she was sure it was her that was going to be Revealed and Reckoned this time.

She and her boyfriend Adam had not asked permission, been inspected, or received approval before they had made love and planted a baby in her belly.

That was at least three Laws they had broken together.

Sage Certainty only ever needed one Law broken to take your head. She never waivered. Rumor had it that in other buildings Sages had been known to turn a blind eye to "minor" infractions of the Laws. But not in this building. Not where Sage Certainty was concerned. She had chosen her name well when she stood forward after the Failing and after the year of near collapse when the remaining People had called out for someone or something to fill the leadership void.

She had said then what she stood for and what they could expect in Building 12.

"Certainty in how this building will be managed.

Certainty that the Laws will always apply.

Certainty that there will be no exceptions.

Certainty that you can count on my consistency.

Until the end of my days," she had recited.

Belle needed an exception to this. Not so much for her, or for Adam. But for this magical growth in her tummy. Her baby.

Turning away from the eating room, she hurries back down the corridor to her and Adam's sleeping room. Not actually theirs of course—ten of them share it, which is the appropriate number according to their Sage. Ten per room. Ninety rooms in this building. Nine hundred Failed and Pure under one roof, just like the twenty or thirty other similar buildings around the Field.

The buildings had once been living quarters for the passengers awaiting loading into the Ships. Of course, before the Failing, the rooms would have been constantly and dynamically shaping to fit the needs of their occupants under the ever watchful and caring eyes of the room Intelligences. Now the rooms are all empty cubes devoid of their former creature comforts. Presumably, those are all still stored away in the walls, floor, and ceiling. But the Intelligences have vanished and no one now knows the secrets to unlock them.

Belle had not been alive then, and had not experienced those more practical and even luxurious versions of these spaces. Born into just such a bare and static space, this was all she had ever known. Perhaps that was for the best. What you did not know could not prey on you. Unlike the Failed, who always entered these rooms disappointed that they were not what they once had been.

In Building 12, there were no other rules about places of sleeping. Just that you had to have ten in your room. Who they were, how you selected them, and they selected you, was left to the ten to decide. How you slept, whether you all huddled together in one spot, using the rest of your room for study and play, or conversely, carving your space into ten equal small rectangles for each was up to the ten.

No Laws was for the most part better than lots of Laws. At least you got to feel that you could be self-determining where the little choices were concerned.

Sage Certainty was big on that in her leadership of Building 12. Self-determination was one of her favorite themes. Except the big choices, she staked out with Laws. She had made them all herself.

There was certainly no self-determination when it came to conception. That was decided a long time ago, when the first Decimation took that choice away from the vast majority. No one, not even the Failed Centimations, got to make a choice on conception. The Law required an application and inspection of both partners, ensuring that no mutation, however slight, went unnoticed where a conception was contemplated. More than once, a couple requesting a conception had ended up with their heads rolling. No mutation went without a Reckoning, so agreeing to an inspection was always a very risky business. Then there was a third Law requiring a formal approval from Sage Certainty—day, time, place etc.—before conception could be attempted. To be fair, she would auto sign a second approval if the first did not result in conception. Though another inspection was mandatory.

Mutations were not contagious. However, the Intelligences had taught in the decades leading up to the Failing, that those with Mutations might also have radiation damage within their bodies as well as without. So the risk of Mutated eggs and sperm was considered highest among those who visibly showed Mutations on the surface of their bodies. The Sage's had taken this lesson to heart, and only the most unblemished of Centimations would be able to get permission to breed. Even then, the moment of birth was a time of great anxiety. As the building Sage looked on, waiting to see if the newborn baby would show any sign of Mutation itself. Perhaps fifty percent of births ended quickly with a Revealing and a Reckoning. Particularly painful for everyone concerned.

Reaching the double doors to their room, Belle opens the left side and slips in. There is no one else inside. They are all eating. She should have been too, but the fear that she was the focus of the Lawenforcers as they came towards the line had brought her stomach into her mouth and driven away any desire for food instantaneously.

She would need to be more careful. If she had run, cried out, or even just flinched, the Lawenforcer might have taken a closer look at her.

Right now, her belly is gently bulging forward, though clever letting out of her layers of clothing—and wearing more layers to create a shapeless bulk—have made it almost imperceptible.

For how long she does not know.

Belle is the first Pure that she has heard of who has become pregnant. So she has no one to ask the obvious questions. A

Pure girl would never think to approach a Failed woman on an educational quest like this other than the Sage. It is Sage work to educate, hear requests, examine, and, once in awhile, approve. But with laws broken, Belle cannot speak to her Sage.

No Pure girl knows the answers to the questions Belle needs to ask.

Were there other ways to tell if a girl was pregnant? She thinks there might be. She does not know. Every morning she examines herself for as long as she can in the communal washroom in the shared long mirror. Nothing seems to have changed beyond a big belly. What else should she expect?

She hurries to her rectangle in the far corner. One wall facing the Field is all windows, the other wall unbroken by window or door. This is the best corner, and as an eighteen-year-old year old Pure, the first to be born by a Failed after the countdown, she has the status to demand the best. Since all the others are Pure too, they have inherited no sense of hierarchy left over from the past.

Adam had suggested they try for an all Pure room in which everyone else was younger, less worldly, less likely to want to lead and exercise their authority. It had turned out well. For the last few years. They had chosen Pure who they were certain would fit in well. Five girls and five boys, a balanced room. Adam and Belle were the eldest. The closest in age to them being Ricky who was fourteen, followed by two girls Cathy, twelve, and Ann, eleven. Then John, who had just turned ten.

Speculation had it that after the Failing on the Field there had been a few months before anyone had contemplated bringing a new person into this world. Presumably Belle and Adam's parents had already taken the required steps before the launch date came around. After a brief burst of births, the Failed had seemingly slowed down on parenting, and now there were few Pure below age ten.

In this room, there are four, which is unusual. Kate is eight, and in many respects a smaller version of Belle upon whom she dotes and models herself. Will, at seven, is a quiet, withdrawn boy. And then there are the two year old twins, Peter and Paula. Their mother had not survived childbirth—not uncommon these days. No Intelligences to guide the process, but more fundamentally, an unhygienic lifestyle makes difficult childbirths more likely to create complications for the mother in the days that follow.

This had been the case with Peter and Paula's mother, who had struggled to birth the twins and then had died of infection within the week. Belle had been on kitchen duty on the day that their mother had expired and she had offered to help with the twins without a thought. Babies are communal property, although typically the mother does the bulk of the work. In this case "Help" had quickly turned into "do everything" and Belle had needed to figure out the mysteries of a pair of newborns with the help of the building's Failed women—most of whom had modest energy for the topic and had succumbed years before to the belief that bringing children into this world was a terrible idea.

Fortunately, Sage Certainty had ensured that the essentials were made clear, and had also provided Belle and her roommates with extra supplies, food, and relief from at least some work.

So, a happy room, for the most part. Though when Maggie had developed a mutation a year ago, it had taken weeks for them to settle back into their rhythm. Their new roommate Cathy was great. But no one could forget that one of their number had lost her head. It could happen to anyone, anytime. The dice rolled every time you went outside to the fields. They all knew that. But losing a roommate made it all too personal.

Maybe this all Pure room had been the biggest mistake of all. If Adam and Belle had shared a sleeping room with older Failed, maybe they would not have felt so confident, so mature. Thinking that they would be able to take the risk, break the Laws, without repercussions.

Belle kneels down on her mattress on the floor, and places one hand above and one below the gentle swelling of her tummy. She begins to breath deeply as she has been taught by Sage Certainty. A way to calm oneself in times of trouble. Her breathing, now slower and deeper, brings with it a state of rest. Belle is almost sleeping. Kneeling here in the corner.

Her mind beings to wander, and then, it gets caught. Caught by a troubling image that begins to form in her mind. Before her stands the Sage. All in white, her sword before her. Looking directly at her. Seeing all. Her keen vision penetrating into Belle Revealing all of her secrets. Belle is unable to move. Trapped in the intense stare from the Sage's eyes. In this vision she becomes aware of the red moon that is rising behind the Sage. Filling the scene with red light. Blood red. Belle tries to protect her belly, the sleeping baby within, but she fears it is only a moment before that sword begins to rise. Begins to fall. Her heart is pounding. Panic rising.

She rolls into a ball and begins to sob.

It takes only a few moments for Belle to recover. Pure bounce back fast. Their young bodies and willing and positive minds recovering faster than the Failed. She lies and thinks to herself. "This is not reversible. Soon it will become obvious. Her own

Revealing weeks away perhaps. A Reckoning as certain as their Sage's name. Belle's own death was one thing, too terrible to imagine. But the baby too. . . ."

A few minutes later the door opens, and she knows that it is Adam coming to find her. She recognizes his tread. She senses his concern. Hears him kneel beside her and feels his slender arms come and wrap her and hold her.

"Belle, Belle, that was so dangerous to leave like that," he whispers in her ear. She remains in a ball, tight, unyielding.

"You can't behave like that. It's too risky," he says.

Belle opens her eyes, looks into his and with a force and rage she has never felt before, grabs his face in her two hands, squeezing hard, not caring whether she hurts him, tears his flesh, makes him bleed.

"It's too risky? I can't behave like that?" she hisses. "You fucked me. You made me pregnant. Where was your concern, your risk assessment, your danger gauge then? You did this. You damned my baby. Fuck off!" The intense, harsh, words pour out of her with no filter.

As quickly as she says it, she regrets it. This is Adam. Her lover. Her darling.

The rage leaves and she falls back. Tears, then sobs, then great spasms shake her body.

She feels his arms again. Reaching out. Bringing her into him. Holding her so tight that they are not two but one. Not three but one.

"You're right, Belle. I was selfish. I am selfish," he says in a voice full of shame and guilt. "But I'll fix this. I swear it to you. I'll fix this." This time his voice tremulous. Halting. At the same time, a touch of optimism creeping in.

Belle feels the rage coming again. "Fix it? How do you fix this, Adam?" she thinks to herself.

So many Laws broken. So soon they will all see. Sage Certainty's blade falling. Baby dying, before it has ever lived.

But Belle says nothing. Just lets the tears continue to flow.

Adam clasps her closer to him. "I love you, Belle," he says. "I love you, my darling".

Over and over again, until her anger has melted away in a wave of his words, washed away from her, then from him, until they lie together quietly.

Two young People, one blonde, one dark haired, old before their time.

It is at least ten more minutes before they move or speak. Only when they hear more steps along the corridor, and their own door beginning to open, do they break from their embrace.

"What's wrong you two?" comes a voice from across the room.

"It was fish and potatoes" says Ricky. "It doesn't get better than that."

"Little Ricky" they had called him for so long, though at fourteen, his voice tells the lie to his nickname. He is growing fast now and his only conversation seems to focus on food. Or the lack of it. Understandable when you consider that his adolescent growth spurt is probably making his hunger unbearable at times.

"What are you up to over there?" he enquires.

"Just some personal stuff. Belle had a hard day. Let's go get the clean laundry from the laundry works." Adam replies.

Adam takes Ricky's arm and they leave by the door.

Belle lies a moment longer, and then, brushing her sleeve

across her wet face she also rises up, but stops short of leaving the room. She knows the other seven will be there any moment, and it will be safer if she tells them herself about her upset tummy. Nothing strange about that. Their diet, while the best they are capable of making, always has issues.

...

Later that night, while the others slept, Adam and Belle left the sleeping room and quietly crept along the corridor to the long abandoned office at the end. Once, perhaps a cleaner or handyman drone's storage cupboard, the room was too small for even a solo sleeping nest, had such a thing been allowed. But like their sleeping room, it had floor to ceiling windows overlooking the Field.

Tonight there was a clear sky. Bad news. It meant that the tropics had temporarily won the battle over the poles, bringing with their victory the heat, but also the days of Capital Mutation. The worst time to be farming the croplands. A clear night lottery was the worst one to win.

Clear nights also allowed the stars to shine down, and sometimes the moon too. This was a full moon night, and the pale red light lit up the Field, and around it the circle of buildings marching off into the distance. Almost all of them quiet now, with their occupants resting as best they could. If they had not already marched out to the croplands.

In the middle of the Field, the moon shone down on the Ships, too. One still perfect, one tarnished at its apex. Enormous they stood, shining with a pale pink lumination. Smooth, unbroken sides save for the escape shoots that still hung from their lower levels to the Field below. Their tops the only difference between them. One still unblemished perfection. The other missing altogether, with black and broken upper edges, like an egg with its top sliced off.

To the Failed, they were symbols of lost dreams.

To the Pure, they did not carry any meaning at all. Like the Field itself, the buildings around it, and the croplands. They just were. Only less useful, less a part of everyday life.

Belle silently went over to the far wall of the room, and sat down side by side on the narrow ledge against the glass. Six inches to perch their bottoms. Narrow bottoms if truth be told. Not enough food to be anything else.

"We need to talk," Belle said to Adam. " We need a plan."

"I know, Belle. I know," he answered her. Belle took Adam's hands and raised them to her lips. Kissed the left palm, kissed the right palm. Held them to her cheeks and whispered "No blame, no shame."

He leaned in. She felt him relax a little.

Adam is black haired and about the same height as Belle. Slight for a boy, but his modest body size belies an inner strength. A strength that comes not from his physical, but rather from his mental attributes. Adam has a wonderful ability to see things others can't see. Sometimes in dreams, sometimes just in his sense of intuition. Adam sees things that give purpose for Belle. Things that help her set her goals and make difficult decisions. He helps her decide on her path.

Sometimes he dreams too much. Sometimes he seems disconnected, or impractical to her. Sometimes his intuition seems flaky. Yet, when she is lost, it is more often than not that Adam is the one that provides the sense of direction.

She goes on. "You are my love. My light. We did what we did together. We made our choice. We knew the risks. No blame for you that I don't share equally."

Adam's face crunched up and she could see tears welling up in his eyes. To avoid an outburst, she drew his face towards hers, and pressed her nose into his warm and red right cheek. Red because she had made it so in their earlier fight. Fortunately no broken skin. That would have drawn serious questions.

"I don't regret making love with you. I love you. But I know what we have done, and we need to fix this. I will fix this," Adam whispered back, even his whispers almost more sobs than words. But she knew his meaning, and her mind filled in the blanks.

This time the rage did not come. She was Pure. Pure were optimists.

"What are the ways then? Let's name them," she whispered.

Taking the initiative. Structuring the conversation. Her role always. Adam so different from her. There was a pause. She could tell Adam's mind was racing.

"Name them, Adam," she said again.

"We run, or we Reveal ourselves," he replied at length. Looking at her for confirmation, validation, maybe forgiveness too.

She did not name the other choice. The one she had heard about when Centimations did the unspeakable of mating without approval. This was her baby. That was not an option worth naming. She appreciated he did not name it either. Loved him for it. She drew him to her even more tightly.

"We don't Reveal ourselves. There would be no exceptions

made by Sage Certainty," she said firmly. Cutting off that stream of his thinking. Bringing his mind into line with the decision she had already made. "No Revealing, Adam," she reiterated, knowing that it would take a moment for him to process her words.

His dark eyes, first roaming from side to side, came to rest, staring into hers. "Then we run," Adam replied, adding after a moment, "When?"

"Soon," she answered.

They both sat in silence for a while, imagining it.

The People said that beyond the croplands were places where you could scratch a living. Stealing from the same croplands that the Field People tended from the Far Side. Creeping in each day, under the hot dangerous sun, when the workers had gone to take a few potatoes or turnips.

Some said these Scavengers numbered all who had run and not risked the Revealing. Perhaps scores, perhaps hundreds, in a handful of small settlements they had made themselves in the deserted buildings found beyond the Field and croplands.

Others, including the Sages and the Lawenforcers, said that was ridiculous. Only those mutated would run, and they would have scant time to live once they knew their mutations were obvious enough to make hiding them untenable. Dead mutants running. The Sages said you would do better to Reveal and be Reckoned, than live for a few more days or weeks with your mutation driving you insane, and your body wracked with the pain it created, not to mention the pains of starvation, dehydration and exposure.

In which case, the Scavengers must be few in number. A

handful perhaps. Perhaps none at all. Just a tale told to give hope to the Runners.

Better a short, sharp shock from the Sage's silvery sword? Or Run, Run as fast as you can. To the other side. Where hope awaits?

The Pure were optimists. Adam and Belle believed they had a plan.

Run then.

Chapter 9

Belle's Dream

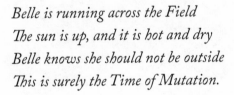

Belle is running across the Field
The sun is up, and it is hot and dry
Belle knows she should not be outside
This is surely the Time of Mutation.

Belle should not be running
Even more importantly, there is something on her back
Something that must not be exposed to the bright rays of
the sun
Something very dear to her.

More dear to her than herself
A small bundle
She can feel it wriggling as she runs
It's alive.

She tries to name it, but can't
It is precious to her
Of that she is sure
She turns her head.

She is not the only runner on the Field today
There are others behind her, to left and to right
Fast runners
Closing on her.

She can't let them catch her
Or the bundle on her back
If they do something bad is going to happen
Something really terrible.

Bright swords arcing down
Slicing through clothing
Cutting into flesh
Dividing bone.

She feels a surge of energy
Picks up her pace
Now she is running faster
The fastest runner in her Flock.

On this Field
Not fast enough
The problem comes to her suddenly
She is carrying another.

That's why she is not flying as fast as she might
That is why the runners are going to catch her
Something nasty is going to happen
What can she do?

She needs to get away
She thinks about abandoning the bundle
So that she can run faster
So that she can be safe.

It's too heavy
It's a burden
Just drop it
She knows the answer.

It is too precious to abandon on the Field
To the runners who are coming up behind
What chance does she have?
Please give me a chance!

Give me a chance
Give my baby a chance
The thought makes her run faster
Still not fast enough.

She can see them now, unsheathed
Silvery swords glinting with the light of this harsh sun
That beats down on her and baby
What are they going to do with those?

"Give me a chance" she cries out
She feels baby move on her back
Baby turns towards the runners
He has something in his little hands.

Baby is dropping things on the ground
She can't see what
Something is happening
She is still running so fast.

Now the others are falling back
She is making ground—pulling ahead
Now almost across the Field
She is going to be all right.

She and baby are going to be all right
She stops running
She is still
No gasping, no heavy breathing.

She feels calm and relaxed
This is the Far Side
She escaped them.
She is safe.

Baby gave her a second chance
She reaches for baby
Pushes the hood away from its face
Adam smiles back at her.

Chapter 10

Sage Caring's Failed Woman

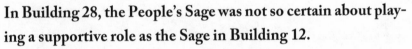

In Building 28, the People's Sage was not so certain about playing a supportive role as the Sage in Building 12.

He had named himself Sage Caring, and for the most part he did. In the beginning he had cared a great deal for his People, his Flock. He had entered into Sageship with an intent to do good.

He had stepped forward that day years ago in a spirit of abundance and goodwill.

However, seventeen years is a long time to lead.

In those years, Sage Caring had discovered the benefits of power. Since his power was absolute— at least as far as the People and internal workings of Building 28 were concerned—he had suffered the fate of generations of politicians and leaders before him.

Today, he was corrupt—absolutely.

He was still Sage Caring. However, now he cared for himself first and foremost.

He cared for his 912 charges secondly—he was clever enough to know that they were his source of power. They gave him his position and they gave him what he needed. So long as he held on to it. Which meant he needed to care a lot about his Flock.

Ensuring that they remained just that—his Flock.

Thirdly, he cared that his People did not break his Laws—particularly if there was any risk that other Sages would find out and hold him accountable.

So in this third motivation to care lay Sage Caring's deepest fears.

If you wanted to know how Sage Caring would behave, just trace the thread back to see how it impacted him, his Flock, and his ability to maintain his position of power over them. If an action increased his power, he would take it. If on the other hand it threatened or reduced his position of power, expect no action. Or sometimes, a violent alternative action.

Sage Caring had learned early on that a little bit extra for him in all things made a great deal of difference for his comfort and way of life. He could get twice as much, or three times as much as his People without much of a difference to them. Spread across 912 others, three times as much for him only reduced their personal share a fraction of a percent each. Not enough for any of them to notice. But for him, three times as much of everything. Much much more of some things—things he cared for a lot.

It had begun with food, drink and shelter. Sage Caring made sure that his Flock understood that his benevolent care might be directed towards those who cared for him.

Pork barrel politics. Except there were no pigs left.

But there was a barrel. Discreetly in an alcove a few doors down the corridor from Sage Caring's very large room, with several of his Lawenforcer's between him and the barrel. Just so that if ever another Sage called to visit, it was not obvious that this was for Sage Caring. The storyline instead being that this was the Lawenforcers food supply, despite the fact that they dined in the eating room with everyone else and only got to dip into the barrel on days when Sage Caring had already slurped his fill.

The People understood the barrel. The rules were not complicated. After your days in the croplands, you stopped by the barrel. You discretely emptied the potato or turnip from your pocket, or dropped a handful of insects, making sure it was oh so quietly done. Fish were of course another matter, delivered by hand, rarely, but the ultimate donation. Won at great risk since it was so hard to smuggle out. The fish farm building was shared among all the others, and its crop was carefully apportioned. Every building wanted its fair share, and the duty managers were blended from multiple buildings to make sure that this fair apportionment occurred each day. It was hard to steal a fish when every other worker was keenly assessing whether the biggest and best fish would come to their building each day. So a fish stolen won a great reward from Sage Caring on the rare occasions it happened.

The only person you wanted to see as you made your donation was the Lawenforcer leaning just there against the wall. He or she would make a mark against your name.

Later, you would feel some benevolence. Not always when expected. Like grace from heaven. Falling your way.

Forget about the barrel, and you should expect a hole to open up in the floor under your feet. A hole that might take the form of another trip to the croplands just when you thought you were about to take your days off. Days that the laws provided for, but which Sage Caring was well able to take away. Or perhaps a bruising tumble down the stairs. No bones broken—at least not on purpose. Enough to shake up your memory and remind you of how Building 28 is supposed to work.

Give and you shall receive.

Sage Caring had known for a long time his personal preferences. As the years went by, he found less and less satisfaction in choosing his personal friends among the Failed, male members of his Flock. Aging like him.

Now a new golden age beckoned. The Pure were growing up. Taller, stronger, handsomer. Just as Sage Caring preferred. Not something to think about very often. But once in awhile. When the weeks become months between the last such thinking, then beware, because the Sage would start caring again.

If you were Pure, male, and in your teens and you forgot to put something in your pocket, make sure you solved the problem before you got to the barrel. Not doing so would leave you very much regretting it.

Sage Caring was not a caring lover. Indeed, he knew enough to kill off his lovers on those rare and infrequent mornings after. Just to make sure there was no risk of someone talking to another Sage. Careless talk costs lives. Under no circumstances would Sage Caring's life, or power, be jeopardized.

Which led naturally enough to another characteristic of the world of Building 28. People did not talk. Not to those outside the building, not to the other nine hundred plus in it, unless absolutely necessary, and rarely even to their own sleeping room fellows. The Building 28 Flock had learned the hard way. Careless talk costs lives. Their own, if Sage Caring believed the talk might cost him dearly. A creative mind would always connect some dots from some carefree banter to a matter that their own Sage would turn an ear towards.

This was why Building 28 stood alone. On one side the main gate of the Field and perhaps half a mile beyond Building 1. On the other side Building 27. Or what was left of it.

Where Building 27 had once stood was now a burnt and broken shell. Shards of walls, and floors, and roof collapsed together at ground level.

One morning, some six years ago, Sage Caring and the Sage of Building 27, Sage Inquiring had gotten into an argument.

In the build-up to this, Sage Inquiring had heard, from her People, that not everything was as it should be next door in Building 28. Rumors spread between People out in the croplands or in the aquafarms perhaps. Whatever the source, the rumors had come to her and she had ignored them until they became so frequent that she could no longer do so.

After deciding that she must listen to the rumors, she had dug a little deeper. Taken the step of speaking to her neighbor's workers out in the cropland during her very rare trips to oversee. While they seemed unwilling to speak, Sage Inquiring had her ways. Some of them had broken and told her their tales. More had kept closed mouthed, but the signs were ample enough.

Enough to go a step further.

In a spirit of seeking the truth, she came to Building 28 to see for herself. That morning she arrived without warning, and maybe that was to be her undoing. She saw more than she expected when she peered through Sage Caring's sleeping room door. What exactly she saw no one ever knew.

"Sage, what are you doing?" she had shouted, her voice echoing into the building, so that it brought those within hearing upright, and quivering. Sages in rage were no good for anyone's health.

The People of Building 28 could not see what happened in that room, as Sage Inquiring confronted Sage Caring. What everyone did know was that the two Sages left the building together in what could only be described as a state of high anxiety. Shouts, threats, counter threats. A final agreement to talk once more the next day.

"A few hours for you to consider your position," was the way Sage Inquiring put it.

Maybe she was a little too generous in making this offer.

That night, Building 27 burned. The screams of those trapped filled the night. Innocent bystanders to a quarrel among Sages? Or just in the building when it had the bad luck to catch alight?

Suffice to say, Sage Caring had agreed to take in his share of those rescued that night. Added them to his Flock. No one the wiser that it was his doing that Building 27 and most of its Flock were no more. The handful of People still alive, too petrified to spread any more rumors about Sage Caring.

Sage Inquiring was not among them.

...

So Building 28 was not a happy place. The People each got a tiny bit less of everything, even though most needed more. Some of them suffered more than others at the hands of their Sage. All of them suffered in silence.

With one exception.

Deep in the basement of Building 28 she lived. In the blackness. Never emerging, never speaking, never entering the lottery, never working the croplands. Never doing what the rest of them took for granted. Why not?

She was an enigma.

Sage Caring protected her. No one understood why. But every day he had them throw her some food to go with the water that she took from the basement sump.

Why he fed her was lost in memory. Maybe it was just a joke he liked to play. "See how much I care for my People? See what you might be like if you don't care for me?"

Perhaps that was the sermon he was preaching to them.

Their Sage would be seen slipping down into the basement at least once or twice every week. Why he went there, and what he did when he arrived no one knew. No one dared to ask. Better to leave him to care for this woman in whatever way he thought fit—the others turned away if they encountered him coming or going to the stairwell that led down to the basement. Don't make eye contact, was the unwritten rule of these periodic encounters with their Sage.

...

The woman smelled. Or more precisely, if you had smelled her, you would have recoiled in horror. Anyone who needed to go down into the basement, on any task, however short in duration, knew enough by now to block their nostrils, cover their mouth, and get out of there as quickly as possible.

It wasn't just her smell. Eighteen years in the dark had made her albino white—if you could see the color of her skin under the layers of filth and excrement.

Smelly, pasty, sick.

Well, not completely sick.

It was true that she had become sick in mind, seemed incoherent when she talked, and always wild eyed. However, by no means was she sick in body. The woman in the basement was perhaps more fit and healthy physically than anyone else in the building. Most days they would hear her going through intense exercise sessions, running around her basement cell, doing calisthenics, counting out loud as she jumped, and crouched, and balanced. Indeed, it seemed that this was the way she spent most of her time.

Stories circulated among the Pure. Daring young members of the Flock who had crept down the stairwell to peer through the crack between the twin basement doors told of this weird white woman going through these elaborate exercise routines. Doing things with her body that no one could even imagine mastering. Those who had tried inevitably ended up with strained muscles or bloody noses where a balancing trick ended in a fall. Not so the woman—she seemed to be able to lift her entire body from any hand, foot, or even finger and hold it motionless in ways that defied their abilities.

She seemed obsessively driven to push herself through these workouts. Her body glistening with perspiration, mixing with the grime and running down her legs into the dirt and dust of the basement floor. The pungent smell of dried sweat mingled with all the other odors of her body and lair, furthering the unpleasantness of this part of Building 28.

Perhaps as a result of all of this working out, her lungs were strong and their capacity enormous.

Every few hours, she screamed and screamed. Filling the first few floors of Building 28 with her pain and suffering. Sharing the blackness of her life with everyone within earshot.

The Failed woman in the basement is the stuff of nightmares.

Chapter 11

Council of Sages

Sage Gratitude stands at the door of Building 8 and watches as the other Sages approach his building in the fading light of this time of Mutation.

Some walking around the Field perimeter, some walking by the straightest routes even though they take them past the two dead Ships. Most taking the former circular paths, and the bravest/stupidest leaving what shadows the buildings throw for the straightest and quickest way.

Sage Gratitude is a perimeter walker. Any shade you can find must surely reduce by a little the impacts of the sun's rays and the dangerous risks they bring. Others disagree, saying that the harmful rays pass through the shadow too. For them, the direct path and the reduced time in the open is more important.

Even then, these direct walkers don't quite walk the direct radii paths—it has been more than a decade since anyone has passed under the Ships.

Years ago, a few of the Failed had reentered through the still open hatches, but little could be salvaged. Apparently the Intelligences had done a good job of sealing up everything useful as they departed. A few handheld objects had been recovered, but nothing worked without power, and it was far easier to scavenge from the buildings than try and go deeper into long closed Ships.

Later, some adventurous young Pures had done the same. Making a game out of daring each other to climb into the Ships using the staircases still hanging down from each open hatch. After one Pure fell to his death on the Field below, the Council had agreed that this must be stopped, and Sage Gratitude had passed the law that said no one should pass beneath either Ship.

So now the straightest route across the Field passed almost, but not quite through the center, the last few hundred paces circling around the Ships that had not been disturbed or visited since. Sage Gratitude appreciated the strict and disciplined way in which this law had been followed by the Flock.

Sage Gratitude had a lot to appreciate.

While all Sages were equal, he was a little more equal than the others.

It started physically. Sage Gratitude was an entire head taller than most of the others around this Field. Once he had been even taller because of his great mass of curly black hair. Now long gone, his shining, dark bald head still looked over the heads of all of the others. With his great height also came great breadth. Not the breadth of the manual laborer who develops a broad back from countless hours of heavy and demanding work. For the Sage, his breadth was inherited. Broad shoulders, broad hips, massive arms and legs and great plate sized hands. In his role he does not use his bulk other than occasionally to intimidate. In his role, however, that is a very valuable attribute.

On the day of the Failing, he had been ejected in the direction of Building 8, and had entered it with a mass of other Failed. Finding that this building was bigger, and it turned out, better than all of the others.

This had been the Field's sports arena and facilities. A great arena in which games of old were played before the Failing. Seats in the thousands. A warren of locker rooms, changing rooms, coaches' offices and more, now mostly turned into sleeping rooms. Often with benches and tables rather than cold hard flooring. Neat lockers rather than piles of belongings heaped in corners and along walls as was the norm in all the other buildings.

Best of all, a world of equipment that was now put to purposes that always surprised him.

Uniforms that worked not as well as the flexible skins of the past, but so much better than the clothing the other buildings preserved until they fell apart into rags. Balls cut into helmets. Pads and braces that protected still. Bats and rackets that became valuable tools. Tape, padding and netting in vast quantities. And so forth.

Sage Gratitude's building was a little bit bigger and better than everyone else's. His People a little less Failed, he felt. Though that was probably just an illusion.

No illusion that he was 'a little more equal' though. For on the night of a Council of Sages, all the others came to him. His arena was their meeting place. Which made him their host. Which over time had made him their Voice.

Controlling the agenda as ever, the source of the leader's

power. He chooses who gets to speak, or whose hand is ignored. Rewarding voices he likes with extra time. Cutting off those he does not with sharp dismissal. Shaping the discussion. Tipping it towards the outcomes he prefers. Becoming the collective Voice of the Sages.

Some might call Sage Gratitude manipulative. Like most politicians he was good at getting his way. However, no one would say this to his face. His level of intimidation, when turned on, was enough to create a zone of fear around him. Which in practice was enough to allow him to spend most of his time projecting an air of calm and quiet confidence. It had been years since anyone had challenged the Sage, though his defensive guard was always ready for insurrection. Win by the sword, die by the sword was as true in the political battles around this Field, as in the skirmishes between Lawenforcers and Far Side residents. Sage Gratitude was a master of both.

Today's meeting is an important one. Not just a recounting of the state of each building and its People. A litany of reports. A discussion of mundane matters.

Instead this is to be a decision meeting. And while he usually knows which decision he wants the Council to make, this time he is unsure.

"Welcome, Sage," he says to each one, taking their hands in to his two strong dark hands and squeezing and shaking theirs.

"Greetings, Voice," they respond as they pass by.

Most wear gowns. Somehow that has become their preferred dress. He expects it has always been that way. People of power in gowns. Of all the People around this Field, only his twenty-seven Sages chose to wear gowns and in time, no one else would dare break that equation. Sages in gowns – cleaned every day to pre-serve their whiteness while everyone else wears the Field's dust encrusted in their clothes. Sage Gratitude has decreed that the Sage's should have water to clean. His own white robe contrasts with his dark skin – such that he almost glows in contrast.

As the final Sage arrives, he turns and follows her in.

Into the arena—the inner sanctum.

...

The arena has been lit by torch light, and over the years modified for just this purpose. Twenty-nine seats have been taken from the banks surrounding the flat playing surface, and brought onto it. They had been arranged in a perfect circle at first. Then on the loss of two Sages (one dead of Mutation, one burned to death), two seats had been removed. It has been a powerful move by Sage Gratitude to take those two seats from either side of his own. Making his seat the focal point.

He is the last to join the circle. Tradition has all the Sages standing in place awaiting his arrival.

He sits first, they follow.

Allowing a moment for all to settle and for the silence to establish the right atmosphere, Sage Gratitude composes himself, stands and begins.

"At your request, I have asked you to come together today."

"Representatives of our People, we join together," the Sages reply, as custom dictated,

"We are equal among ourselves and equal among our People," Sage Gratitude says.

"We know our burden, received not asked for," the others respond.

"We come here to protect our charges. Our Flocks."

"We know our task," the twenty-six Sages confirm.

The formalities over, Sage Gratitude sat and began his prepared words.

"Each time we come together, we begin our meeting with building reports, then health and mutation reports, and then with the cropland and aquaculture reports. Today, I have asked you to provide those in advance, because we have all become aware of changes that we must address. I thank you for your diligence, and I now will share today's report in summaries so that we can move quickly into our discussion."

The twenty-six Sages leaned forward. Sage Gratitude could sense the tension and allowed it to develop with another pause.

"The Building reports sum as follows:

23,597 Failed Non Breeding

3,455 Failed Centimations, 51 with child

1,699 Pure, none with child

27 Sages

Today, our People number 28,805."

It had been a good idea of his to compress this part of the meeting by asking for the reports ahead of time. Tradition allowed for each Sage to report their building numbers at the outset of any council meeting, and twenty-seven such reports, and the frantic adding up that was required to create the total, always accounted for at least a third of their time together. Dispensing with this also removed the Sages' opportunity to speak at the beginning of the meeting. Now they would need to wait for him to call on them to speak.

"Health and Mutation reports have also been prepared. These I will not recount in detail. You know their findings because they have been the same for every meeting we have had in recent times. Our numbers continue to fall both through natural causes and because we have had an increasing incidence of Reckonings. There have also been an increase in unfortunate self Reckonings since last we met."

There was a slight rustle around the circle at this last comment. During a normal council, each Sage would be expected to name all those who had taken their own lives and would expect the censure of their peers for allowing self Reckoning within their Flock. Reckoning was a Sage responsibility, and not one to be shared.

"As we have discussed at prior meetings, our Failed have aged, and many among them are becoming unproductive. Some no longer have the strength for the croplands. We are concerned that this will worsen. Some of the Pure are becoming productive workers, but they are too few in number to make a material difference."

Sage Gratitude looked around the circle, his dark eyes intense and searching. He pauses a little longer before continuing.

"I have asked those Sages overseeing the croplands and aquaculture tanks to summarize their findings, too. Each of you have held those positions in the past, and you know the critical nature of what I am about to share."

Raising his voice, he says, "We have never had plenty, but we have ensured that none go without sufficient."

These words were tradition too, and the other Sages responded, "We are the leaders of our Flocks, and their care is our task."

"The reports are bad. Very bad," Sage Gratitude says gravely. "Yields have fallen in the croplands. The second Field in our

Western section had to be abandoned altogether as a result of worsening blight. While the insects hold up well, we have not seen such low crop yields in a time of Mutation since the season after the great winter. Most concerning of all is that the carp are no longer breeding. We do not know why, but only the catfish are still spawning. We expect to see dramatic fish yield reductions within the next few months if this cannot be rectified."

Now the Sages are moved into voice, and the outcry ripples around the circle. Only the aquaculture team themselves had known this latest piece of news, and they, and Sage Gratitude, had been careful to ensure that no rumor of it left the tanks. A shock indeed. Protein has always been the greatest challenge—fish and insects. Never enough. Now even less? How would a Sage ensure their Flock receives sufficient? How to complete the sacred task if the fish fail?

Sage Gratitude raises his voice over the hubbub and, after one attempt, is able to speak over the quickly quieting crowd—long trained by custom to never speak when the Voice speaks.

"I have considered this carefully. There are two options that present themselves for our consideration."

There is silence, as every Sage leans forward, all focused intently on Sage Gratitude.

"We must reduce our Flocks. The choice we have is only how. Not whether to do this. Only how to do it."

There are sharp intakes of breath and rustling of robes as Sages squirm in their seats. A muffled gasp or two. All eyes still on the Voice set back a little from their perfect circle.

"We can either reduce our numbers randomly, or reduce our numbers by Reckoning those who are least able to contribute.

This is our choice. I have decided that we will not make this choice today. Return to your Flocks and consider the options well. I will call you when I determine we must vote."

Without another word, Sage Gratitude stands and walks across the circle towards the arena doors. This the signal that the counsel is over. Much as the others would have liked to discuss and debate, this action brooks no opposition.

When Sage Gratitude leaves, custom demands they do the same.

So they do. A line of twenty-six Sages passes Sage Gratitude standing at the main doors of his building. Only once they have all left does Sage Gratitude let the rigidness seep out of his face and body, slumping a little as the burden of formality leaves him.

Just one more aging Failed confronted by the inevitable. They are all dying on this Field. The only decision: which ones will go first.

Chapter 12

Overhead, Overheard

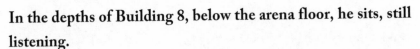

In the depths of Building 8, below the arena floor, he sits, still listening.

Listening to the footsteps as Sage Gratitude walks around the floor, dowsing the torches.

Listening for the doors to slam as Sage Gratitude closes up the arena and leaves to join his Lawenforcers and Flock in Building 8's eating room.

He waits until all is silent and he is sure that the arena above is empty.

Then he slides the panel back over the floor vent which had once been used to channel away the cleaning fluid and waters used to scrub down the playing surface after each game.

Stepping down from his chair, which he has perched on a desk to bring him closer to the ceiling, just feet below the arena floor. He climbs down to quietly stand on the floor of the former janitor's office.

This room is his secret place. Long ago, he found ways to keep it hidden. Building a false wall to hide the entrance, cleverly concealed so that only he knows the way to slide it up and reveal the doorway into this space. All that Engineer training has its benefits—even if his teachers never expected him to use their knowledge quite like this.

In this secret place, he has gathered everything he thinks could have value in his future.

Everything he ever needed to be an Engineer is here. His manuals, tools, equipment, all carefully preserved. A tiny proportion of course, of what once was. So much was stored virtually by the Intelligences, and lost as they went away. In the first year, he had gone back to basics—pencil and paper, no less. Jotting down everything he could remember while it was still fresh in his mind. Binding those bits and pieces together into precious manuals on every topic he could recall.

So little, but still the most valuable jewels of his training captured and laid down. He can't say why. He just feels that a good Engineer would do this. Catalog everything, organize everything, make sure nothing is lost if it can be retained. His disciplined training applied to this work. Everything meticulously managed and organized.

Just like he is himself, his slight body is well maintained – he still follows the daily practices that the Intelligences taught him so long ago. His chestnut hair is cut short and he brushes the stubble each day to keep it clean and tidy. His nails are clean and clipped, his body beneath his tidy clothes is as clean as he can make it given the scarcity of washing water.

This has become his life's work – attending to himself and

to his journaling and recordkeeping. So little to show for it. He sits back into his armchair. His favorite place to rest and do his thinking.

Tonight, he has a lot to think about.

The Engineer has listened to these council meetings for years now, never expecting to hear Sage Gratitude say words like these.

He replays everything back to himself. Going over what was said about Earth, the croplands, and the aquaculture buildings. Checking and rechecking their numbers regarding yields and shortfalls.

Then the Flock. He jots down in one of his manuals the most recent numbers shared tonight. Long ago he had created his own census of the buildings and the People in each. For no particular reason but because the mental mathematics kept him engaged. He had created his own population model, and now he runs the Sage's new numbers into it. His mind straining to keep all the numbers synced up. Mental mathematics comes easily to him, but this is a complex set of equations to work in his head all at once. He does some forecasting, some scenarios. Adjusts some critical assumptions about life expectancy by cohort and mutations by age and gender. He is more right than wrong, but it is still good to have objective data to refine his own calculations.

Then he combines the two. Carrying capacity model meets population model. This he plays with, trying a few different approaches, and running a handful of different scenarios. He enjoys seeing the curves in his mind's eye and watching as they approach and then cross each other.

He eventually comes to the same conclusions that the Sage reached, but by his own much more intricate pathway.

The bottom line is the same.

They are out of equilibrium.

The falling carrying capacity, and the failing food sources, demand a rebalancing. If the denominator of carrying capacity can't be changed, then the numerator of the size of the Flock is the only way to make the equation come back to its proper place.

The Engineer does not like it, but all his training brings him to the same place as the Council of Sages.

Time for a cull.

He thinks about this. Imagines what it might be like. Slowly slips into a deep sleep in his armchair beneath the arena of Building 8.

Dreams his solitary dreams for another night.

Chapter 13

The Engineer's Dream

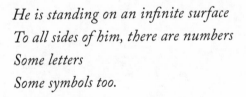

He is standing on an infinite surface
To all sides of him, there are numbers
Some letters
Some symbols too.

He turns and realizes that in every direction the surface
is curving up
He is at the minima
That seems fitting to him
He is the minima.

He is at the lowest most point
It is just what he deserves
Yet he does not want to stay here
How can he get out?

His feet are firmly bound to this point
Maybe he can lift a foot, but he can't
The answer must be a different equation
He looks around.

Picks up some numbers, letters, and symbols
Maybe if he can put these together, he can move away
from this minima, this low point
He hangs the numbers and letters and symbols in the
air
The sequence he creates does not make sense—that is
obvious to him.

So he changes some things
Moves some symbols around
Drops one back to the surface and picks up another
A new equation - this one does make sense.

As soon as he confirms this, the surface changes shape
It tilts up more steeply in front of him
He turns and sees the gradient has become even more
gradual
But in both directions, it still slopes upward, leaving
him at the lowest most point.

He has to try harder.

He reshuffles the equation. Adds numbers. Changes
orders. Flips two symbols
Again, a good equation
Still not the right one

He is desperate to get this right.
He was always good at this.

That is why he was chosen
The best
No longer
In this dream, he can't get it right.

He tries again, hanging a new equation in the air.

A last chance.
This time, the surface becomes very steep, and his
minima drops downwards
The sides are coming closer towards him
Closing around him.

With more force than he had expected.

Squeezing him
His head is held now, he can't turn it
He wants to try again, but his arms are held tightly to
his side
His minima drops downward, ever lower.

Now he is suffocating
His face and mouth are covered by this mathematical
surface
That he created but which he can't undo
He is at his lowest most point.

He does not deserve anything else

His mathematics won't get him out of this one
He needs a smaller head
Or a helping hand.

Chapter 14

A Plan

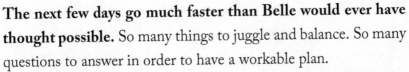

The next few days go much faster than Belle would ever have thought possible. So many things to juggle and balance. So many questions to answer in order to have a workable plan.

How to make sure she and Adam get a little extra food to build their strength for the coming trip across the croplands? What to take with them? How to make sure they have the opportunity to go into the croplands during the next cycle? Then how to make sure that they will not be noticed for a few days when they did not come back in the morning? They needed that time to scout out the Far Side and decide whether it was livable. Not that coming back was an option if it was not.

Then there were all the practical issues that come from not sleeping alone. There was no way that they would be able to cover up their absence. Their roommates would know they were not there at sunset when everyone gave up trying to read by torch light. So then, when and how should they let the others know? How much should they share? They could tell them that they were taking a visit to the Far Side, perhaps. That they expected to be back in a couple of days was probably the easiest white lie to tell.

But what was the explanation for why they were going?

The last thing Belle wanted was to have eight others share the knowledge of what she and Adam had done, and the implications that came from breaking such fundamental laws. Belle could only imagine the panic and fear that would come into their eyes if they connected the dots. Revealing and Reckoning were bad enough when it happened in another room. In your own, it would be traumatic just to imagine. Belle lost a lot of time and energy worrying about this part.

Belle worked through her lists, systematically checking off items, and adding more as they came to mind. She also found herself spending time thinking about how to make sure Adam stayed strong. Stayed on course. It had always taken all of her powers of persuasion to keep him on track. Adam was a dreamer, which was one of the things she loved about him. That he was also a bit flaky and unable to maintain focus was not such a desirable trait. Certainly not right now, when so much was at stake.

Right now Adam seemed ready to give up on their plan. Every time they whispered together, he raised new issues, and each time she had an answer, he only dug deeper for other reasons why their plan was not good enough.

Was he trying to put her off? Trying to lead her to the conclusion that running could not work?

He had not mentioned the other way, but she expected him to at any moment. Which was not an option she would let him share—even if she had to hit him in the mouth just as he began to let it out. She would if she had to. She knew just how she felt about it.

Just then, as Belle mulled over the plan one more time, Adam entered the room and came to her corner to sit with her. It was growing dark in the sleeping room, and all ten roommates were readying themselves for sleep. Going about their close of day rituals. None of them would be leaving for the croplands this night. No one a lucky lottery winner.

"How are you feeling, dearest?" Adam asked in his quietest voice.

"I think we are ready now," she replied. Intending to end run another round of doubt and confusion.

"I agree," he whispered.

Belle looked at him in surprise, and grasped his hands in hers. She could see the tears in her eyes mirrored by the tears in his. Silently they wept together.

This was it, then.

She reached out and ruffled one hand through his dark hair while the other touched his cheek. She let the wetness rub off onto her forefinger. Smiling, she first touched her wet finger to the end of her nose and then put it into her mouth, tasting his salty tears. After a momentary pause he did the same. Smiling. United.

"I was worried you would not come with me," she said in a tremulous voice.

Adam admitted, "I wasn't sure myself until just a little while ago."

Belle's hands, now white knuckled, are tight around his. Squeezing hard.

"I was in the eating room and saw Sage Certainty and her Lawenforcers meeting and it just became clear to me," Adam says. "This is our only choice. We have to go before they find out."

She does not respond. Good that he had come to a certainty of purpose of his own accord. Caught up with her before she needed to pull him into reality. They were running. Even if they included in their plan a return option, realistically this would be their last night in Building 12, and perhaps their last alive. Running was risky business.

"Then it's decided," she says.

She kisses him on the cheek, and her hands relax, now soft around his. He feels the difference and knows he has said the right thing, and that she is with him.

"Let's go over the details," she tells him. "I have managed to collect together a few extra bits of food and some other things I think we will need." Ever the practical one, she has done much more than gather a few bits and pieces. She has worked down a precise list, created in her mind.

Items rated by value, accessibility, weight, bulk, and half a dozen other variables. Ordered by overall ranking. Then, after adjusting for new variables, and final thoughts, she picked the top of the list and focused on it. Making her mental list into reality by hard work and discrete thievery. Until she has checked off the 'must haves', and even a few of the 'would be good to haves'.

"I have a knife, a mirror, some cord. Not much but hopefully it will help" she says modestly. "They are under my mattress and tomorrow night when we go out for the croplands I plan to put them into the pockets of my inner clothes. I was able to scavenge a few extra potatoes, but best of all, when cook was not looking

I took some dried fish and have it in a bag along with some dried grasshoppers—although we should not be short of those," Adam responds proudly, with a smile. "I don't have much more than that. Some bits of tinder, a flint and steel and like you my knife."

Belle is pleased. She had asked Adam to focus on food. Knowing that if she did not give him something to focus on, he might come back with a random selection of 'we don't really need' items. Even then, he had surprised her. Especially with the dried fish. Protein was always the most difficult type of food to obtain.

Of course, it was not enough to live out there. She knew that. But then there was nothing very sensible about this plan. Go out with the others to work in the evening. Find a way to hide when the long night came to an end. Endeavor to get to the other side under the harsh sun, when sane People hid indoors. Hope to find someone who could help them once there.

"We have what we need for our plan," she tells him.

Knowing as she says it to him that it is not much of a plan at all.

...

They were not the first to have run. Not by any measure.

Running was what a few of the Failed did when they could not face the Revealing. Failed they might be, but those few that remained clung to life. Otherwise, they would have passed away along with the others years before. There might not be much meaning in life, but that did not mean that you gave it up without at least a little fight. For a few, it became the decision to go. Go meant Run since no one would go slowly once their decision was made.

The most common reason to run was of course a mutation. Something growing upon you until you knew it was too real to pretend it would go way. Too obvious now for you to be able to continue hiding it.

The Runners who left before a Revealing were the exceptions. The few. The many just waited to be caught. Waited to be Revealed and put to the question. Then and only then would they make the final choice. Stay and face the ultimate penalty that Sage Certainty would surely demand if they were Mutated or their Law breaking serious, or Go and control their own destiny.

When the few ran, they did it in many ways. Some, like Belle and Adam developed their plan in great detail. Others just ran. Straight out the door, around the back of the building and into the cropland.

No one knew which strategy was the better one. No one followed the runners. No one saw them reach the other side. Those that did not make it might be found in the croplands the next day or two. Sometimes begging to be brought home. Sometimes face down in the mud. Either way, they would not last much longer. That was the Law.

Few Pure had run. Mutations had been the cause in the past—always. This time, the running was for reasons deeper than self-preservation. Belle knew that Sage Certainty would consider the Laws they had broken cause for only one outcome – their head taking. But this was not only about Adam and Belle. In this case, Belle was planning for another too.

Maybe that would make a difference.

...

Later that night, once the building has settled down, Belle and Adam make the rounds of their roommates.

"Ricky, wake up," she says gently.

"Ann, we need to talk to you," he whispers.

Soon there are ten of them, in a huddle in the center of the room. Confused but aware that this is serious. The grim faces of Belle and Adam are making that abundantly clear. Most of them are old enough to understand something important is about to be shared.

"Hush now," Cathy tells one of the twins, Ann rocking the other.

The twins cannot have understood, but the mood of their elders has affected them too, and they are quiet.

"What is it, Belle?" Kate asks anxiously. "I can see that you have something you want to tell us." She is trying to appear grown up and calm like Belle, but is inside melting down as she prepares for the worst—she has overheard talk from her bed next to Belle and Adam and thinks she knows what they have planned. Her intuition marks her out from the rest who are none the wiser regarding what is to follow.

"Adam and I have got ourselves into a mess and we need to explain to you what we have done and what it means," Belle says.

The group leans in as Belle outlines why they are leaving. Not ducking or avoiding at all. This is what we did. These are the consequences. This is what Adam and I have decided to do. This is what we expect from you.

She pauses, and then goes over it all a second time.

"Any questions on any of that?" she asks after they have the essentials.

"Why aren't you allowed to be together?"

"Why does this mean you need to leave us?" from another.

The inevitable "Why are you going to have a baby?" from one of the little ones.

Belle answers them, Adam chiming in from time to time. It takes a while, but she is patient since they will need to understand to the best of their ability before she moves to the next step.

When she gauges they are ready, she says, "So Adam and I have to leave and we need you to help us with our plan."

They are quiet. Focused. Listening.

"We don't need you to do much, but you need to do a few things really well," Adam adds. Belle nods, and goes on, "Yes, there is one big thing we need you to do. You are all going to play a game, in which you pretend that we are upstairs here in the sleeping room."

"A game?" Cathy asks. "Like hide and seek?"

"Not quite," Belle explains. "It's more like a game in which we all pretend something is happening, even though it is not. Like telling a story. We don't want anyone to try and find us."

It takes a while for the younger ones to understand, but they do eventually seem to get the point.

"So we tell everyone you are upstairs sleeping?" Ann reiterates. "That's right." Belle replies." "We can do that, Belle, don't worry" from Kate. "I will make sure nothing bad happens" from Ricky who has been quiet throughout but now that the plan has been shared, joins the conversation.

Adam and Belle go over a few more details with the group.

Cover for them for a couple of days—cropland workers are allowed their week off when they return from the fields, and many do just that, curl up and rest, especially if the heat has been intense as it has been during this time of Mutation. Belle makes her roommates no promises. They do not know what lies on the Far Side. So she doesn't pretend it is something that it probably is not.

"Don't promise to come back," Adam had said to her hours before as they went over the game plan. "I don't want to lie to them."

Belle had concurred. Just make sure they know not to be surprised in the following morning. Just make sure they kept the rest of the building believing ten, not eight, live here together.

When Belle has finished, she is surprised but happy when Adam speaks out. "I love Belle and want to be with her," he says. "We did this together and we will see it through."

Not much. But it means a lot to hear him say it.

Then he says, "I love you all, too. My brothers and sisters. Take care of each other, and take care of yourselves."

The group comes closer into a tight huddle and clasps each other for a while. Adam and Belle side by side. Ricky on the other side of Adam. Kate nestled into Belle. Cathy and Ann, trying to be grown up, are keeping stiff upper lips. The younger children seem confused. The twins are still quiet, which is a blessing.

After a few minutes, Belle breaks the moment, leaving the circle to return to her corner, laying down and trying to sleep.

A moment later she feels Adam join her. Without looking, she lets him under her blanket, and leans into him as he puts his arms around her.

She really needs him now – as always.

Chapter 15

Run For the Far Side

In the morning, they begin the longest day of their lives.
Waiting for the evening when they will leave for the fields. If
they can win the lottery that is.

"Adam, I can't figure this out. How will we win the lottery
and make sure we get to go out to the Croplands?" Belle asks.

It is a question they have both been wondering. Ironically,
most People don't want to win the lottery. Night work in the
fields being one of the harder forms of work.

For Belle and Adam their plan requires that they do win
this time.

Then, when Belle is beginning to see her hopes slip away,
Adam has come up with one of his moments of inspiration.

"Let's watch and see who pulls the winning tickets, and if we
know them, then trade with them," he says. "No one will say no."

Like so many of Adam's moments of clarity, it is obvious
when spoken out loud. But Belle had not seen it until then.

They watch carefully as the lottery is played out. Cathy from their own room is the first to pull a token that says she has won and it is of course easy to switch her token for Belle's. It takes a while for them to see another opportunity for a trade. This time, it is one of the older, and most tired of the Failed women of their building who, on looking at her token, drops her head and turns away. Adam can see why. She has won what she least wanted to win. He sidles up to her, and a second exchange takes place in a hurried moment. The woman confused but grateful that someone else will do the work.

"We have them Belle," Adam whispers.

They have won the lottery as easily as that.

•••

As the day comes to an end, down Belle and Adam go to join the line of lottery winners.

Out the door, around the building, and into the croplands. A long night ahead for all of them. A longer one ahead for Belle and Adam. They fasten their clothing tightly around them, and pull their protective goggles down over their eyes.

"This is it," Adam says as they leave their building, and begin the long walk across the Field and into the croplands.

Walking on the Field is easy. The daily patterns of People have kept the remaining asphalt clear of blown dust and debris, and in the places where the asphalt has been worn away, many feet have scoured hard packed paths into the earth below. The only challenge is to watch for the step up and the step down each time asphalt meets earth and vice versa.

Then as they reach the edge of the Field, they pass under the dark and menacing silhouettes of the wind machines. Looming above them. A row of six, massive, black, man-made trees holding their limbs above them into the night sky.

Symbols of the People's backward slide into the past of technology.

After the Failing, and the abandonment by the Intelligences, the Engineers and mechanics had turned their attention straight away to power sources.

First came the salvaging of solar panels stripped from rooftops, vehicles, and even the backs of robots. Cobbled together to catch the sun's rays and channel them into whatever battery packs could be linked together into storage systems.

That yields a couple of years of power, lost as the panels themselves felt the harsh glare of the sun's rays, made more lethal by the high quotient of radiation allowed through the thinning atmosphere. Without the means to manufacture new solar panels, this first energy solution was short lived.

Then to wind. Again the Engineers and mechanics went back to first principles, digging into old records of technologies from the past that they had never needed to learn. They found images of windmills long gone.

Then a year of hard work collaborating to build first one, then six windmills with salvaged metal beams, carbon fiber arms and wings tailored from wall panels (too heavy), plastic sheeting (too easily torn), and eventually flooring materials pried up from buildings no longer in use.

For a while, it worked. The arms turning together. Six tall, irregularly fashioned windmills providing power that could be converted and stored and which, insufficient and precious though it was, could still turn on the most important tools when needed.

More human ingenuity, and one of the windmills, connected to newly fashioned grindstones, was able to speed the process of crushing and grinding insects and dried fish, quickly turning heaps of the indigestible body husks and bones into calcium and protein rich flour.

Until one night, during a time of mutation, the great winds had come and undone all of their work. One night to shred the wings, bend and crack the arms, and entirely blow down two of the windmills.

This Earth, tortured by humankind's demands, turned its own malevolent intent in their direction and tortured them in turn.

Until, eventually they gave up and returned to their most basic of energy sources.

Their own collective human power.

...

Usually the furthest away working stations in the croplands are the ones that no one wants. As a result, it is easy for Belle and Adam to take these. Marching outwards to the very edge of tonight's work section.

The workers tending and harvesting the root crops spend the night with backs bent, their hands in the soil, seeking out the precious bounty and taking it to the end of their rows to fill each box and sack.

The insect gatherers have a very different task. Each of these workers carries a long net sack with a round hoop mouth. The job is simple enough—pass up and down the rows all night long holding the hoop of the net just above the ground. As the hoop disturbs the leafy tops of each plant, a small cloud of insects is launched into the air, and hopefully a number jump through the hoop and into the net. At the beginning of the night, the job is easy. But after five or six hours of walking, the insect gatherers will be fighting both their own fatigue and the weight of a heavy net of crawling insects dragging out behind them. Not until the end of the night will the nets be emptied after first dunking them into a tank of water drowning the harvest before dumping them out into collecting bins for later processing.

Tonight Belle and Adam collect root crops. He turns the soil, pulling out weeds and revealing the precious bounty that lies beneath. Each root made red by the light of the moon, like a small ball of some red ruby like material. Almost as precious to this age as those now useless symbols of wealth – rubies, emeralds and diamonds - from a past that makes no sense to anyone in this terrible present.

Belle is one step behind Adam, brushing off the soil and filling the crates. The two roles suit them. Adam discovering something, Belle taking advantage of it.

A long and hot night, working row after row. Carrying the heavy boxes to the perpendicular paths that lead back to the Field, so that others can come and collect them and carry them back for the People in the buildings. Returning with the same boxes filled with night soil, which Adam will spread over the rows as Belle empties them of their crops. Enriching so that others can plant again another night.

Most of the cropland is flat, without interruption of tree, or bush, or man-made structure. However, here and there are dotted simple sheds in which the workers tools are kept, cobbled together from scraps of wood, plastic sheeting and rusty metal sheets.

It is getting towards the end of the shift now, and both Adam and Belle are tired, but their minds are fully awake. Adrenalin is pumping now in each of them. This is the moment.

"Come on Adam, it's time," whispers Belle.

"I'm ready, lead the way?" comes the response.

Belle looks left and right. Takes note of the position of the other workers who are now beginning to make their way back to the path that leads to the Field. Their long night of work completed.

Belle begins to follow, making sure that she sets her pace a little slower than that of the others. So that as the minutes go by, she and Adam drift to the back of the line. The light is not yet good, the sun still below the horizon, so that as the gap grows between Adam and Belle and the others, so they become lost in the gloom.

A few more minutes and they pass one of the sheds.

"This one," Belle whispers to Adam, and taking his hand she quickly leaves the path and squats down behind the shed. Its bulk between her and the others who are now invisible down the path towards the buildings around the Field.

"Now we wait," she says, and Adam squeezes her hand. "Your plan is working," he answers.

Belle's plan is simple. Work all night. Wait until just before the collection time. Make sure to be in the vicinity of one of these sheds when the workers stand up, turn around and head back to the Field. Duck behind the shed out of view. Wait until the others have left the croplands. Wait a little longer until dark is giving way to sunrise. Then run for the Far Side.

A simple plan, made feasible because no one will expect it. Everyone has worked all night for the chance to go back to the buildings. No one needs to count the heads. They went out, they come back. As simple as that.

This time, two did not.

As simple as that.

Chapter 16

The Scavengers

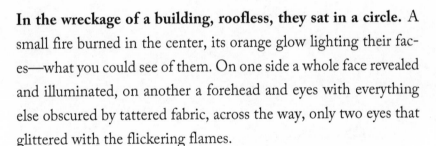

In the wreckage of a building, roofless, they sat in a circle. A small fire burned in the center, its orange glow lighting their faces—what you could see of them. On one side a whole face revealed and illuminated, on another a forehead and eyes with everything else obscured by tattered fabric, across the way, only two eyes that glittered with the flickering flames.

Around the fire there were twenty in number, though in the corners of the room were other bundles of fabric, flesh and bone. There might still be twenty-three if the three who could not summon the energy needed to join the fire circle were still alive. But by morning, it most probably would be just twenty. The other three were in bad shape.

One had external malignancies that had grown to such size and coverage that he had begun to look lumpy and deformed even when swaddled by his outer clothing. Those mutations were distressing to everyone, a constant reminder of what awaited you if you also had a small but irritating lump, extrusion or rash. Growth the common factor for all such gifts.

One had internal mutations. She said that her stomach and intestines felt full and expanded within her stretching skin. She found it harder and harder to eat and now only liquid seemed to find its way through her failing system. At least she could put some food down her throat.

Four weeks ago another had said his throat was seemingly getting narrower. Three weeks ago he stopped speaking. Then, days after, his breath had come in shallow and harsh, difficult gasps, he had found himself unable to take down anything at all. They had buried him two days ago—more a skeleton than a man. At least his bundle of skin and bones had not aroused the hunger in any of the others.

Not that this leader would have stood for that. Burning or burial, but never that. Whatever the momentary benefits of some additional protein and much needed minerals in their diet. This leader believed in treating his circle with respect whether they were alive or not.

The third had just laid down today. Said she was ready. Courageous to come to the conclusion in a graceful way. They appreciated her calmness and equanimity. It made things easier for all of them. Usually deaths came much less frequently out here. However, seeing two passing had brought out the decision in this third.

So three were leaving now. Who would join and fill their places?

...

The Scavengers were all the same in one respect: They had all fled when their mutations became apparent. Some left that same day, fearful of the wrath of the Sage and Lawenforcers in their build-ing—and some buildings checked every day for signs of the fearful afflictions. Others hung on as long as they could before they too left the comfort and security of their building for the unknown of the Far Side.

Every year, a few score mutated would make the journey and seek out the Scavenger camps, which the Scavengers themselves called circles. No one knew how many there were. Not many for sure, since they were so hard to find. Perhaps 100 or 200, mostly organized into a handful of small bands.

Finding a circle was of great importance, since living alone on the Far Side was usually a quick path to death—no circle of friends to share the task of crop and fuel foraging and water collecting meant exposing oneself to the harmful environment every day. Sure to accelerate the final stages of your mutation. At least circles could share the work, perhaps reducing the harmful exposure.

Even with these realities, the Far Side still had its individual Scavengers.

They were the dangerous ones. Loners who would cut your throat and slake their thirst and hunger with anything you car-ried—including anything you still carried on your bones. Even the Scavenger circles avoided the loners.

The rules of the circles were varied and depended upon the beliefs and preferences of the respective members. Some were based upon the theme of one person one voice. Others were ruled by a single voice—tyrannical or benevolent or unpredictably oscillating between the two.

Change came fast. The modal life expectancy of the Far Side Scavengers was less than a year, since mutations could move fast. So each circle was constantly trading out existing members for new arrivals in the Far Side. In the past, circles had come together in the belief that numbers created additional security and strength. Just as often, larger circles had fractured into two or more smaller circles as some sought their own way to live and die.

Conversely, in a few cases mutations moved slower. Seeming to linger or even cease their progression— a false impression, since no one had ever seen a mutation depart entirely. But this did mean that there were some few Scavengers who had lived in the Far Side for years, and in many cases, they had risen to be the leaders of their respective circles.

So, an odd mixture. The old and the new blended together, all living under the constant threat of their personal nemesis. Their own mutation.

Scavenger life proceeded according to a pattern similar to that of the Field buildings. Perhaps a little looser without the Sages and Lawenforcers, but nonetheless the pattern was driven by the need for the essentials. Food to eat, water to drink, fuel for the cold nights, shelter from the days of Mutation. A degree of discipline around waste disposal—including the disposal of fallen circle members.

After so many years, the Scavengers knew the Far Side around the Field and had scouted out its secrets. No stone had been left unturned. Most of it was no longer usable. Warehouses of machines and equipment, supplies and parts, maintenance items and tools. If you could not eat it, it was of no great value. The Scavengers had found it all, and in most cases left it to slowly corrode and stagnate.

This was the world that Belle and Adam had decided to enter.

...

Back at the circle, one reached out to the fire, holding a hard won dried fibrous root. He dropped it onto the fire in the center where the coals were hottest. It flickered as the flames rapidly heated it to combustion point.

"This root is good fire," he said.

"All fire is good fire," another muttered.

"Thanks for fire," the rest responded. Heads down, but awake and ready to participate in their rituals and dialogs—this one more a superstition than a belief. Without fire, Scavenger circles were hard to make work. Tending the fire a vital task that their leader only entrusted to the most able and disciplined among them.

The fire, now fed, sent up flames and in doing so, a flickering light now illuminated the furthest corners of their room, exposing its secrets.

Bundles of clothing, some old and dirty mattresses, boxes and containers along one wall, some tools along the other. Everything Scavengers needed for their daily routine.

By the door, the most important tools of all. Twenty-three blades. Each one crafted lovingly by the circle member who had found the old steel or titanium, ground it down to a sharp edge, polished it on long nights such as this, found a way to add grip and guard.

In Scavenger stories, it was told that the first arrivals on the Far Side had just used their hands and clubs, but that one day, an arrival had come bearing a sword stolen from their building Sage as they ran. That sword had been the model upon which all others had been crafted.

Every Scavenger had a blade. Regardless of circle, every runner, on arrival would learn this most fundamental of laws. To be a Scavenger, you needed a blade. Most were given one left behind by a circle member now departed. By definition, this gift would be the least effective blade in the circle. For some, it was enough. For those who began to master the art of swordship, that first blade would be given up once a better one could be crafted.

Originally, blades had been a defensive necessity, to protect against the loners when Scavenging in the croplands and when foraging for useful items including firewood and the like. A blade could dissuade and in most cases that was all it was needed for. Quickly pull it from its wooden or plastic scabbard, drop into the stance that you have mastered best, and let the other know that they won't get what they want without coming through you. Most challengers leave, and if this one does not, at least you or they will pass with honor.

A few had gone further. Sparring with each other, learning how to move their blade with its unique characteristics of balance and swing. Learning where it cut best. Where it could block, and where it was weakest.

Learning what not to do with their blade as important as learning what to do.

In this circle, one of their number had a very special blade handed down more than a decade ago and then made as perfect as it could be by long hours of work. For ten years, this Scavenger had lived by his sword. Had made it as much a part of him as his hands or feet. Perhaps more so, because his blade gave him purpose as well as status.

This blade brook no opposition—never had.

...

The dawn broke to find the circle putting on their protective clothing—those with the energy and health to do so.

"Are you going out today?" one asks of another.

"Not today. My leg won't hold me," comes the response.

"Can I take your hood? the first enquires. "It's better than mine, and the sun is going to be unbearable today."

"Take it."

There is more discussion around the room as the circle gathers up their tools and containers and prepare to go out into the croplands.

They may not have Sages and Lawenforcers to set their tasks, and call the hours, but the discipline of survival is just as real here on the Far Side.

Those able to leave the room march down the stairs before assembling at the main door where their leader checks them each. Two are sent back—one because their leader views her as unable to cope with a hard day in the fields. The other to retrieve forgotten goggles without which a day in the sun is impossible.

Then they are outside. In single file, approaching the croplands from the Far Side. Doing almost the same work as those from the Field the night before. Only quicker, less systematically, and leaving less trace. Sure to depart the fields before the lottery winners and their guarding Lawenforcers arrive to harvest their crops.

Of course, this is not the best way to do this. The day is to be avoided. The sun so harsh, their Mutations will only be accelerated. There is now choice, however. At night the croplands belong to the Field People. So that only leaves the days for the Scavengers to do their own harvesting.

"Which crop today?" one asks of their leader, who strides out in front.

"The second field. They worked it last night. I think it should be easy pickings with the soil so recently turned," he responds.

"Potatoes?"

"Yes, I think so, though they seem to have been planting more of the sweet ones this last cycle," their leader answers. Always on top of what they can find and where—true Scavengers.

They take what the others have left, and poach a little of what the others still plan to take. But not too much.

Too much, and their scavenging will become a burden and a squad of Lawenforcers will show up one night to dispatch their pocket of People. It happens. Those nights become clashing skirmishes of swords fighting swords. The Lawenforcers less proficient in their bladework, but stronger and healthier given their superior diet and living conditions.

Better to make sure there is no reason for the Lawenforcers to come out at all.

So Scavengers have learned and passed down their rules. Never more than a handful from any row, section or crop field.

Leave the Field dwellers the 90%, and they will turn a blind eye to what the Scavengers take.

...

"I am hungry," says one Scavenger to another in the circle.

"Not long now," comes the response.

The Scavengers are preparing their reward. On the fire, a large black pot warms. Scavenger stew. Sweet potatoes, some bits of broken and discarded vegetables, insects, and water. Not much different from the Field food, save for the absence of fish.

The same Scavenger who has being feeding the fire now reaches out to stir the pot. He is their leader. He is just a bit stronger, more vital, more active. His mutations are perhaps a little less severe, although he has shared them with no one. He has not been here the longest, but ten years have gone by since he arrived. Maybe lucky. Maybe more resilient. He does seem to make more decisions, completes more work for the group, takes the lead at times like this.

"It's ready," he says, and the room bursts into life. They come to him, their bowls in hand. No rushing, no pushing. They know there will be enough for all—strong or weak, worker or rester, it makes no difference. Everyone gets to eat.

"It's good tonight. We found some extra roots the others missed," he says, and it is true. Each of their bowls is fuller tonight by a slice or two of thick steaming sweet potato, mixed into the soup.

"Thank you, leader," they say, as they take the bowls and sit down around the fire.

He takes the last of it and divides it into four bowls. He delivers all but one to the corners of the room where those too sick to stand wait for their nourishment.

Then he returns to the fire with his own bowl.

"This food is good," he says.

"All food is good food," the rest respond. "Thanks for food."

They begin to eat.

The leader looks around at them and is pleased with what he sees. They may be an unlikely lot, but they are his People.

This circle is his, and he has trained them well. They are good at what they do. Scavenging, cooking, tending fire.

In one respect they are more than good. They are the best.

Bladework.

After dinner, they will do their sharpening and polishing. Every blade must be worked on every night. What tools would have done quickly, now their hands must suffice. A hundred thousand caresses with a soft cloth brings each blade to a mirror-like polish. Good enough to see the reflections of their tortured skin. Those with facial mutations don't look too closely. But the blade sees everything.

He looks over towards the door, and there it is. His perfect blade. He the master Sworder among a circle of Scavenger Sworders.

He is their leader.

He is James.

Chapter 17

Across the Croplands

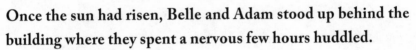

**Once the sun had risen, Belle and Adam stood up behind the
building where they spent a nervous few hours huddled.**

"It's time to go," Belle says.

"I am ready," Adam replies, picking up the last of their
supplies.

Deep breaths, a long hug, and they begin to move towards
the Far Side.

Both had assumed they would be able to move faster, but
that is just not possible. Within a few yards, first Adam and then
Belle have stumbled and in her case, fallen.

"Are you okay?" he asks.

She gets up, brushing off the dirt, careful not to let him see
how much it hurt as her knee drove into the stony ground. "Yes,
I'm fine. Just a little trip."

The ground here is uneven by design with the soil that
covers the rows of crops built up into long low humps. But what

also becomes increasingly obvious as they move forward is that the orderliness of the cropland is fast disappearing. Out here the fields are not maintained, and in some places, no longer cropped at all. As a result, the ground is uneven and treacherous.

"Belle, slow down," Adam whispers. "The last thing we need is a twisted ankle or worse."

Belle is tiring of Adam's protective stance. He has spent the last few hours worrying over her. She suspects that it is partially genuine concern, but more his own need to cover up his fear with some other form of expression.

But Belle knows he is right. After all, it is only perhaps a mile to the Far Side. They have hours to creep there before the sun goes down.

"Okay, Adam. I'll go slow," she says. Then for good measure, "We are going to be alright. We are almost across."

"Thanks, Belle," he says. He reaches out and takes her hand in his.

...

Eventually they reach a place where there is no cropland left at all.

"I think we are across, Adam," she says.

There are piles of wreckage on hard beaten ground. Nothing useful grows here. Some scrubby bushes and thistle, but without the tending, the night soil, the watering, this land is unable to make itself fertile under the harsh rays of the sun beating down incessantly.

Ahead they can see scattered buildings still standing. The first thing the People had done after the Failing was to create their perimeter of cropland. This meant that not only were most man-made structures within one or two miles out from the Field demolished, but in addition, debris, wreckage, and usable materials had long ago been taken from the cropland for use back at the Field.

Now Belle and Adam are entering the area beyond. The 'real' Far Side.

They begin to pass ruined buildings. Eighteen years of abandonment, when compounded by the increasing ferocity of the weather patterns, have taken a tough toll on these buildings, and most are partially or almost entirely falling into disarray.

"Can we take a break?" Adam asks, and looking ahead, it seems to Belle that it is exactly what they should do.

"Yes, let's do that. We need to have something to eat," she says, sitting down just where she is.

Adam sits, and reaching into his pockets he brings out some of their dried fish and a small root. Belle adds another, as well as a handful of mangled crickets—the latter looking even less appetizing than usual having spent hours crushed in the bottom of one of her inner pockets.

As they eat, Belle can tell that Adam is not himself.

"Adam, tell me a story," she says.

He looks at her in surprise "A story, now?"

"Yes, tell me a story about how it's all going to be alright."

Intuitively, Belle knows that this is the best thing to help him right now. Let him fantasize a little and escape from this bleak setting.

"Once upon a time, there were two young People living together in a paradise," Adam begins as Belle settles into his side and leans her head back on his shoulder.

"His name was Adam and hers was Belle. Their paradise was

beautiful, and peaceful, and bounteous."

"Adam and Belle lived by a stream on a green bank. The stream was made of clean water they could drink whenever they wanted and full of fish, and the green grass was full of the largest, juiciest grasshoppers you had ever seen. They were so easy to catch they could just reach out and take a handful anytime they felt hungry."

Adam knows Belle likes insect paste, but the crickets that live out in the croplands are too skinny and hard shelled to be eaten easily, and he has always imagined a world in which softer, juicier insects abound. Belle goes there too now, imagining mouthfuls of soft sweet chewiness.

"The fish too were large and juicy. They were so numerous that if you stood in the stream, which was shallow and cool, you could just reach down and tickle a fish and it would come into your hands and you could just take it from the water. The flesh sweet and soft and good to eat."

Belle takes a deep breath and letting it out, settles even more deeply back into Adam.

"One day, Adam caught a big silver fish, and he and Belle ate it sitting under the shade of a boojum tree which had great big fruit hanging down for their dessert."

Adam has no idea of what a fruit tree looks like, but the mental image is one that the Failed have passed down, and in the stories of the Pure, trees full of rich and sweet food feature centrally. So now he embellishes a little on this idyllic scene.

"Belle climbed up on Adam's shoulders and reached up and picked two with the softest skins. They were both pink and larger than her hand. She brought them down as Adam carefully lowered her to the ground."

Belle smiles at this. Naturally, in Adam's stories he is always careful.

"Belle takes one of the fruit and breaks it open and it is full of sugar and honey, and she offers half to Adam and eats half herself. It is so delicious."

Adam pauses here and lets them both imagine this sugary, honey treat.

Like the trees and the fruit, Adam has never seen a bee, but the Failed tell stories of a time when harvests were made fuller by the work of clouds of these gold and black insects which no one ate because they were much more valuable as pollinators for the crops and sources of a thick yellow nectar called honey.

Adam does not really know what that means, but he pictures clouds of insects bringing their honey to the crops, and so he also imagines that fruit must benefit in much the same way.

"The honey is sticky and by the time Belle and Adam have eaten it all up they have filled their tummies with the most delicious feeling."

Belle takes Adam's hand and puts it on her tummy.

"My tummy is full of the most delicious feeling," she says, and laughs.

Adam laughs too.

"You make me feel happy, Adam," she tells him. "Your stories, your dreams, your intuitions are just what I need," she goes on. "I am so happy we have each other."

Adam smiles from ear to ear.

"And I need you even more than you need me," he replies. Hugging her closely.

His stories often have these images of a world that is more paradise than reality. Belle knows it was not always this way.

The Earth did not always hate them.

...

They continue their journey among the standing buildings. They hope to find Scavengers living in these relics, but this in turn means they have to go even slower, zig-zagging from building to building, exploring each one as they pass. At first they did so carefully, gingerly, scared of what might be inside.

But after one, then ten, then twenty, their worries begin to subside. These buildings are all seemingly empty.

"Is there anybody in there?" shouts Adam into one gaping doorway.

"Hello, hello," Belle shouts up into the broken windows of the next. A particularly tall building that stands above most of the others around them.

The echoes of their voices are all that come back to them.

"Let's go inside this one," says Belle. "I think we may get a better view if we can go up to the top floor."

"Are you sure, Belle?" Adam asks nervously. But Belle is already through the doorway, disappearing into the dark interior. Adam follows, more afraid to be left alone outside, than to enter into this dark and frightening space.

Inside it is not as bad as Adam had feared. Just beyond the doorway is a large open entry atrium, and Adam can see Belle standing in the center of it. Light is coming in through large open windows high up that must once have been glazed, but which are now just open to the elements. Across the atrium, Adam can see a line of doors, and to either side, flights of stairs.

"Wait for me!" he shouts, and catches up with Belle. He takes her hand in his, and together they cross the atrium.

"Which door should we take?" Belle asks, but it turns out that none of the doors seem to open. They are each completely immovable. Little do the two know that these are not doorways as such, but rather a line of what were once elevators. Long sealed shut as the power was turned off and their Intelligence deserted them.

"Let's take the stairs up," Belle says after they have spent a few minutes trying each door in turn. Again holding hands, they begin to climb the stairs.

It is a long climb. Flight after flight, turning again and again as they ascend the floors of the building. For the most part the stairs are empty save for the occasional debris of broken glass and bits and pieces of masonry that have fallen over the years. The stairwell is lit by large open windows at each landing, so Adam is less nervous. Following Belle hastily up the stairs.

Suddenly Belle stops, and Adam bumps into her.

"What's the matter?" he asks her.

"There is something on this landing that I don't like the look of," Belle replies.

"What do you mean?"

"Stay here."

Belle is moving before Adam can respond. Walking up the last couple of steps and onto the next landing. Adam feels his fear rising, but is able to take enough steps to also be able to see the landing. Unlike the others they have passed, this one is covered in a jumble of boxes, mattresses and what appear to be blankets and other debris. Belle has already stepped into the middle of it all, and is looking around.

"Adam, don't come out yet. There are bones here," she says.

"Bones?"

"Dead ones," Belle says with a chuckle in her voice. She knows her Adam and it is important that she not spook him.

"Nothing to fear. Just dead bones," she says.

Adam wants to see, but can't make his legs move. He is grounded to the penultimate step, his feet just below the level of the landing. His eyes, much higher, can see Belle and where she stands among the debris.

"Are you sure it's safe?" he whispers. "Come back here."

"It's safe Adam. These bones look really old," she responds

She is looking around, her eyes to the floor, when she hears Adam come up alongside her. He has mastered his fear.

"What sort of bones are they?" he asks.

"Human bones."

...

It is Adam that eventually makes the discovery. While Belle works her way through the piles of stuff lying on the floor, it is Adam that looks around and sees the writing on the wall.

"Belle, look at this!" he cries.

"Just a minute Adam, I am nearly through here," she replies

"Come Belle. I have found poems," Adam says in a voice full of awe.

"Poems?"

"Come see," he says again.

Belle goes over to stand with Adam, and is also struck by a sense of amazement. Covering the entire wall on this side of the landing, is the most tiny, carefully aligned writing. From ground level to just above eye level. Lines and lines of writing, in columns some two hand widths wide.

"What does it say?" she asks.

"There is so much of it. I can't begin to know," he replies.

But ever willing to do Belle's bidding, he begins to read some lines out loud.

"Why did they go?

Where are they now?

My head is quiet without them

My life is my own, but I need so much help

I wasn't prepared for this

This was not the way my life was supposed to be,"

Adam pauses.

Then he begins again. This time closer to the ground.

"We are all dying

Just it is taking us longer than it took them

William's mutation was too much for him

He took the easy way.

I won't do that.

But it hurts so much."

This time Adam stops with his voice choked off suddenly.

He turns to Belle.

"These poems must be those bones talking to us Belle," he says in a quiet voice.

...

They spend another hour or two on the landing. Reading and sharing. It is not an easy task. The wall is covered by the thoughts and fears and recordings of a group of people who must have known they were dying on this landing. There are various hands at first, far to the left, but by the final stanzas on the right, a single hand, first strong, then wavery, is all that is left to journal the final days here. Some of the poems are frightening to the two Pure. Others have a calm beauty to them. Eventually, when they have had their fill, it is Adam that says, "Belle, it's time we left and went up to the roof."

"Okay," she says, and taking his hand, she leaves the landing and its records and climbs the final flight of stairs to an open doorway that leads to the roof.

There is less to see than she had hoped. Just a panorama of wrecked buildings, unused roadways, and debris everywhere.

"This doesn't help Adam. Let's go down and keep on walking into the center. I think we should go that way," she tells him pointing down a particularly broad thoroughfare.

They don't hesitate to go back down the stairs. Ignoring the landing with the remains of a Scavenger group. Quick to start the next flight down, without a second glance. Down and down until they are back in the atrium, and out the main door. Back onto the road and into the Far Side.

...

They continue walking until dusk.

"Belle, I think we need to stop," Adam says. "I'm worried we will trip on something in the dark."

"We need to keep going as long as we can," she insists. "The sooner we find a Scavenger circle, the sooner we will be safe."

Adam wants them to be safe, but is not so sure that the Scavengers represent the safety that Belle assumes. At the same time, he does not want to speak out against their plan.

This time, Adam prevails and they stop in what might have been a former garage.

Another light meal of some of the stolen food, but they both finish almost as hungry as they had begun. Adam only then sees the wisdom of Belle's earlier preference. If they do not find a circle soon, their food will be exhausted.

In the deepening darkness, Adam and Belle huddle together and silently gave each other what support they can.

Suddenly, Belle jolts forward. Then a moment later she jumps to her feet.

"Adam, I think I see a light!" she cries. "Over there, where that large building is."

Adam jumps to his feet too, staring with her into the darkness. He takes off his goggles in order to see better, freed of the smeared and scratched protective lenses.

Yes, a soft glow, rising and falling in intensity against the otherwise black outline of an old building. One of many here that punctuates the horizon against the slightly lighter night sky behind them.

Adam stares, and as he does so, his eyes became more dis-criminating of the subtle variations in color tone. Now he can see that this particular building is not as dark as the others to either side of it. On the second floor, an end window is lit from within. An orange glow.

"Do you think that's them?" he asks.

"Let's go and see," she replies.

Holding hands, they walk together in the dark, perhaps a little quicker now that a specific destination drives them forward.

Fears of falling forgotten.

Chapter 18

The Circle's Prophecy

Around the fire circle, the twenty are eating. This night they have made enough for twenty-three with seconds for all. Most are on their second bowl but the pot still holds enough for those that have not joined the circle.

Food has warmed them, and they are talking. Simple matters. What they have each found in the fields today. How they found the food. How they are feeling tonight. What they hope for tomorrow.

Some nights, their conversations are more profound. About the meaning of it all. Of values and beliefs. But the leader of those conversations is huddled against the wall, and none of the others feel a desire to take the conversation into deeper and more philosophical directions. At least not yet, though they know from experience that in time someone will step into the role of facilitator of the circle's discussions. They all need that person to step forward, whoever it will be. They need to talk, and not just about the fields and the grind of daily life.

However, just the simple things are being talked about to-night. Everyone is being respectful of the discussion leader as she slips away from them, over by the wall.

They all have known they have visitors long before they arrive.

Scavengers live, for the most part, without fear of others—just fear of their own mutations. Even so, other, and sometimes desperate Scavenger groups will come raiding. Then too, the Lawenforcers are a distant threat they need to guard against. So their leader has sprinkled the entrance hall and staircase of the building with the husks of dead insects—in particular the dried thoraxes make a particularly loud snap or pop when trodden on.

When, as tonight, visitors tread on them, only a deaf person will not be woken.

After the first snap, they had all come to attention, nervous and frightened of what the night was bringing them. Their leader had risen silently and taken his blade from the wall near the doorway. Then had walked by memory along the zigzagging path he had left free of insect alarms to the top of the stairs. There he had paused, listening with increasing comfort to the noises from below. Lawenforcers did not fear the night—they would have stormed right up. But these visitors seemed more frightened than all-conquering. Indeed, he worried they would not conquer their own fear, and would instead turn and flee. However, they came on.

James smiles to himself. Time to get ready for them.

He returns to the room and puts back his blade against the wall.

"It's okay, put down your swords," he tells his group in a quiet but firm voice.

He gathers up a large armful of wood kept solely for this purpose, and throws it onto the fire. As it lights and the flames jump up, James says to his circle, "We welcome what the night brings us. We welcome new friends to our circle."

The traditional words of preparation that Scavenger leaders use to encourage their circle members to sit up tall, bare their faces, and shape their mouths and cheeks and eyes into welcoming smiles—if their malignancies still allow them to do so.

...

Adam surprised Belle by being the one to enter the brightly lit doorway first. He dropped her hand, and walked forward two or three paces ahead of her. She figured that he was protecting her and she felt a wave of emotion rise in her by this simple action of his.

She follows, and over his shoulder sees the room.

The Scavengers are many in number, sitting closely together in a tight circle around a brightly burning fire. All their faces are turned towards the door, and as she enters, she sees their smiles.

Then with one voice, they say, "We welcome you to our circle. Come join us, friends."

One stands. Walks towards them, holding out two hands. Takes Adam's left hand in his right, her right hand in his left. Holds them up high.

"We greet our new friends. See them. Welcome them," James declares.

He steps towards the circle as a space opens up. He sits, taking them both down with him. Until the circle is complete again.

"Tell us your stories and why you have joined us," he says.

Without thinking, Belle begins to tell them, and cathartically, and uncensored, it all comes pouring out.

To her twenty plus new friends.

When she finishes, Adam is asked to tell his story, but he is short in the telling. Her story is his story, and there is little more to add.

The Scavengers thank them both, one by one, beginning with the person sitting just to the left and going around the circle. A simple thank you, then their name, and how long they have been in the circle.

Too many names to remember, but a common pattern in the stating of their tenure. Mostly a couple of years or less. Only a handful who claim longer.

Then their leader speaks.

"We now know your names and your stories," James says. "We thank you for your sharing."

He looks into the fire, and is silent for a while. The flames flicker, making his features bright and dynamic. Shadows highlight his nose and mouth and the deep sockets of his almond eyes. The light makes his cheeks shine.

"We understand your quest, your hopes and your dreams," he continues. "We too came here with hopes of a better life and freedom from those who gave us the choice to stay or run."

There is a rustle of agreement around the circle.

James pauses, looks at Adam and Belle. Then back to the fire.

"Know this. There is no hope to your quest. There is no escape here," he says loudly. "We know our truth."

"We know our truth," his circle responds.

"Our only escape is death and we wait for it to come and take us. Our circle makes our waiting bearable. We support each other in compassion and with equanimity, and we will support you too."

Another pause.

'You have joined our dying circle, and we welcome you"

...

The next day and the one after, Adam knew Belle was living in disbelief. She did not speak, but he saw it in her eyes. She had come to escape, and instead she had been told to accept a graceful end. He knew she would not accept that. His intuition of Belle's feelings a step ahead of her realization of them. It made him feel warm to know that he was one with her thought process. Knew her as well as she knew herself.

It took two full days before she said out loud what he already knew.

For two days, Adam watched the Scavengers go about their work. Scavenging for food and fuel for their fires. In small groups of three or four, moving out in different directions and at varying times of day, but all returning burdened down by their finds.

After watching the first few teams depart, Adam called after one, "Can I come too?"

After first one, then two groups had rebuffed him, he gave up asking. This was not work they wished to share, and perhaps the secrets of their preferred paths and buried caches were not meant to be shared with outsiders. Life on the Far Side was tough enough without sharing your secrets with others from outside your circle.

Later, Adam noticed that some of the returning teams were also bringing back sacks that were being taken around the side of the building and which clattered when dropped to the floor. Clearly not food or fuel.

Curious, he asked a Scavenger who had just put down such a load,

"What's in these sacks?" expecting to receive no answer. However, this time he did receive an answer. "Metal for the swordsmith."

Coming closer, Adam watched as the Scavenger emptied out the sack onto the floor. A pile of shiny round objects – some smaller than his hand, some as large as his head.

"What are those?" Adam asked.

"Drones," came the response. Then, "we use drones because they are made of the best materials and there are small amounts of steel and titanium that we can use mixed in with the plastic and carbon fiber."

The Scavenger bent down, picked up one of the larger examples and handed it to Adam.

"Take a look and tell me what you see."

Adam took the drone, and held it up. It was about the same circumference as his own head, but flatter. More of an ovaloid than a sphere. Smooth and perfectly symmetrical when viewed from one direction. When turned over, the other side was a mass of divots and ridges.

"Which way is up?" Adam asked.

The Scavenger reached across and rotated the drone in Adam's hands so that the smooth side was up and the other side down.

"All the legs, eyes, equipment and everything else used to come out of the bottom, but we can't get them to work anymore," explained the Scavenger.

"Nowadays what we want is inside them."

The Scavenger took the drone from Adam, and carried it, along with the others from his sack, around the corner of the building. Adam followed.

Here they found three other Scavengers standing to either side of a brick furnace that was full of a hot fire that one was blowing on with a crude pair of bellows. Each time she worked the bellows, the fire intensified and burned with a brighter orange/white flame. The other two were in the process of breaking apart one of the recently found drones. Swinging a heavy hammer made from a block of concrete fixed to a wooden shaft. As Adam watched, the hammer came down and neatly split the shell of the drone. The other Scavenger took the broken shell, and pried it further open. Adam leant forward, and was amazed to see a mass of shiny shapes inside the recently broken open object.

"What are all those bits for?" he asked.

"These are the workings, but all we want is the metal," came the reply.

Adam watched as the drone was pulled apart, most of it thrown to one side, until all that remained were a few small bright metal parts. Within half an hour, and with the addition of the new sack of drones, the Scavengers had a handful or two of metal parts, and a much larger pile of discarded shells and innards.

"Here comes the good part," said the Scavenger who had brought Adam to the furnace. Adam watched as the woman stopped working her bellows, and using a long pole, opened the door of the furnace. A wave of heat erupted from the now open furnace, and Adam was amazed to see the air shimmer and dance. Without a moment delay, the woman took the pile of metal bits and fed them into a container at the base of the furnace, before quickly closing the door again.

"We are now melting the metal in the crucible. It will take a while, but if you come back in an hour or so, we will show you something wonderful."

Adam could not wait to get back to the furnace an hour later, and watched as the group reopened the furnace and, with great care, took out the crucible that was now full of a pulsating white liquid. With the help of one of the others, and moving very slowly, the woman poured a stream of the intensely hot liquid metal into a wooden form about four feet long and about two inches wide. The metal flowed slowly into the form, making the wood steam and smoke.

"We leave this to cool, and then we work it into a sword on the forge," explained one of the group. "It takes days of work to fold and refold the metal, heating and reheating it, but eventually we get to a point where James takes over."

"What does he do then?" asked Adam.

"He is our swordsmith," came the reply. "Only he knows how to complete the final stages that takes the folded metal and tempers it into a sword."

...

Later that day Adam was amazed to see the passion and dedication that the circle put into their bladework and sword practice.

It seemed that hardly a moment went by in which at least half the circle's number weren't either grinding and polishing their blades, or practicing their stances, their attacks, their parries, their avoiding moves. An obsession if he had ever seen one.

Across all of this practice, the Scavenger leader James stood out above all.

He had a level of accomplishment that was peerless. Adam had seen other swordsmen of great capability including Sage Certainty, who was considered the greatest Sworder of all by those living around the Field. However, even she could not match the perfection of this Scavenger's work. Adam watched in awe as James' sword shifted into a whirling silver field of light and his body now still, now in blurring motion, moved through the exercises. His play was magical, and Adam was entranced by its beauty and deadly perfection.

While Adam watched, Belle seemed to turn inwards. He was worried for her, but left her alone. It was clearly what she wanted.

Belle had no time for swordplay. Her mind was preoccupied with her own body and the growing presence within. Refusing Adam's advances, offers of food or drink, or companionship. She was still. Hands to her belly. Eyes closed. To the outside world made of stone. Within, a private world of kicks and pressure was her entire focus.

At their third nighttime circle, after two days in which they had buried three new friends, and worked alongside the twenty, Belle came alive again.

This night, after a new facilitator had been appointed, and the circle had turned to talk about what should happen next, Belle joined in their discussion.

Brutally, and disruptively.

"You sit here and talk as you die. That may be enough for you. But I am not ready to. I am not ready to scribble poems on the walls as my life slips away."

She paused. Looked around. Then continued, "My belly is full of life, and I will live and my baby will live too."

There was a sound of gasps as each of the circle took in what she had told them. However, Belle was not finished. "What can you teach me that can help in my quest? Tell me now, for Adam and I leave tomorrow."

Their new friends broke into a babel of sound and some cried out, but not the leader. He knew this was coming. He had seen so many die around this campfire, including his own wife years before, that he understood the insight that underpinned Belle's outburst. It was true, that this circle was not the place for one such as she so full of life.

"Belle friend, we have welcomed you on your arrival, and we will welcome you as you leave. I knew it as you told your story, and I know it now," James responded. "Your time is not yet, and you will leave us tomorrow. You are not the first to come and go, but let me tell you that all have come back who left us before. You will come back too. But before then, let us share the Prophecy with you. Friends, join me now."

As one the twenty rose shoulder to shoulder, Belle and Adam stood too, until the circle was complete.

James stepped forward, thrusting his hands out and as he did so, the fire burst into bright green and blue flames, casting an eerie hue over the faces of his People.

"We are the circle. We are friends together. We share with you the Prophecy that we have been taught to pass on," he intoned.

The circle responded, "We are the circle. We are friends together. We are dying together. Now we share with you the Prophecy that we have been taught to pass on."

James turned now with his back to the flames and standing just in front of Adam and Belle, he said, "We are here to die, and we do so in our calmness and compassion. We see you and we see that this is not your time. You are free of mutation. You are Pure and we see it. We have waited for you. Here is our Prophecy that has been handed down to us since the Failing and the arrival of the first Scavenger out here on the Far Side."

He paused for a moment, and in it only the quiet crackle of the fire was heard.

"We don't know where this comes from, and yet all Scavenger groups know they must share this prophesy with those who arrive from the Field. Some of us wonder if this is not a message from the Intelligences left to guide us" he shared, and then, in a formal voice, reciting:

"There is an escape, but we know not where to find it.
Search for those who know the secrets of the past
They will know how to unlock it
The doorway through which you wish to pass
They are the keyholders, though no key do they bear
Go to them if you seek your escape
Go."

On his last word, the flames lost their color and returned to their soft orange glow. The circle sat, leaving Adam and Belle standing a step outside of it. The circle began talking again, but the two of them were no longer a part of it.

No eyes tracked them as they left the room for the darkness outside.

...

She wakes in the dark and reaches out for her blanket. It is stiff with dirt and the odor is strong, but it is her blanket and she wraps it tightly around her. Hers. She comes onto all fours and slowly crawls across her room. To her bowl, which is full, as it is every morning.

She eats the protein first. Hungry for the lumps of chewy substance. Rich in essential materials that her body demands. Even with the limited exercise she affords it, her body always wants the protein first. Then she works her way through some boiled, cold potatoes and roots. By now she is fully awake, the munching and masticating shaking away the remnants of sleep.

Finished, she creeps back to the sump. Dips into it with two hands and slakes her thirst, washing down her meal with gulps of brackish water. More and more until her belly is full. She wipes her hands in her hair, ironically making them dirty again.

She rises to her feet. Tilts back her head. Pauses.

Then her morning routine. Stretching, flexing, bending, balancing, until every muscle is fully activated and ready for the next phase. She launches into a furious whirlwind of activity, bouncing from wall to wall, jumping, pumping, whirling, and twirling. Finally, phase three. Acts of strength that stress to the limit every body part - neck, shoulders, back and chest. Arms, forearms, hands. Bottom, hips, thighs, calves and feet. Every part doing its utmost to meet her demands.

Once this third phase is complete, she seems to relax. Her breathing is slowed and her body is at complete rest. Her eyes closed. She is in a deep meditation or perhaps a trance.

Minutes pass by. Could she have fallen asleep?

Suddenly, her blue eyes snap open. Her head tilts back. Her mouth opens. Her lungs fill.

Then she starts screaming. Long drawn out wails, each rising and finishing on a very high note.

If they were not already up, the People of Building 28 now are.

Their morning alarm shocks them into a new day of unrest.

Chapter 19

Back to Building 12

After the circle had delivered its Prophecy, Adam and Belle had talked for hours about their situation and what to do next. Huddled together in the darkness with their backs against the building, facing towards the Croplands.

"Let's go over this Prophecy, and see what it means," Adam had begun. "I feel that there is a very important message here for us."

"They said that they don't know where the Prophecy comes from but that they must tell every visitor about it," Belle replies. "I agree that seems important."

"I couldn't help but notice that it is for People who are trying to escape something," Adam goes on. "It's a message for People like us."

"But who left the message and why?" Belle asks.

"I don't think we can ever know that Belle," Adam says.

They both become quiet for a while as they go over the words in their heads. Hugging each other tightly, together in their shared need to understand this Prophecy that they have been given by a group of Scavengers that seemed to think it was vitally important that it get shared and passed on.

It is Adam that breaks the silence first.

"Belle, I think we have to go back to the Field"

He feels her become rigid in his arms.

"Are you crazy, Adam!" she declares, pulling away from him.

"We just spent all this effort leaving, why would we ever decide to go back?" she demands, staring at him wildly.

"You know what will happen if we go back and Sage Certainty and her team Reveal me."

"I know, I know," Adam says, reaching out towards her again. His advance rebuffed, as Belle refuses to be held.

"I know it is terribly dangerous, but the Prophecy makes me think we have to go back," he says. "Remember what they said."

He sits up straight.

"Search for those who know the secrets of the past."

He pauses, then again more loudly, he recites;

"Search for those who know the secrets of the past
They will know how to unlock it
The doorway through which you wish to pass
They are the keyholders, though no key do they bear
Go to them if you seek your escape
Go"

"I am sure that is a message for us, Belle," Adam continues.

His voice becoming more excited as he shares this latest, and perhaps most important of intuitions. "We need to find those who know the secrets of the past, and they have to be among the

People at the Field."

"Why not among these Scavengers here?" Belle asks.

"Because they are the holders of the Prophecy, which means they can't also be the keyholders," Adam responds.

Belle doesn't quite see the logic of this conclusion, but if she knows one thing about Adam it is that his intuitions and dreams, when they come, are much more often right than wrong. She waits, thinking. Her fears loud in her head. Drowning out her ability to reason. Baby, Sage, Lawenforcers, Revealing, Reckoning, Swords, Failure. The thoughts swirling in her head. Fear, panic, flight.

Adam succeeds in wrapping his arms around her, and as he does, she feels her mind calming. With the calmness, comes her own ability to reason, and with that in turn, acceptance.

"Adam, we will go back," she says at last. Knowing that she is heading back into the greatest of danger, but that Adam is convinced that their escape can only be found among the People they have left.

"Thank you Belle," Adam whispers.

"Let's not wait," she continues. "Every day I feel myself getting bigger. The longer we take in finding our escape, the more the risk that we will be found out first before we do."

"We will escape Belle." Adam says with confidence. "We have a Prophecy to guide us, and the ones who left it want us to escape."

With Adam's confident words in her ears, Belle knows what to do next.

...

That night, the third since they had left their room in Building 12, Belle and Adam crept back into it. Their journey across the fields had been uneventful. Belle marched with purpose, Adam followed. They just retraced the route they had taken three days before – making sure to hide and avoid the workers when they came across any.

This time, Adam did not seem worried about the risk of a turned ankle. He did not dare to slow Belle down. Only once they began to approach the Field did she reduce her pace and turn to Adam.

"We need to go quietly now, Adam. Let's get back into our room unseen and then we can talk about what to do next."

He did not respond. He had felt a curtain of darkness come down over him as they were closed out of the Scavenger circle, but it did not blind him from the obvious truth that they needed to re-enter their building without Sage Certainty or her Lawen-forcers realizing they had been gone.

Assuming that their absence had not already been discovered.

This time of night, it was easy for them to sneak in unnoticed. Quickly and silently, they entered their building and crept down the corridor and back to their sleeping room.

Belle paused at the door, and together they both took a deep breath. If they had been found out, someone would be in the room waiting, and the results could only be a Reckoning. Most probably in front of the entire building, and perhaps accompanied by the lives of those who had abetted their departure—their roommates.

Still, Belle went ahead and opened the door. Inside it was

quiet, with just the muffled sounds of a group at rest. Belle crossed over to her corner, Adam following.

He whispered, "Shall we wake them?" But it was already decided.

"So you are back," Ricky said from his place on the floor, and as he spoke, there was a rustling as the other roommates sat up to greet them.

"Yes we are," Adam replied. "We will tell you all about it in the morning. Did anyone find out that we were gone?"

"Don't you trust us, Adam?" Ricky enquired. "We are not hopeless without you...but we did miss you both." There was a flurry of similar comments from the other roommates welcoming them back and expressing happiness to see them.

The two little ones, Peter and Paula, toddled over and hugged Belle's legs.

Belle felt a warm surge of emotion. She had been fearful of the dangerous position Adam and she had put their roommates in ever since they had left days before. To hear that their absence had gone unnoticed by Sage Certainty, and to hear the pride in Ricky's voice as he declared both their self sufficiency and their happiness to see them reunited filled her with a powerful change that she had not anticipated.

To have the two little ones hugging her legs was something else. Suddenly her strength drained away, and she collapsed down to their level, hugging them, and bursting into quiet but powerful sobs that wracked her body and shook their tiny frames on either side of her.

Belle's motherly instincts woke within her, primal and deep, as she held their small bodies she felt the kicks within her for the first time. Telling her that the baby within her was as real as these two who were now in her arms.

"I love you all," she said

In moments, the room was filled with the muffled sounds of joyful weeping.

Nothing else was said that night. They were all too emotional, too relieved, and too tired. None of them had been able to get much sleep in the nights since Belle and Adam had left. In the absence of their own parents, and in a world in which the family unit had ceased to exist, the younger in the sleeping room had all become reliant on the older. Without it ever being expressly acknowledged, Belle and Adam were like parents to this little group of children, living together in Building 28.

Now they were back.

...

In the morning, they resumed their normal routine. Cathy and Ann went out to the croplands. Ricky and Will were on kitchen duty and had been up even earlier to prepare the morning food that day. Kate had been asked by the instructors to come and be examined for her ability with math.

So it was relatively quiet when Belle and Adam awoke. The twins were sleeping deeply side by side and as Belle looked down at them, she saw them for the first time, not as charges that she was caring for, but as her children. How had she failed to see it before? While not their natural mother, she was their mother all the same. How had she left them without a thought? So focused had she been on her own growing presence. As she watched their little chests rise and fall, she swore to herself that she would never abandon them again. Whatever happened, she would put them, and her unborn child above all, including herself.

Just then Kate came back into the room.

"What were the tests like?" Adam asked

"It was the strangest thing. There wasn't a test today. Instead Sage Certainty wanted to talk to me," replied Kate.

At the mention of the Sage, both Adam and Belle turned their attentions fully to Kate, who had now sat down on her own mattress.

"What did she want?" asked Belle.

"It was odd. When she first said she wanted to meet with me, I admit I was concerned."

"Did she ask about us," demanded Adam

"No, don't worry. She did not seem at all angry or anything, and in fact she never mentioned you or any of our group."

"She didn't really ask me anything at all," Kate went on.

"I don't understand – what did she want?" asked Belle.

"She sat me down next to her, and asked me to ask her questions."

"What about?" asked Adam

"She didn't say. She just asked me to talk to her," replied Kate

Belle's senses were fully alert by now. This was truly unusual and with everything else that was going on, the Sage's curiosity might not be a good thing for any of them.

"What did you ask her?" she demanded of Kate.

"I asked her about the Sages and what they do and why," came the response.

"Was that alright with her?"

"More than alright. I think she was really happy I was asking and she told me a lot that I didn't know. Things about how they were selected, and the meetings they have and how they have to look after their Flocks and stuff like that," Kate went on. Her eyes alight and her face full of her own interest.

"Are you sure we are safe?" asked Adam.

"Well you are not safe, and time is against you Adam," Kate said in a quiet voice.

"But I am sure she does not suspect anything yet."

...

Adam and Belle were meant to be recovering from their time in the fields and so it was unsurprising that they had not gone to the eating room and day rooms for a while. Many People chose to spend their rest days in their own rooms. Today they knew they should show themselves just to make sure no one missed them, and also because they were coming closer to the time when they would be placed back into the lottery for fieldwork and would be assigned building work for those days when they drew a blank in the lottery.

So around mid-morning, the two of them left their room and the twins in the care of Kate and went to the eating room.

The line was long enough to extend into the hallway when they arrived. Every sleeping room was assigned a mealtime, which was supposed to sequence their arrivals over a one-hour time-frame. But few adhered to the schedule, and their Sage turned a blind eye. So those who could tried to arrive early, their theory being that the early bird would catch the best worm. In practice, that was unlikely to be true. The biggest potatoes and other roots tended to drop to the bottom of the large cooking vats, so it was arguable that arriving later got you the largest portions—though you also risked an infrequent, but nonetheless real, risk that the food would be running low.

Belle and Adam arrived at the end of the first wave, when the line was probably as long as it would be today. It meant a slow shuffle down the hallway, into the eating room, and past the serving counters where today's stew, insect paste and hopefully some dried fish (what a treat) would be distributed.

It also meant a slow shuffle past the Lawenforcers in their regular positions at the door and at the beginning and end of the food counter.

In front of Belle was another Pure teenager who she knew well, and had grown up with. He was an odd boy. He was one of the few with jet-black hair and almond eyes. Michael was his name, and even though he was one of the oldest of the Pure, he had taken on the demeanor of the Failed. Belle found it hard to deal with Michael, but Adam seemed to have a better connection with him. Adam was intrigued by Michael's ability to make, polish and wield knives. While only the Sage and Lawenforcers possessed swords, Michael had crafted his own, long, curving and beautifully polished blade from a kitchen knife. It made him stand out from the other Pure most of whom went without any weapon at all.

These days Michael rarely spoke, keeping his head hung low and eyes on the ground. It was nearly impossible to engage him in conversation. They called him 'Strange Michael'—not that his persona was that different from most of the People in Building

12. But because it was remarkably strange for one of the Pure.

Today, Belle did not try to engage him.

The line moved forward, and before too long she and Adam were picking up their bowls and spoons and holding them out for the stew. After many years of working shifts in food preparation, Belle could smell that this was going to be a good meal. The building's head chef had clearly used some of their precious herbs and the smell of dried rosemary and thyme was easy to make out several paces away. The color was less special—dirty brown, as always.

Past the stew station with her bowl full, she put out her hand for a moist square of insect paste. Today Belle's square looked especially appetizing. However, her body, hungry for protein, cried to her, and unable to wait, she began to eat it, while still in line.

No fish today.

As she stepped past the end of the counter, munching and swallowing her insect square, she looked forward and found herself in direct eye contact with the Lawenforcer on duty.

He glanced down at Belle's mouth, and then her hand. A big smile broke out across the Lawenforcer's face as he took a step forward, saying, "Hey Adam, your friend Belle's looking porky—you been bringing back extra food from the fields for her, or just giving her some of yours?"

Belle swallowed hard, almost choking. Her face turned red and her hands trembled and she dropped both the remaining section of insect paste and her bowl of stew.

With a flash it came to her that she had made the most obvious of mistakes—she was too far gone in her pregnancy, and now it was showing. She was caught. Done. The Reckoning would start now. Her head would roll and her baby would never see the light of day.

Panic, exhaustion, despair all came now fast. How stupid she was.

Then she felt an arm around her shoulder and Adam was there beside her.

"Look what you've done now," he said to the Lawenforcer. "We have little enough food and you have made her drop hers just because you find it funny to tease her."

Belle felt the danger building. She needed a quick response to finish this now.

"You may be a man, but even you should know what time of month makes women swell," Belle managed to say.

She tensed expecting the worst, but the Lawenforcer takes it in stride and with a laugh throws back at her, "You may be right about that, but you're no woman yet—just a sweet little Pure girl, and don't you forget it."

Then Adam hurried Belle to a table, and put his food in front of her.

"Don't go anywhere, just breathe and keep your eyes on the food. Take it slow, relax, eat a little and I'll be back in no time," he whispered to her, and then he was gone.

She felt the panic and despair still threatening to overwhelm her, but Adam's words were there too. She repeated them to herself, and they carried her along.

"Eyes down, breathe deeply, eyes down, breathe deeply."

The mantra worked and she felt the panic leave, and her heart became less like an angry animal trying to tear its way out of her chest.

She took a small spoonful of stew.

Another drop in tension, and she had the fortitude to look up at the person sitting opposite her. It was Michael, staring straight back at her, his black eyes unwavering.

She gulped, but could not break the eye contact. He held her gaze.

"I see you, mother," he said.

Chapter 20

The Scavenger's Dream

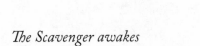

The Scavenger awakes
In a hole in the ground.

A deep hole.

He looks up, but he can't see much
Just the walls of the hole and the night sky far above
He thinks the moon must be up somewhere
But he can't see it.

Down here, in the hole, it is cold.

He has just woken up, and the ground is damp
Its cold dampness has leached through his clothing and
into his body.

He feels alone and it makes him sad.

He sits up and feels cold wet sand slip off the back of his head
A stream of sand that slowly pours down his spine
He brushes the rest of the sand off his head
It is too dark down here to see anything.

His eyes begin to adjust and he can make out his surroundings
He is sitting on a flat round disc of ground perhaps ten feet across
There is nothing on the sand apart from himself, and a long bundle beside him
The wall in front of him has a hole in it.

Narrow and tall
A black doorway through which musty air is blowing
He looks down at the bundle
He can see a narrow thread running from it towards the doorway.

He can't remember what is in the bundle, but he knows it is important
He reaches down and picks it up, carefully laying it across his thighs
It is maybe three or four feet long, and light
He begins to unroll the bundle.

*As he does so, he can feel that there is something long and
hard inside
He gets to the end of the length of cloth
The contents of the bundle drops onto his lap
It is a sword and scabbard.*

*The thin thread is tied to the pommel
He picks the sword up in both hands
Feeling its heft and balance.
Despite its length, it is light.*

*He stands up, carefully making sure not to let the tip
touch the ground
Standing there, on the sandy floor of this hole in the
ground, he feels alright
With this sword in his hands
He feels less alone.*

*The doorway is black and the air is blowing straight at
him
He knows he must enter this doorway
He needs to follow the thread
Then, all of a sudden, he unsheathes the sword.*

*It comes out smoothly and with a flash of light
Without hesitation
He moves into action
The sword whirls above his head.*

Around his shoulders, down one side and to the other
Twirling, arcing, thrusting and cutting
The air is rent by the sword
He warms with this work.

He does not stop until his skin is covered in tiny beads of
sweat
The damp is now driven out of his clothes in waves of
warm mist
Finishing, he stands motionless with the sword pointing
directly at the doorway
He walks in, gathering the thread as he moves forward.

The tunnel he enters is dark, air blows towards and past
him
His sword cuts the air to either side and he marches on
One hand carefully winding up an ever increasing ball
of thread
He doesn't know how long he walks.

He is aware of a growing sense
That something is ahead
That needs to be found
No, someone.

He is alone here with his sword
There is a chance he might shed this aloneness
If he can find the someone who is ahead
Nothing is as important.

More walking.

Then he is aware of a light
A slowly pulsating light
His sword gleams brightly
The light is in a place where the tunnel widens.

A room of some sort
Before he knows it he has arrived
In another round room
Just like the one he left.

The pulsating light is coming from an oval shape floating
about one foot off the ground
The thread extends from the base of this oval shape to the
ground below
The man slowly comes closer
Winding in the last few feet of thread.

He sees the oval is actually a big ball of thread, just like
the one he holds in his hand
A big ball of thread floating in this circular chamber
The light is coming from inside
He is right beside it.

His sword touches the edge of the ball and is lit by it
A shiny bright length of bright steel
Pulsing with the same rhythm
His feeling of aloneness is there, but a voice is in his head.

"This is the way out of your aloneness," it tells him. "This
is the answer."

He carefully pushes the edge of his weapon
Against the pulsing ball of thread
It yields, and he knows with a rush that this is not a ball
of thread
This is a cocoon.

Something bright and pulsing is inside
He gently, but firmly uses his sword to separate the
threads
The light brightens
His heart is beating furiously now.

He reaches the object hidden within
He brings his face closer to the source
Of no longer aloneness
His face is bright with reflected light.

He stares into the ball
A face looks back at him
His son's face
Michael's face.

Ties that bind.

Chapter 21

Council of Sages: The Choice

Sage Gratitude stands at the door of Building 8, and once again watches the other Sages approach. This time they come the straightest and quickest way from their buildings to his.

He had sent the messengers just a couple of hours ago and had stressed the urgency of their meeting this night. He did not give any explanation, and he expected none was necessary. They knew this was the time to make the choice he had outlined at their last council. Purposely, he had called it at short notice, hoping to catch them off guard. At least to the extent that was possible.

At the last meeting he had been brutally honest. He had said that they needed to cull the People and the Sages were coming expecting a vote on the two options he had outlined: decimation by productivity, or by random allotment.

Of course, those were not the only options possible. There were many other ways. They could let the Sages volunteer their picks, they could call on the People for volunteers, they could wipe out three buildings from top to bottom, and so on.

The real surprise tonight was that he was going to let them bring up and discuss other options. Their options.

He wanted the ultimate choice to be theirs entirely, to remove any risk that in the future the People would look back and assign the blame to him, as the Voice of this time. This was not a matter of democracy. It was a simple matter of self-preservation.

In the arena, the twenty-seven Sages now stand in their allotted positions around the circle. Sage Gratitude looks around and sits. The rest follow.

A momentary pause and then, as usual, he speaks the customary opening words. Then he says, "As we have discussed, our resources are not maintaining at the level needed to support our People. We have no choice but to cull our Flock."

Here Sage Gratitude pauses just long enough to create a sense of gravity. Then he continues, "Some among you have come to me and asked that we consider all of our options. These Sages think there are more ways to reduce our numbers than I outlined at our last meeting."

This is not strictly true. But it serves his purpose to seed the thought that some others have initiated this change of plan. Let them think this has come from among their own number.

"So today, let us pass around our circle, and each Sage who wishes can suggest the approach they favor for carrying out this terrible, but necessary passage in our history. This is not yet a vote. Let us first simply hear from the Council and see what options present themselves."

Another pause, and then he adds, "We are the leaders of our Flocks, and their care is our task," knowing that this touch of ritual will position him well in their minds when eventually they think back to tonight and what has transpired at this Council.

Sage Gratitude looks to his left and nods at Sage Blessing from Building 9.

"I favor culling the oldest and weakest," she says. "I know it is a difficult decision, but I believe that for many this will be a gift."

Sage Gratitude has to catch himself—he almost thought she was going to call it a blessing. He glances one seat to the left, and nods at Sage Harmony of Building 10. She too suggests culling the least productive. However, she wants to explain her thinking. Always the one for creating consensus, she reminds them of the ways in which the Failed are beginning to age and, in many cases, fall into depression. She brings into her monologue the reality of the rising rate of self-Reckoning. Sage Harmony's style is inclusive as she looks around the circle engaging each Sage by eye contact, and delivering her words carefully and calmly. This creates a nodding of heads, and contributions from other Sages who want to share their own experience and thoughts. Eventually, Sage Gratitude brings the discussion to a close. He appreciates the work Sage Harmony has just undertaken. At least the worst of this meeting is behind them. No one now will resist the need, and only the how remains unresolved.

He thanks Sage Harmony and nods to the chair to her left.

Sage Truth of Building 11 suggests a random culling. This is the only way, he says. Randomness means fairness, and fairness is the only true path. He means well but his dogmatic approach always creates resistance and Sage Gratitude can sense it building as he thanks Sage Truth for his contribution.

Which brings him to Sage Certainty.

There is something special about Sage Certainty of Building 12. Had he not been quite so blessed by the size and purpose of his own building, Sage Gratitude expects that this Sage would have become the Voice. She has a clarity and purity of purpose, a discipline and consistency of operation that is praiseworthy. Other Sages take note of her views, knowing that she will only ever suggest things that she has carefully considered and which she can be relied upon to implement. When Sage Certainty offers a solution, it is clear she has carefully measured its feasibility and that she will stand behind its implementation.

Sage Certainty has never overpromised and underdelivered. When she makes a commitment, you know that it will be carried through.

In a strong, measured, and calm voice Sage Certainty begins, "Sage Gratitude, I have considered the two options that we heard at our last Council, and I believe there is another way."

As she says this, a palpable collective intake of breath can be heard around the circle. Most Sages must have thought that only the two options would be raised. Sage Certainty is making clear that she believes Sage Gratitude is being authentic in asking for another way.

"I believe we can ask for sacrifice—ask for martyrs," she continues. "I believe we should engage our Flocks, let them know our circumstance, explain that a 10% cull is needed, and then ask for volunteers. I say this because I know that more than 10% of our People are ready to pass. Let them do so in grace.

Let them do so in a way that provides benefit to our Flock and makes them each worthy in the eyes of all. I have no doubt that 10% will step forward."

This is what Sage Gratitude wants. Viable alternatives raised by other Sages. This will ensure the decision when it comes is clearly not of his making.

"Thank you, Sage Certainty for your important and well considered contribution," Sage Gratitude says looking directly at her, sitting so poised that he can imagine her springing into action and beginning this terrible task as soon as the vote is over. She really is impressive and it takes him a moment to pull his gaze away.

He does so, and looks around the circle. "Sage Certainty has shown us all the importance and gravity of this decision and has come with a well thought out alternative that we should consider carefully. Perhaps this is the best option, but let us see."

Sage Gratitude nods and then looks one more seat to Sage Certainty's left. Building 13.

So the process continues. Each Sage puts forward their preferred approach. Most choose from the two options outlined in the last Council, some prefer Sage Certainty's more inclusive option.

Nothing dramatic until the process reaches Building 28. Sage Caring.

Sage Gratitude knows that Sage Caring is a little different from the others, but his suggested option is more radical than anything Sage Gratitude would have predicted.

"I think we need to go further than this 10% that we have heard Sage Gratitude propose. We know that our resource issues may not end here, and this is not something we want to do more than once. Let us grasp this nettle firmly. Let us do this once only, and let us do it right," Sage Caring declares.

Sage Caring waits as the circle fully absorbs this first point.

Finally, several Sages cry out, "What do you mean?" and "Explain yourself," and "What do you propose?"

With a smile, Sage Caring goes on.

"Hear me now. This is my proposal. We do all three of the options we have heard. We do them all right now. We ask for volunteers as Sage Certainty has proposed. Then once those step forward, we also cull the old and incapable. Then, we also randomly cull the Flock until we have reduced the People by a quarter. Only the Pure and our Lawenforcers will be left out of the cull."

Sage Gratitude is shocked. This is quite a dramatic option. Much more than he was planning. There is a certain logic to the Sage's words though. They don't know how bad things might become, and it is true they don't want to do this more than once. Yes, the Pure should be left out—they are so productive, so young that their value is becoming greater every day. Even the eight-and nine-year-olds can be relied upon to do better work than most of the older Failed. The Lawenforcers are a different question—they are themselves aging, but Sage Gratitude can see the reason for exempting them from the cull. Of course, no mention of the Sages themselves, but Sage Gratitude knows how Sage Caring would respond on that topic if asked.

For a moment, Sage Gratitude's mind wanders into less positive terrain. Three quarters of the People, all the Sages, all the Lawenforcers, all the Pure. Surely a much healthier Flock. Much more for everyone who remains. He stops himself. This is not about what they will gain, but only about how to avoid Harm. However, he has to acknowledge that perhaps this is worthy of consideration?

"Sage Caring, we acknowledge the boldness of your proposal, and the point that our resources may fall more is something we must consider. Have you thought about the 25% and why you think this is the right number at this time?"

Of course Sage Caring has, and Sage Gratitude knows that. Let him have his moment. Let the Council remember his name if, and when, one day they look back and wish to apportion blame.

"Yes, Sage Gratitude, I have considered this carefully. Let me share my reasoning."

So he does. In great detail. By the end, he has laid out a case that has a certain brutal logic to it.

The other Sages are not only taken by surprise by Sage Caring's case. Many are shocked to their cores. The circle erupts in voices. Sage Gratitude lets them continue in disarray for a while, before clapping his hands for silence.

He waits until he has all eyes turned his way, and all voices silent. Then he turns to the next Sage.

"Let us continue. What is your view?" he says, maintaining his posture and tone as if Sage Caring's proposal is no different from those that have gone before. Thoughtful, open, balanced, and mindful is the impression he wants to leave.

The process continues, but now it is quicker and little new is added. Sage Gratitude can tell that the remaining handful of Sages to speak are confused. Most express no proposal at all, some side with the selective culling. None adopt Sage Caring's approach as their own.

Now the Sage to his right finishes and all but Sage Gratitude himself have spoken.

"We have heard from all the Sages. Thank you. For myself, I will defer from commenting about my own views. I do not want to influence your personal opinion or encourage you to vote one way or another. Let us first reflect on the options we have heard in silence. Then we will vote."

That should nail it, Sage Gratitude thinks to himself. Now no one can say he proposed any option or even influenced the final outcome.

He stands and waits until the others are standing too. Then he turns his back on the Council and walks, apparently in deep thought, away into the darkness of the arena.

...

In his listening station below the arena, the Engineer has been attentive to everything that has passed between the Sages as the discussion has moved around the circle.

This Engineer is good at the numbers—as all Engineers must be.

After the last Council of Sages, he had run the numbers backwards, forwards, sideways, every way and had already come to the same conclusion as Sage Caring.

A 10% cull would not be enough. The resources would not slow their demise anytime soon and indeed the catastrophic failure of the carp indicated that other sudden failures might be on the horizon too.

The Engineer's number crunching had more scenarios in

which carrying capacity plummeted all the way to zero, than scenarios in which a meaningful population would be maintained.

It did not make it any easier to accept, but the Engineer can see the logic of Sage Caring's proposal. His own analysis indicates that further culls will still be needed to ride down the curve of reducing carrying capacity. Until no one will be left standing.

Unless there is some other solution to the mathematical equations he has run and run again.

He didn't see one yet. Which was really something to think about.

Not right now, however.

He can hear the footsteps of the Sages above him as they converge back towards the circle.

...

In the arena, the Sages are settling into their seats. Their faces are grim. A few are close to tears. They are, for the most part, true to their mission of caring for their Flock. Yet this does not feel like caring at all.

Sage Gratitude goes straight to business. "Based upon our discussion, we have four options to vote for:

1. Cull 10% from the old and unproductive

2. Cull 10% randomly from our Flock

3. Ask for volunteers from across our Flock as Sage Certainty proposes

4. Combine all methods above to cull 25% as Sage Caring has suggested

We will now vote."

The Sage of Building 17 gets the big urn while two others bring the big bowl full of twenty-seven paper slips and the table. They place all the items in the center of the circle—the urn in the center of the tabletop and the bowl on the floor in front of it.

Sage Gratitude waits until the three sit back down, and then he nods to the Sage to his left, who walks to the center of the circle and takes a slip. She writes a number on it, folds it and drops it into the urn.

So it goes, Sage after Sage casting their votes.

Once all the other Sages have voted, Sage Gratitude stands and says to the group, "I will not vote, but now I will tally your votes."

He goes to the table and opens the slips one after another.

Finally, once all of the slips are counted, he stares for a while.

It is a shock. Not at all what he had expected. But it is an overwhelming result.

He walks back to his place.

"You have voted. The Council has spoken. I am the Council's Voice and my only role is to speak on your behalves."

He pauses, but not this time for effect. Rather, he hesitates because of the enormity of what he must share.

His voice cracks as he says, "The Council has voted for the 25% cull as proposed by Sage Caring."

As he walks to the door to close the Council, the more attentive Sages can see that tears are shining brightly on his black cheeks.

This is not the Sage Gratitude they have come to know.

...

Sage Caring has returned to his building and has made sure all is in order. Just for good measure he has been particularly stern with those his Lawenforcers have at the bottom of their lists—those who have not been sufficiently attentive to his needs.

For this purpose he keeps a stout cane and he knows how to wield it just right. Hard to make them regret greatly that they did not drop off anything at the barrel this week. Just lightly enough that he will not give them good reasons to claim an inability to work for the rest of the week—for work they will. At times like this, he makes sure that the whole building understands the consequences of insufficient attention to the needs of their Sage.

First the ritual humiliation in front of the several hundred members of his Flock. Sage Caring calling out three names of those who are judged to have done the least.

Second, the caning. Each of the three brought to him in turn by a pair of Lawenforcers. Bent over so that Sage Caring can apply his cane optimally.

Finally, the announcement that these three will work in the croplands each night for the remainder of the week. This the toughest punishment since a single night's work is normal in the lottery rotation.

Finished, Sage Caring has returned to his room to contemplate the results of the Council. He feels that they have come to the best answer—his answer. Taking a bigger cull of the Flock will ensure that there is more for everyone and of course that reduces any risk of him not getting his full share. Not that there was any likelihood of a personal shortfall, but he likes his abundance to go unnoticed, and a smaller Flock should make that easier to accomplish.

As he sits and ponders, he feels the need to speak to someone else. To share his thoughts. As usual he knows the answer.

He pulls on his outdoor boots—because where he will now go is a place of dirt and damp—and leaves his room. On the way he picks up a fish oil lantern. He will need that too.

...

Sage Caring comes here so often. He can't explain why. But sometimes his feet bring him this way, and when they do, it is always for the better.

By the light of his lantern, he can see her. Long blonde hair turned dirty black. Skin caked with grime. Nails grown long, broken and cracked.

Only her eyes, while wild and erratic, are still beautiful as they mirror the light of his fish oil lamp. She is quiet now. Lying on her side in the dirt. He thinks that perhaps she is not even aware of his presence.

He begins.

First he tells her what he has been doing. He recounts his practice. Tells her of his devotions. Of his sword play most of all. Then he goes on to talk of his Flock. The good and the bad of it. He hides nothing.

He tells her of his recent actions. Of bad things he has done to innocent members of his Flock. Of bad things he has done to bad members who have broken his laws. Of recent Reckonings and of those who have stayed and those few who have run.

He tells her of his feelings too. His shame. His guilt. She seems to absorb it from him and he lightens as she accepts his grim litany.

She has heard his confession a hundred times before. Does she even hear it? He can't tell, but it does him good to share these truths.

Then he moves on to the future.

He tells her of the burden that the Sages are carrying. The reduced carrying capacity and the need to make the equation work. The decision to cull the Flock. Of his own belief that they need to cut deeply now.

The plan.

She doesn't respond. She never does. Her eyes are intently focused on him. She appears to be absorbed by his monologue.

Perhaps she is.

He rather hopes she is not. Just let him get it out and then let him leave unburdened. He does not want any reaction. He just wants the catharsis.

Then it is over. He has said it all, and has nothing more to tell.

He gets up, turns away from her, and leaves the basement.

Sage Caring goes back to his Flock.

And to the sharpening and polishing of his sword.

It will soon see much work.

Chapter 22

Michael's Wakening

"I see you, Mother," Michael says.

His dark almost black almond eyes stare at her from under the ragged fringe of his jet-black hair.

Belle feels her stomach enter her mouth. Her heart begins to explode again. Her bowels about to empty too.

She begins to stand, is about to run. Escape now is the only thought in her rapidly whirring mind.

Go.

Michael is quicker still. He reaches across the table, grasps her shoulders, and pushes down.

But it is his words that make her sit again.

"You have nothing to fear from me."

She sits and crumples. Just as she does so, another sits down beside her—Adam.

"What's going on?" he asks worriedly, looking across at Michael and then back to Belle.

She does not respond, but Michael answers for her. "Belle has made a mistake. I let her know that I see it. Soon everyone else will too. Let's talk about that shall we?"

Adam's jaw drops.

"I assume you already had a part in this?" Michael asks Adam with a smile on his face.

Belle and Adam sit absolutely still. The enormity of Michael's observations now hit home with force. Someone else has seen the truth that they have created together. The Revealing cannot be more than a moment away.

They are frozen. Rooted in their seats.

"Come to my room, now," Michael tells them, and they do—following him and his leadership as it fills the void that has just opened up and swallowed both of them.

...

Michael's room is on the second floor, and as they climb the stairs it feels to Belle as if they are climbing up to a terrible fate. Unbeknown to her, the feeling she is experiencing is that felt by a host of those who have climbed the steps up to the hangman's stage or the executioner's chopping block.

The slow climb to a quick end.

Michael hurries them along. "Come on, keep moving," he tells them. This is not the Michael they know. The quiet, withdrawn Michael.

This is something else. Michael with purpose. Michael taking the initiative.

Michael the Strange has become Michael the Mover.

Once inside his room, the good news is that they are alone—just the three of them. His roommates are still eating their meal, or on duty elsewhere.

Michael's roommates are very different from those that Belle and Adam have chosen. Michael lives with a room full of Failed. Mostly female, but a few men too. Among the oldest of the People. Michael's mother and father had been the first to choose this space as their own, and he had been born into it almost straight after the Failing. They had lived here together as a family of three for most of his formative years supplemented by a stream of Failed who had come and gone. Michael's family the only constant.

Then some years ago, first his father, and then his mother, had succumbed to mutations. Michael's father had run to the Far Side first. His mother the same a few months later.

Michael remembers those terrible days when he had been held in tight arms by parents in tears as they told him of their love and of their upcoming abandonment. He had begged them to take him, but they were resolute that his better future was in Building 12 under the leadership of Sage Certainty.

They had not listened to his pleas, his begging, his sobbing. Just the understandable unhappiness of a young Pure whose parents had met their end. A not infrequent occurrence. Mutations came often and those that were left behind after the inevitable Revealing and its consequences always went through a period of mourning. Michael was just another such, left behind by runners.

That was when he had turned inwards, and became 'Strange Michael'.

It has not been without its benefits.

Perhaps more than most of the Pure, Michael has been fully

accepted by the Failed in his room, and in this building. His persona makes them feel that he is one of them. His pessimism, his lack of initiative, his down at heel demeanor, and his constant slow shuffle.

He is one of them, and they have let him in completely.

He knows their attitudes, their beliefs, their moods. Along the way, over the years, he has also learned their histories, their legends, and has absorbed a good part of their knowledge. Even though it does not all make sense to him. He nonetheless has heard it so many times.

The good old days.

How things worked before. What it was like to live back then. What the Intelligences had been able to make happen. Which of their helpers, their tools, their equipment, had been best at this or that task that the Failed were now required to do themselves.

The days leading up to the Failing were their favorite stories to tell. So they have each shared their experiences in the months and weeks before the launch day.

Michael has listened and absorbed everything. Hungry for something to replace the emptiness he felt as an abandoned child. Hungry to learn about the world before and beyond.

Especially the world beyond. The Far Side.

Because, beneath his negativism and passiveness, Michael believes that somewhere out there his parents still make a life together.

That they are Scavengers together.

For Michael there is no other option. He can't imagine the scenario in which the Lawenforcers catch up with them out in the croplands. He knows but does not want to think about how that story would have finished beneath their swords. It happens so often when the runners don't run fast enough.

If Michael ever dreams a colorful, happy story, it is always the same.

One day they will come back to reclaim him.

To give him a second chance.

Reunited.

...

"Sit down."

Michael points at two places and Belle and Adam sit. He does so too just across from them. His first question stuns Belle because it is so unlike the Michael she knows, and because it is so to the point and so direct.

"What does it feel like to be expecting a child?" Michael asks. "What do you feel?"

Belle pauses, looks into his eyes and sees the honest curiosity staring back at her. His questions allow her to speak for the first time with someone other than Adam. She has unconsciously been waiting for this moment. A cathartic release has been needed for a while, and once Michael provides her with the opportunity, it comes flowing out. The words coming with a rush.

"Before I didn't understand. Now all I understand, and all that fills my mind, is that I am carrying a life and that I must protect it. I feel so fragile and yet so strong at the same time. Fragile, as my body gives me challenges I have never experienced before. Strong in my mind as I become more and more resolute about how I will protect and defend my child against anything that might threaten to Harm it."

Adam puts his arm around her shoulders and squeezes her hand in his but says nothing. Michael just watches.

"Emotionally, it is not like anything I have experienced before," she goes on. "I thought I had loved before, cared before, felt emotion before. Looking after the twins these last two years I felt new emotions for them, as a mother should."

Here Adam turns to her and is about to say something, but she is quicker. "And I always feel deep love for Adam too," she says. "None of this compares to what I am feeling now. This is different."

"How different?" Michael asks.

Belle pauses. She did not mean to say so much. She has not put any of this into words before. She wonders if she can. Then goes on.

"It is like a melding together of my body and my emotions. Perhaps it is something deep that is being released as the baby grows. I am not sure, but it is very primal and fundamental. My whole being is here for one purpose right now, and nothing can threaten that purpose."

These last few words she speaks quietly but with an intensity that is almost frightening.

Adam gasps, and she turns to him. Without realizing it, she has dug her fingernails deep into the palm of his hand, and now he takes it back, the red welts dug into the skin beginning to bleed.

"I'm sorry Adam," she says but already he has put his arm around her again, while sucking the bleeding palm of his hand in his mouth.

She looks at him and sees a little boy, and also a strong and protective man. Her man.

She turns to Michael. "I don't know if this makes any sense to you?"

Michael pauses, then says, "I don't understand it. I don't understand how they could have left me, if they felt even a little as you do now."

He says it with such sorrow, such pain, that Belle understands immediately why he has asked his questions.

He is the abandoned boy, left behind when first his father, and then his mother ran. He is asking because he wants to understand what might have made them go.

Belle knows exactly what to say. "Michael, I would leave my baby if it made my baby safer. If I was the threat to my child, I know I would sacrifice myself."

She pauses. "If I had a mutation, I would run if it made my baby safe."

Michael is instantly focused, "What did you say?"

Belle pauses, then repeats her words.

Michael's demeanor changes instantly. Belle can't see inside of him. She doesn't know what he is thinking. But on the outside the change comes quickly and she can see a metamorphosis occur before her.

The down and broken boy is cast off, and Michael straightens and seems to shine with an inner light. His face looses its frowns and creases. Relaxed now for the first time in years.

"I see now," he says out loud but to no one in particular. "I was so loved that they left me in safer hands rather than risking me in theirs." He falls silent in thought.

The three of them sit for a little while longer, and Belle is not sure she should interrupt Michael's deep thoughts.

Then, anyway, she says one more thing.

"I just know I am already a mother and that I would die to protect my baby. I will never let them take it, and that is why I made Adam take me to the Far Side."

As she says it, Michael snaps out of his introspection.

"You were in the Far Side?" he says.

"Tell me everything."

...

Later, as Adam sleeps, Belle gets up and quietly goes to the bathroom. She closes the door and makes sure the lock is secured so that no one else can surprise her. Once the Intelligences would have made this a wonderful place full of light, steam, calming sounds, and personally calibrated experiences.

Belle has no knowledge of that, and all she had ever known is a bare room, with a long mirrored wall, basins that the Failed have placed for water, and other basins that they use for their waste. Other containers hold sand with which they clean their bodies when the communal showers are off as they are more often than not. For water is precious and reserved for only a few uses—rationed by honor, but used sparingly all the same.

Belle moves directly to the mirror. She has work to do.

She quickly sheds her layers of clothing, dropping everything to the floor. In a moment, she is bare.

Eighteen years old, scared and worried, and for the first time, looking carefully at herself and the changes that have been taking place.

She is not exactly sure of her date of conception. She and Adam had fooled around more than once, after the first time. It had been an intense few weeks as they explored each other and how to make their bodies work together. Her best bet was that they had started about six months ago and maybe that was when it had happened. Certainly four months ago she knew her body was moving into a new phase of life. So six months or five.

She looks critically at herself in the mirror. Like an outside observer would. Ignoring her freshness and beauty that would be the image that most would see first. Her blonde hair and her blue eyes first and foremost. Instead she goes straight into a physical examination of shapes and sizes.

Her face is bloated and blotchy, but not significantly changed. She has noticed that her gums are swollen and have been bleeding a little, but she has no reason to think that this is connected to the changes lower down. Most People's teeth have issues in this world of insufficient vitamins and minerals. Belle's mouth, while better than most, is not perfect by any means. So ignore the gums.

Her shoulders the same as ever. Her arms too.

She moves down to her feet next. Keep the good news coming as long as possible, her unconscious mind tells her.

Feet the same, though a little swollen. Legs still long and graceful as ever.

Now the hard part. The changes.

Her hips are broader, she is sure, but it is her abdomen that she now scrutinizes—turning sideways so that the full effect hits her squarely.

Unavoidable.

Her tummy is huge to her mind. Her formerly flat stomach now almost half a head width larger than before. A semicircle of additional girth centered on her navel and from the side so obvious.

She turns back to face the mirror head on, and sees the good news. From the front - and back could she see it - her profile is almost unchanged.

While her whole body feels enormously bloated and extended to her mind, she sees the truth in the mirror and begins to feel a little calmer. Not as big as she had imagined.

She turns sideways again.

Still focused on her abdomen, she tries to make it smaller. Breathes in, but it changes little. Squeezing her diaphragm even more, but no material change.

Then she sees if bending forward makes a difference. It does seem to. The ball of her tummy looks less obvious as her upper body hunches over a little.

As she bends forward she sees in the mirror, for the first time, two large breasts come into view. She has known their tenderness and swelling, but this is the first time she has seen them reflected back to her.

She gasps as she focuses on them.

So intent has she been on her belly and the baby inside, that she had missed the obvious signal. Her breasts have suddenly become large and pendulous.

She touches them with one hand, and then holds them in both. They feel full and the nipples are tender.

This happened fast. Unnoticed a week ago, but in their time going back and forth to the Far Side, this change has taken place.

She holds a breast in each hand and squeezes a little.

Looking down she sees a sight that first scares her, and then with a rush, excites her.

Small drops of yellowish liquid have appeared from each nipple and more is coming. She stops squeezing, and watches closely.

"Baby food," she thinks, and with that thought her excitement increases.

She, Belle, is getting ready to feed her baby. A joyous emotion overtakes her and she quietly begins to weep.

A soon to be mother, learning what motherhood will mean for her.

In a terrible place, experiencing a moment of wonder and joy.

...

A few minutes later the practical and sensible Belle has taken over again. She needs to figure out a better way to cover her secret. At least until they decide what to do next.

She had thought Michael must have noticed her bulging stomach, but now she is not so sure. These new breasts would have shown themselves to anyone who cared to look their way. Altogether easier to see than her stomach, which would have been covered by her baggy clothing as always. In fact, now that she thinks about it, the top buttons of her shirt had been open and maybe he had seen more than just her breasts. For a moment she wonders if her special liquid might have wetted her front, but no way of knowing now. In the morning she will ask Adam and maybe Michael too.

So what to do? The easiest ruse would be to wear her big outdoor coat all the time. However, wearing outdoor work clothes indoors all the time would eventually draw attention to itself. That is not the right answer.

Instead, Belle now tears an old sheet she had brought into the bathroom with her into narrow strips and begins to wrap them firmly around her chest. Breathing in to make herself as small as she can, and then using the material to bind her breasts.

Thankfully this works. Her large and full breasts disappear as she wraps herself. She feels that perhaps more liquid has been squeezed out, but she can't tell for sure. Under several layers, she hopes any wetness will not reach the surface.

Maybe this will work on her tummy too.

She tears more strips. Already this sheet is almost used up— and sheets are precious. If this strategy works, she will need to find another to steal and convert into a coverall.

She holds the end of a strip of cloth on her belly with one hand as she wraps the rest around. It is going to be harder to cover her belly than her chest. She will need some way to attach the ends of the sheet so they do not come loose. But for now she completes one circuit of her abdomen, and prepares herself for another.

She breathes in, trying to suck the belly back to her spine as best she can. As she does so she says, "Sorry baby, I hope this doesn't stop you moving and kicking, but I have to keep you safe. Please forgive me for squeezing you so."

She laughs as she feels the baby kick her back in acknowledgement.

It's going to be alright then.

For a little while.

...

In his room, Michael is going over everything he has learned that day from Belle and Adam.

Some he already knew, but much is new to him. Including some very important details that now fill his mind to capacity.

That Scavengers live beyond the fields is well known—although this is the first time Michael has had the direct confirmation of this from Pure he has grown up with and who he trusts.

This same story has been told to him by older Failed, and so much of what they say he finds hard to believe, confusing in its setting of a world now long gone, or unworthy of his acceptance. Mostly the latter. The Failed are so negative, so pessimistic, so ready to see the dark side of every matter, that Michael tends to devalue what they tell him. Ironic given his own tendency to see the dark side of things.

That the Scavengers on the Far Side are not all dying immediately, but some among them are living long after they run, is truly news. Indeed, there was a broadly held view that a mutation was itself a death sentence with the final moment weeks or months away at best. Hearing Belle and Adam share that some of the circle members have been there for years is a shock—a shock that he wants to view positively, but for now dares not do so. He has long hoped that his dreams of his parents might be true. Perhaps.

The final, and most important piece of information he has not yet directly addressed.

He has looked at it out of the corner of his eye, approached it cautiously, but has chosen not to look directly at it to this point.

For years now, Michael has sought out every morsel of information about those runners that have gone before. He has interrogated every Failed who knew his father and mother. Has soaked up everything they can tell him. About their heights, and weights, and coloration. About their looks and distinctive mannerisms. About their preferences and those things they avoided. Details to confirm his hazy ten year old memories.

It is one of the things that had branded him as odd. This constant dwelling on the past and his parents who are long gone.

Now, as he slowly approaches the new information that Belle and Adam have shared, there is one part of it that is very hard to look at directly.

He wants to, but fears the disappointment that is so likely to be the result. He doesn't think he can take the pain of looking closely and finding that this slimmest of hopes leads nowhere.

But his unconscious self will not be denied.

He looks.

It seems so clear.

Adam says the leader was a master Sworder with almond eyes.

Michael's father was the Sworder who first brought this gift to the Failed. Who showed them how to turn their despair into practice, and their lack of motivation into a constant search to better themselves in this one regard. More importantly, Michael and this James share the black hair and almond eyes of their race.

Michael slips into sleep, his conscious mind refusing to accept this thin thread of solace.

However, all night long his sleeping mind celebrates.

At last a chance.

Chapter 23

Council of Sages: The Plan

The Sages are back in Building 8, but this time they are hard at work, and the arena is noisy and informal.

Each has been asked to come today with a census of their People. Something they have done many times before, since tending the Flock is their principal charge. They have lists of every building member, with personal details, working history, strengths and weaknesses.

All scratched down onto the hard found paper and cardboard scavenged from the buildings. Using precious pencils if they still can be found but more usually making marks with charcoal sticks—precious too in this world where most wood has long been burned or turned into tools. Had they only known how to, they could probably have done better by mixing the Field soil and making their own clay tablets—without bees, wax tablets were not an option.

Only Building 8 has a better way. The large coaching boards have been brought up to the arena floor. Sage Gratitude does not share out his writing materials, but he has an invaluable stock of color markers that can still draw color if wetted. Better yet, he also has white chalk that looks beautiful on a black background. Much more impressive than the other Sage's scratchings on their miscellany of recording surfaces.

This time, each Sage has been tasked with a new addition to the report.

"For each of your Flock you have age, sex, working status, and health status. Now you will add their mental disposition," Sage Gratitude has begun. "We need to assess how many we believe will volunteer themselves, and then we will need to put those that we might need to cull into groupings."

This has generated a lot of discussion and some confusion. What are the groupings? How to define them?

Sage Gratitude suspects that there are deeper strategies at play now. Some Sages trying to move the definitions in ways that may benefit their Flocks, Allowing them to reduce the number they put into the cull columns. The discussion is long and complex and is becoming heated when he decides to close it down.

"I expect each of you to divide your Flocks into deciles with those you can't imagine doing without at the top, and those you know are at the end of their productiveness at the bottom," he says.

At first it had seemed a simple task. But as each Sage got to work, it had become harder and harder. How do you assess the mental disposition of your Flock? On what dimensions? What predicts who will step forward and martyr themselves for the good of others?

Most Sages have come to a common realization. That those

most likely to volunteer themselves may not be those who are least valuable to the Flock. The correlation with health is one thing. Yes, it seems that the very least healthy may be expected to wish to end it all. But too often Sages are discovering that they find that those who they predict will seek to pass, are also those with invaluable work skills. They are the oldest, but also in many cases the most skilled too.

So lists have been drawn up and redrawn. Deciles calculated and recalculated.

Too much precious paper and charcoal have been used up, and still most Sages are not sure they have this done right. But time is running out and they need to be ready to report in just a few minutes.

So this is why the Arena is full of noise. Sages comparing notes, asking questions of each other, hoping to find an easier and better way to do Sage Gratitude's homework.

Only there are no better ways.

Finally, Sage Gratitude declares this meeting open. It is not to be a formal Council so he does not use the ritual sayings. Just tells them, "Let's get started," in his most authoritarian voice.

They begin as usual to his left, and Sage Blessing of Building 9 does a good job detailing her work. For her, the first decile was not too hard to find. She knew enough of those in deep despair to be able to predict more than ninety who she thinks will step forward when asked. Almost all are the oldest of the Failed. Some exceptions that she briefly recounts, but no need to name the ninety. They are there, and she is quick to move through this decile.

She does, however, for the first time raise the issue of skill loss, and here there is a flurry of agreement around the circle.

They need to be concerned that some knowledge and skills will not be transferred if they allow the holders to all pass. How will they ensure knowledge transfer? Sage Gratitude can see that this will be a common theme, but he has predicted this already.

"Thank you Sage Blessing, I hear your concern about the loss of our most skilled. Let's continue and we can revisit this at the end of the reporting."

The second decile is mixed for Sage Blessing, in that she can't find another ninety likely volunteers. She expects that by decile two she will be into a cull. She has kept things simple and crafted her second decile by infirmity, which broadly correlates to age but not completely.

By decile three, Sage Blessing is in distress. Now the names in front of her are productive, valuable members of her Flock. She turns to Sage Gratitude as if to ask for his permission to stop, but he is resolute.

"Sage Blessing, we understand your dismay. I myself felt it at the Council, and it is why I did not vote at all. I was amazed at the boldness of Sage Caring's plan, and the courage of each of you who voted for it. But I knew that in its detail we would find this terrible reality."

"If you ask me together to revisit this vote after we have done today's work, I will consider your requests. However, now you must do as you were asked. Share your deciles. You must get to 25% as agreed in our vote."

So Sage Blessing continues, though now her eyes are dim with tears and her voice has become cracked and waivers. Her deciles reported, she slumps back.

Sage Harmony is next.

It takes a long time. Overall, most Sages conclude that volunteers will be few, the cull will have to start soon, and skills will be lost in almost every building.

By the time the Sage's reports reach the other side of the circle, Sage Gratitude has assumed there will be nothing new to learn from this process.

But he is wrong.

Sage Caring reports the possibility of fully two deciles of volunteers while those before have never got beyond one. Sage Gratitude wonders how Sage Caring can so easily declare this in his report—surely he understands that every other Sage will see the clear implication.

His building is an unhappy one.

Sage Caring seems unaware or uncaring. He simply reports it as a fact. "I expect two deciles of volunteers before we need to cull," he states.

Then he diverges from the approach of all the Sages who have gone before. They have all taken the first cull by focusing on infirmity of the old. Sage Caring has quite a different approach.

"My cull is clear in my mind, but I think it is a better way than the work reported to date. So let me explain my logic so that you can all perhaps find it easier to create your deciles," he says.

"When we stood forward and took up our responsibilities, we knew a time like this might come. We knew we needed to protect our Flocks, but that we also needed to make the hard decisions. The decisions that must be made. We carry our swords because we know that we have to be the Reckoners. We recognize our obligations and we never shirk from fulfilling them."

Sage Gratitude nods. He still can't quite see Sage Caring's plan, but this is a good way to engage the Sages and bring them into alignment. Reminding them of their obligations and everyday reality of their positions. All the Sages around the circle are masters with their swords, and all of them take heads as a duty. Connect this cull to that sacred duty and perhaps it will still their fear of the unknown, attaching it instead to something they have come to accept and even to excel at.

"We know the signs of the Mutation. We are familiar with the ceremony that accompanies the Revealing. We know that it is always followed by the choice. The Flock knows its choices, and whether they stay or go, all know that it is their choice mindfully taken," Sage Caring continues.

"So far, we have awaited the Revealing. Waited until our Lawenforcers have called upon us. But we know the truth. Many members of our Flock have little Mutations that they hide from us long before they become the subject of a Revealing."

Here he pauses. Let it sink in. Looking around the circle, there are more heads nodding now.

"I suggest we make our first cull based upon an acceleration of Revealings. Let us each go to our Flocks and ask them to come to us unveiled in their natural form. Let their own bodies determine the cull and let the cull be according to our ceremonies." As he says this, his voice has become quieter but also more formal. More like Sage Gratitude, perhaps.

"This is the way that we have learned—let us not depart from it now," Sage Caring says as his voice rises to declare, "Let us stand and say it together, the sacred words that we all have used so many times before."

He begins, but within a syllable they are with him in one voice:
"We are the People, I am the Sage.

I protect each one, I protect the whole.

You have brought me to this Reckoning

I did not ask for it, I do not want it.

But I see this Mutation. I incur the Law.

Your choice is yours alone.

Go or stay

What is your choice?"

The Sage's plan is made. Only the details take their Council late into the night.

By then Sage Gratitude has stepped back into his traditional role as Voice. Happy that the hardest part of the meeting was delivered by another. A little concerned that he, for a moment, let another lead. But the end seems to justify the means.

They have a plan.

...

Under the arena, the Engineer is overwhelmed with emotion.

Volunteers taken first then a mass Revealing and a Cull by way of a Choice for all those showing even the smallest Mutation. Reckoning of all those who chose to Stay.

He can't have heard that correctly. Surely the Sages did not agree to this.

The Plan: Volunteer, Reveal, Choice, and Reckoning.

Not one or two as tradition had it, but hundreds and most probably thousands all at once.

Masses of heads falling as sharp swords come down in

silvery arcs.

The Engineer's mind is full of this image.

A wave of heads falling and rolling away.

His very precise and quantitative mind calculates those curves.

The arcs of the swords. The curving fall of the heads. The rebound curves quickly dampened.

As he sits petrified in the imagining of this plan, his hands move of their own free will. Touching his torso, his legs, his arms and head. Searching himself unconsciously for a first sign. Perhaps he has one somewhere. A telltale lump that will add his own curves into this equation.

Then he finds it. Just behind his right shoulder. The smallest of lumps.

His own little Mutation.

Chapter 24

The Long Slide

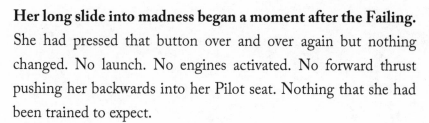

Her long slide into madness began a moment after the Failing.
She had pressed that button over and over again but nothing
changed. No launch. No engines activated. No forward thrust
pushing her backwards into her Pilot seat. Nothing that she had
been trained to expect.

Simply nothing.

She had become aware in a fraction of a second of the vacuum
left as Launch Intelligence vanished.

Her suit had disengaged her from the console and had gone
dark. As it did so, she felt the Intelligence draining away from her.

She felt it with all her senses.

Her blue eyes first, as the lights went out. The augmented
reality data feed had gone dark in a metaphorical blink of an eye.
Electric blue, pulsing red, cool green, bright white, all gone. Letters,
numbers, symbols no longer in her line of sight. Her augmented
reality display flicking off and replaced by a clear view of her new

reality. Her eyes suddenly adjusting to almost black—lightened a little as the emergency lights activated throughout the Ship. Eyes that had been well trained to absorb a myriad of Intelligence fed detail, now confronted by one static image of her external surroundings. The plainest of views.

Almost as quickly, her skin felt the change too. The pulsating, probing Pilot skin died and all of its intricate interactions with her own skin stopped instantaneously. In a heartbeat, her body was encased within a now dead membrane, devoid of all of the Intelligence's adjustments to her own bodily functions. No gentle touches, probings, sensings. Her body, long accustomed to that continuous and careful interrogation, now alone. Her golden skin crawled in response.

Her hearing and sense of smell came next. Less impacted by this sudden vacuum, but nonetheless changed. Her ears felt the dull dead silence of the Pilot skin and her cockpit—but at the same time, they were assaulted by a wave of mechanical noises as the fail-safes kicked into action. Replacing the familiar sounds of her training, with the sounds she had hoped never to hear. The sounds of failure.

Her nose almost at the same time became aware of a new smell as her terror rose to the surface. Her fight or flight response system activated and began the generation of alarm pheromones. Sweat to her skin brought the steroidal, endogenous odorants that were evolved to act as human alarm signals. High anxiety elevating as her nose sensed these new self generated compounds. An almost startlingly quick reflex as her right amygdala moved into action.

Run, run, run.

And with that terror came the taste of Failure. Her body, seeking to eject this panic, created its own counter attack—nausea and a rising mass of vomit filling her throat and mouth. Her body quickly seeking to void itself of this horror that now assaulted all her senses.

She bent over double and gagged and spewed out her breakfast and all of the additives and supplements that the Intelligences had filled her with for this launch day. Wave and wave of matter leaving her as her mind opened to the reality that they were not leaving the Field at all.

Dead on departure.

Long after, she still sat in her Pilot seat. By then the Ship had dumped its other passengers out onto the Field in waves of automated evacuation. For herself and the Engineer deep below, there was no such fail-safe system. An oversight? Perhaps. But it was for her to rise, leave her seat, and pass through now dim and deserted corridors down to the central hold.

Walking without thought. Her feet moving her down pathways she never imagined she would tread. Down to the last hold, through the hatch, and to the top of the stairs now hanging down from the Ship to the Field below.

Zombie-like, she descended. Physically down flight after flight. Mentally into the deepest, darkest despair of human trauma so sudden and so absolute as to absorb her mind completely.

Gone.

...

The rest of that first day, she was numb.

Her body took her into the flow of humanity now on the Field. For a while she sat with the many who were giving up. Sat among them as they closed down. Unable to cope with the death of the hub behind their ears. One after another, lying down to die.

Her training, however, was too ingrained to allow her to simply succumb as they did to the grim arms of death which were reaching out and taking so many in a dark and final embrace.

She sat among them, but was not one of them.

Perhaps a few hours later she rose and walked away towards the perimeter buildings. Her feet guided her back towards her own quarters. Taking a turn after they entered Building 28, towards the stairs down to the basement.

Walking down. Into the blackness. Down to where her mind had already descended. Into the basement of her soul.

That was when the primal screaming had begun.

Down in the dark of the basement.

Now become hers.

...

Even in this darkest of moments, a glimmer of light.

Seated beside her on the Field was another.

As she wrestled with her despair, so another also faced his own failings. Beside her physically, but remote mentally. Going through his own journey. Grappling with the enormity of this Failing.

First fighting, then running, then fighting again. A moment of black despair, flicked away subconsciously. More flight, fight response. More black despair. Panic, then cold calm numbness.

Then, as she rose, so his conscious mind flickers on again. "Who is this rising, when others are lying down to die? What is she doing? Where is she going?"

A lifeline thrown to him. Questions to be answered still.

And as she rises, so he does too. As she begins to shuffle towards Building 28, he does so as well. Following her lead. Away from this place of doom. His unconscious will carrying him forward in her wake.

Daring to care.

The man that will become Sage Caring.

Chapter 25

Adam's Dream

Adam is standing on the Field
The moon is high and full
A ghostly red light illuminates everything
He looks up and sees the red disc above
Beautiful in a cold harsh way.

Something wants him to hide
Just out of reach in a corner of his mind
Some reason why a clear sky and a bright shining moon
should be avoided
He tries but each time he gets close to this idea, it
vanishes.

Flitting away
His mind can't catch it
He turns away from this inner chase
Looks around

The moon has changed everything.

His feet seem to hover just a little above the ground
Which he can't quite feel beneath him
It is quiet, he can't hear anything
He can't smell anything
Only his eyes seem to be working.

He tries to utter a sound, but nothing comes out
He looks around from side to side, and then again up at the sky
As he stares at this moonlit night, a shiver runs down his spine
He is convinced that something malevolent is
approaching
Something is creeping up on him.

Something he wants to, needs to, run away from
He needs a chance to escape this feeling
He tries to name it but he can't
More than a feeling—a certainty
Something wicked this way comes.

He is desperate to name this threat
Without being able to, he can't move into action
He is stuck
He looks down at his hands
Bunched up into fists.

He stretches them out
The light of the moon illuminates them
Ten digits of pure pink extend from his palms
Beautiful and somehow calming

A power over the unnamed threat.

He imagines his face is pink too
Turns it upwards to the bright disc in the heavens
The moon looks down and he knows it is telling him
something
Something very important
About a second chance that it wants to offer to him.

He can't fathom it
Adam holds quite still and thinks very hard
But his head is full of the red light
Fears, uncertainties, doubts
All crowd out his thinking mind.

The moon calls
Adam gives up the battle to answer his own questions
Instead, he gives himself up to these moonbeams
Opens his arms to make more space in his chest for this
light to fill
As he does so, he realizes he is floating.

He watches as the Field falls away from him
His pace of ascent accelerating
He is rising on a moonbeam
Rising towards this moon that has something so
important to tell him
He is happy.

Happy to be leaving
Rescued from that unnamed and threatening

malevolence below
Then suddenly he is not so happy
A little voice in his head tells him not to leave yet
He can't go by himself.

Where is she?
This is too soon
He can't go alone
He needs to leave with her
Where is his darling Belle?

He looks to each side
Hoping that perhaps she is rising beside him
He struggles now
He must escape from this inexorable pull of the moon
It is taking him too soon and without his completeness.

Without his Belle
He struggles more
Then, like a thread suddenly breaking
He feels the moonbeam release him
He falls.

Down he goes
Head over heels
Black night, purple ground
Then another bright red disc
His whirling head tries to make sense of this.

On the next rotation it all makes sense
This red disc is the nose cone of Ship 10

Illuminated by the moon above
With a rush, he wakes and sits up
Of course!

Chapter 26

We Can Escape

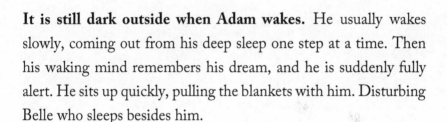

It is still dark outside when Adam wakes. He usually wakes slowly, coming out from his deep sleep one step at a time. Then his waking mind remembers his dream, and he is suddenly fully alert. He sits up quickly, pulling the blankets with him. Disturbing Belle who sleeps besides him.

She wakes too.

"What's the matter Adam?" she mutters, one arm thrown out to pull him back down beside her.

"I have the answer," he replies. "It came to me in a dream."

She sits up immediately, her blonde hair messy and clothing rumpled, but her face fully alive. Blue eyes intense and focused.

"What, Adam?" she asks. "Tell me."

So he does. Recounting his dream. Taking his time to let her imagine it just as he experienced it. He gets to the final image, and she too sees it immediately.

"That's it, Adam. The Ship."

"Yes, exactly. We can escape on the Ship," he says, hugging her to him.

They look into each other's eyes. Full of brightness and optimism.

There is a chance.

...

They are not the first to think about making Ship 10 work again. In the early days after the Failing, no one had dared to suggest the possibility, the communal trauma of the Failing lay so heavy on their collective shoulders. Later it had been the Engineer of Ship 9 who had suggested that they visit Ship 10 and determine its condition and the possible opportunity that it might represent. He was able to get the support of the Council of Sages and had gone out with the Engineer from Ship 10 to take a look. They had run through the basic checks and had concluded that the Ship was in good condition but that the onboard Ship Intelligence was inactive. Try as they might this was not something they had been able to further diagnose or correct. Meanwhile, the manual interventions all required the combination of an Engineer and a Pilot, and try as they might it had proven impossible to get the Pilot of Ship 10 to talk to them.

In the end, they aborted any idea of using the Ship beyond stripping its hold of those supplies and pieces of equipment that seemed usable in the buildings and workshops around the Field.

With all their training, skills and capabilities, the two Engineers are unable to imagine moving forward without the essentials as laid down by the absent Intelligences. They, instead, focus their minds on the immediate task at hand. Survival in the terrible world of the Field and its Flock.

···

For Adam and Belle, once the concept is established, the rest follows quickly. Adam and Belle are Pure. The practicalities are not their concern. Never having seen the Intelligences at work, never having experienced the wonders of technology, they cannot imagine the complexities that any Failed would see from the outset. The Failed would have rejected the idea as ridiculous. Knowing no better, Adam and Belle, Pure in heritage and outlook, accept the dream at face value.

The Ship will take them to the moon and beyond.

They have no idea of the enormous emptiness of space, the destination of the fleet, or how to navigate this Ship towards it. All they know is that out on the Field stands a spaceship. Flying into space was what it was built to do. They will just make it do so now.

Wake the Ship, tell it to leave, sit back and enjoy the ride. Simple. Until the complexities enter into the picture. For them, these are not the complexities of a technological, Intelligence driven world. Not the issues of how to get a long dead spaceship to wake up from its slumber. No, instead Adam and Belle begin to discuss the only complexities that they can imagine given their experiences and upbringing.

"We can't leave them behind. We have to bring them all with us," Adam says for the sixth or seventh time, his hands gripping Belle's tightly. "We can't run away and leave them in this mess, especially since the Lawenforcers will blame them for what we are doing."

"Easy said, Adam, but we can't have a group of children relying upon us—we have enough on our plates right now just figuring out how to look after the three of us," Belle responds firmly.

"The twins, Belle. How can we just walk away from Pete and Paula? And Kate, and Will...." he pleads, his voice quivering as tears spring to his eyes.

She leans in, holding him, her voice tender as she responds to his emotion.

"You are lovely to care so much, and I love them all just as much as you do," she says quietly. "But right now we need to stay focused, Adam. We need to focus on ourselves and our baby. I can't risk being Revealed. You know that."

She goes on "It's like Michael's story, Adam. The twins are safer left behind than with us. I feel they are like my own children, but with me they are in great peril. With the rest of the group they are safe. It's our baby who is in danger," she ends.

He does not respond, and he has lost eye contact with her.

"Adam, look at me," she says. "I need you to hear this."

His face comes back towards her, his cheeks now shining with tears. His eyes are again locked on hers.

She reads them. Sees the pain and the struggle. Understands how her sensitive, dreamy Adam is tortured by this part of their plan.

But also, she sees what he needs from her. He needs her strength. He needs her to make this decision so that he does not have to.

"We will leave, just the three of us," she confirms. "But I promise that if we ever can, we will return for the others."

"When shall we leave?" he asks.

"As soon as possible," she says.

...

Beyond that, they are into a world of speculation. All the questions they want answers to are beyond their experience.

How best to enter the Ship?

How to do so unseen?

Where to go once within its hull?

What will they find there?

How to start it up?

How to make it fly?

Of course these questions, and a handful of others, are naive and insufficient. Ludicrously so. But they know no better. They get to the right realization in the end, anyhow. They need to find someone who knows. Gazing into each other's eyes, it is the Scavengers' Prophecy that they utter at exactly the same moment.

"Search for those who know the secrets of the past

They will know how to unlock it

The doorway through which you wish to pass

They are the keyholders, though no key do they bear

Go to them if you seek your escape."

"We need to find the Pilot or the Engineer of Ship 10," they say to each other.

For a moment, it seems that simple.

Chapter 27

Questions and Answers

Their search begins.

Within a short while they realize that they can in fact search for three not two. Everyone knows that the Engineer from Ship 9 escaped as well.

In the months that followed the Failing, the central players – Pilot and Engineers – had been lost in the crowd. Capabilities, training, titles no longer relevant to this first chaotic, and then newly ordered society. The blame of the Failed launches, and the shame of not having fulfilled their purpose of Pilot and Engineer, had led them to embrace anonymity. Now almost twenty years later, Belle and Adam would need to resurface identities long hidden.

They begin with the most direct route. They visit one of the most elderly, and most trustworthy of the Failed in their own building and take him aside after breakfast. Probably unwise and unsafe. But they are in a hurry, after all.

They ask him their question straight out.

"What happened to the Pilot and the two Engineers?"

And just as quickly he gives his truth.

"I don't know about the Pilot and Engineer from Ship 10," he begins as they wait breathlessly. "In this building, we are all of Ship 9."

He pauses.

"Our Engineer was Reckoned by Sage Certainty just a few days ago. Don't you remember?"

Belle does.

She remembers all too well. The head falling in front of her, as she backed away, in fear of her own Revealing.

That must have been the one that this Failed is talking about.

"That was an Engineer?" she asks in disbelief. Living her life just thinking of him as one more Failed. Unaware of the old title he had carried.

"Yes."

And just like that, their chance is dramatically reduced.

One down, two to go.

...

It is harder for Belle and Adam to agree on the next step.

"What do we do now?" he asks as they recover from the shock of the realization that the Engineer that has lived with them their entire lives is no more.

"We have to find the other Engineer and the remaining Pilot," Belle says matter-of-factly. "We will need to visit the other buildings and track them down."

"But isn't that dangerous?" Adam asks, his worry apparent.

"Yes, it will be but we have no choice," she tells him, and with just as much certainty, she takes his hand and squeezes it.

"Trust me, Adam," she says slowly, calming him with her strength of purpose. "We can do this. Stay with me Adam, and stay strong."

He nods, but says nothing.

Asking one of their own has been easy. To leave their building, and seek out Failed from Ship 10, and then ask them about the past will be much more difficult. They simply do not have relationships with the People from other buildings.

If they are seen asking questions like this of People they don't know, there is a risk that the Lawenforcers will be suspicious of their curiosity. Or even that a Failed will alert their Lawenforcers and perhaps their Sage about these Pure seeking answers to strange questions.

"We need to be clever about this," Belle says. "There must be ways that we can do this without setting off alarms."

One that will not raise the obvious counter question: Why do you want to know?

Belle suggests a host of options, but it is Adam that comes up with a simpler and better one.

"Let's ask People why the two Ships are different," he suggests. "Let's say that we want to know why Ship 9 is missing its nose cone and Ship 10 is not. Once the People we ask give the obvious answer, we will ask for more details."

"We just go on asking questions until the Failed don't have answers for us. Then it will be natural to ask who has the answers, and then this will lead us to the Engineer and the Pilot. Then we can ask the question we really want to ask. Where are they?"

Belle is impressed, and tells him so. It makes sense to her.

"So if you agree with this plan, who shall we take it to?" Adam asks.

Belle's answer to that question is also straightforward.

"Let's volunteer for fish pool," she says.

"Every building has to volunteer People every day for aquafarm duty," she continues. "We will be able to find a Failed from Ship 10 for sure with so many People working together. Then we can ask them our questions."

...

Often the most direct path is not the quickest. But this time it is.

Their building duty manager has no issue with extra fish duty for the two of them. If they want to work a little more this week, that is fine. The aquafarms are always seen as a fun place to visit by Pure, who love the lively waters filled with their active, swimming charges. And two of the Failed who have todays' duty will gladly relinquish it. So the trade is quickly made.

Adam and Belle put on their outdoor clothes and goggles and out they go.

Adam notices that Belle looks stiffer and also thinner than usual but does not say anything. Last night, she shared her approach to hiding her now full breasts and belly, and even let him put the fabric around them.

Adam found her full breasts very exciting, but did not let her know. His physical excitement got them into this mess in the first place, and he really did not know what leaking breasts meant or if touching them would be good or bad for the baby they were preparing to feed. So he just wound the fabric around them and felt a little disappointment as they vanished from view.

On the way to the aquafarm building, Adam holds Belle's hand but says nothing. For her part, she seems wrapped up in her own thoughts, and so it is in silence that they arrive at their destination. The aquafarms are housed in one low structure that stands a little back from building 17. Neither Adam nor Belle knows the original purpose of the building, but the older Failed do.

Originally this was the sewage treatment plant. The Intelligence-driven bathrooms and toilets of the living quarters were all pumped into this one building. Human waste driving multistage, multipurpose processes. Here tanks of varying size and shapes slowly converted the human waste into usable products that were then recycled again and again. Gases for combustion for heat and cooking. Oils for lubrication and burning. Solids that once concentrated and matured and mixed became powerful fertilizers. Nothing lost. Everything utilized in one way or another.

Since the Intelligences disappeared on the day of the Failing, this original purpose had ceased to function.

The precious energy from solar and then wind had been rationed and used for the most critical of purposes, and the energy hog pumps were low on the priority lists.

No longer was human waste moved by a network of pipes, pumps, and valves from each node across the collection of Field buildings into this one collection point. All of those pumps silent, their toilets and baths hidden behind now immovable walls whose secrets had died with the Intelligences all those years before.

Over eighteen years, the static matter in the network of pipes had dried and hardened, so each one is now clogged. The valves impenetrable. The pumps and all their moving parts sealed and silent.

Now the People carry the bulk of their waste to the croplands. Their approach to recycling much more basic than that of the Intelligences. They simply throw the pails of matter across the planting rows—night soil no different than that used thousands of years before by the first human farmers.

Now, the former waste recycling tanks are used for aquafarming. Each of the building's two stories are organized in the same way. The tanks on each level are connected to each other but no longer to the outside world and the other buildings. In each tank is some combination of water, algae, water plants and fish. In some tanks, only algae are at work cleaning and filtering. In other tanks, the workers put the eggs stripped from the mature fish, ensuring the highest possible hatching rate. In the largest tanks, mature fish move sedately, eating the water plants and other materials, including crushed insects brought from the croplands.

Water flows downhill from tank to tank, first purified sufficiently to support the aqua pond fish life, then used in hydro ponds for plant farming, and then cleaned again through plant tanks until drinkable. Finally, pumped again into the highest tanks to begin the cycle again.

Constant water losses made up with human waste in moderation, and the occasional addition of rain captured by rooftop tanks acting as backup reserves for the dry season. The aqua and hydro ponds much too precious to be exposed to the risks of a long dry season.

The People have refined this system over eighteen years,

understanding from the outset just how fragile their protein balance is, and how reliant their community has become on their gilled friends. Every little part of the fish treasured and used. Flesh eaten fresh or dried. Skin, fins, tail dried too and eaten in crunchy snacks or ground down into flour along with the bones, head, and whatever insects can be added in.

Bones used too for all those purposes that existed before humans discovered the skills to work metal. Pins and needles, fasteners, and sharp points all crafted from the bones of the bigger fish.

Fish blood and anything else treasured as fertilizer. Gathered up and applied at the base of each plant. A precious drop of fuel added each night to each plant to increase yields. More food harvested, more plant waste and vegetable scraps for the fish in the tanks. Full cycle.

In this most important of buildings, one level housed the Carp and one level the Catfish. Each a delicate but productive ecosystem carefully tended by a host of workers. Just why the Intelligences had chosen these two species was unknown, but without access to the oceans and the fish below, these were the only types now bred in the aquafarm.

It was into this space that Belle and Adam now walked.

They are quickly assigned to the Carp tanks on the second floor with the task of grinding down buckets of insects into small pellet sized pieces for the fish to eat.

The work is hard.

For years now, the process has been refined—ironically evolving to a process that any early hunter-gatherer would have known ten thousand years before. The field workers have brought back sacks of insects which have then been dried in big troughs outdoors on the roof at night, covered by nets to keep away fresh clouds of insects brought to the drying corpses of their brethren, indoors in the winter months when moisture is the great enemy.

Once dried, the insects have been sorted and graded by size. The smallest are directly fed to the fish. The largest and medium sized (mostly locusts, grasshoppers and beetles) have been further prepared for today's work. They must be crushed and ground into parts small enough for the carp to manage.

Elsewhere, further steps are taken to reduce the crushed particles to flour for human consumption. But here in the aqua-farm, the smallest particle required will be a little smaller than the finger nail of Belle's hand. Pellet sized.

To accomplish this, the workers are lined up, each sitting on the ground with a large stone mortar between their crossed legs. Just behind them to their left is a basket of unprocessed dried in-sects. To their right, a container into which they will periodically empty their mortar.

Other workers are constantly moving along the line, filling baskets with more insects, emptying boxes of completed pellets, and occasionally bringing water for the workers.

The clouds of dust that the grinding create are impossible to avoid. After just a few minutes work, Belle and Adam are covered in dust and insect pieces that coat them from the top of their heads to their shoes. Their goggles protect their eyes but their vision is compromised by the dust on the lenses and the need to constantly wipe it away. Unfortunately, the goggles don't help with breathing. At the outset, they keep their mouths closed and rely upon their noses to limit the intake, but soon this no longer works as their noses fill with clogging dust. Then their mouths open along with a long line of others, and, as the work becomes harder, so their breathing becomes louder.

Then the water becomes more than valuable—an essential part of the process. Allowing the workers to clean their mouths, spitting out white paste, and then clear their throats so that work can resume.

Left hand takes insects, drops into mortar. Right hand thumps down pestle and with the aid of left, begins the grinding. Check once, check twice. Then, once no large pieces remain, two hands scoop the pellets into the box to the right. And repeat.

Adam is good at this work. He finds that he can disconnect his mind and let his body do its work, while he goes off to dream. Hands in motion. Mind somewhere else. Once he finds his routine, his flow, he almost enjoys this work.

Not so Belle. For her, every minute of grinding seems like an hour. Every hour like a year. The monotony of this work almost grinds her down. There is nothing in it to keep her engaged and unlike Adam she is not a dreamer. However, knowing that this phase will lead to the next sees her through it. She looks across at Adam and sees his smiling face, and his eyes gazing to some far horizon. She smiles. She knows her Adam well. He is in his dream world while she is firmly here in the room grinding a never ending supply of dried insects into powder. She smiles again to herself. "Maybe his way has its advantages," she thinks.

...

It's break time.

This work comes with advantages. One advantage are the frequent breaks. Another is that the snacks always include some fresh and some dried fish as well as glasses of pure water—the purest that the People now have is here where the recently filtered water leaves the algae and plant tanks and enters the first of the fish tanks.

As Belle and Adam arrive in the break room, other workers are leaving, and for a moment they both fear that they will be on break alone. However, shortly after they sit down, eight other workers arrive.

Two of them they know from their own building. Both are Failed but presumably as Ship 9 members, they will not have the precious knowledge that the Pure seek.

Two others are Pure, and much younger than Adam and Belle. They will not have the answers, either. The other four look more promising. Neither Adam nor Belle recognize any of them, which is itself a good start.

"Which buildings are you from?" she asks after each of the others have quenched their thirst, and begun their snacks.

They answer in turn, that they are from Buildings 3, 17, and 23.

"Which route do you take when you come here?" Belle asks one.

It is a slightly odd question, but she makes it less so by explaining that she needs to visit another building and is wondering whether the perimeter route is quicker than passing by close to the Ships - passing beneath them being unlawful.

One of the four is not interested in the discussion and turns away, eating her fish. But fortunately, the three others seem more willing to engage.

"My building is three away from here, so we just walk the perimeter—there is more shade and you just can't be too careful," says the first one, a grizzled man who must have been old when the Failing happened, and is now bent over and stiff with age.

"I live across the Field, but I always walk the perimeter. I feel it is safer that way," says the second.

"I am in Building 3 which is almost as far from this one as you can go," says the third, a grey haired women who must be in her fifties but looks older by at least a decade. "We always walk close to the Ships."

"It must be strange passing by the Ships every time you come here," Belle comments.

"I don't even see them anymore," the woman replies.

"Why does one have a hole at the top?" Belle asks.

All four of the Failed who are gathered close by, and the two Pure glance up at this. They know Belle knows the answer already, but assume she wants to hear the story again.

The women pauses, and Adam can see that she is uncomfortable and unsure how to continue.

After a moment, she says, "Dear, you know as much as we do about that. One Ship had an explosion, and we don't know why, but it was damaged and the top of it shows that clearly."

She takes a pause. "Our Ship just did not work."

Belle looks at Adam and nods. First task completed. They now know that this women is from Ship 10.

Belle nods to the woman, and goes back to chewing her

dried fish.

Enough for now.

...

After break, it's back to the line and their mortar and pestles. More grinding. Over and over again. Adam wonders at the quantities they are creating. So much work to feed the fish and to refill the supplies created for times of mutation when fresh insects can't be gathered.

Of course, some of the boxes of pellets are being taken to the flour line and perhaps it is the People more than the fish who will consume the results of their labor.

Lunch seems to take forever to arrive, but when it does, they go to the eating place again. They find the same group as before, now sitting down to their lunches of fish stew and water.

Belle sits as close as she can to the woman from Ship 10. Adam follows, sitting on the other side of Belle. He can hear Belle beginning to engage the woman in chit-chat, talking about the fish and the apparent reduction in eggs that they are getting for the hatching ponds. The Woman is very concerned about this, and says it is her impression that the only eggs they are getting now are from Catfish.

"How do you know the difference?" Belle asks.

"Our Catfish lay orange eggs while our Carp lay bronze ones," the woman responds. "Now I only get orange eggs for my tank even though it has always been a Carp hatchery."

She seems troubled, but Adam is not sure of the implication of this. Surely a fish is a fish?

Belle takes a moment, and then asks the planned next question. "You said at break that Ship 9 had an explosion. Why did it have one?"

"I don't know," the Failed responds.

"But there must be a reason. We are Pure and never received your education. Didn't the Intelligences explain this to you?"

The woman recoils, and Adam sees Belle's mistake straight away. She has mentioned the Intelligences, and every Failed knows they left at the time of the explosion. Left everything that each Failed viewed as so precious and necessary to a normal way of life.

The woman turns to Belle and her face is grim.

"Stupid girl. You know nothing. The Intelligences left when the Ships failed to launch, and we lost everything then." She is visibly distressed, and the other Failed at the table drop their eyes as she goes on.

"My own husband laid down and died, and I don't know why I didn't too. If our fool Engineer and Pilot had done their jobs, it might have been different. But they failed us, and we have lived with the consequences ever since." The woman's voice has raised in volume and intensity, and she is leaning forward her eyes staring into Belle's from a distance of inches.

"The Pilot from Ship 9 deserved what she got, blown up in her Ship, and I hate her for her failure." The woman is now visibly angry, her face red and the words spat out in a fierce and threatening diction.

Adam is scared and turns away, but his Belle is made of sterner stuff.

"What of the other Pilot?" she asks. "The one from Ship 10?"

"The Pilot of Ship 10?" the woman asks back. "Don't you

mean the crazy woman of Building 28."

Belle and Adam both breathe in deeply, surprised at the answer they have just received.

"But she is no good to anyone anymore," the woman continues. "Lost her mind and who knows why Sage Caring keeps feeding her. He likes his pets I think, and everyone says she is his favorite, living in her dirt in his basement. She deserves just what she got as well."

Belle tries to ask another question, but the woman has had enough, and she falls into silence.

Adam nudges Belle to stop, and she does so.

At least they have one tracked down, even if she appears to be almost the worst possible candidate.

A Pilot who has lost her mind and an Engineer who has lost his head.

So near, but so far.

For the rest of that day, they continue working, and find times and opportunities to probe for the location of the Engineer from Ship 10 with the other fish farm workers. However, either no one knows, or the Failed are simply tired of this Pure asking awkward questions that stir up painful memories.

They learn nothing more and return to their building at the end of the day half resolved. Half pregnant with an unanswered question.

Where is the Engineer from Ship 10?

Chapter 28

The Ship

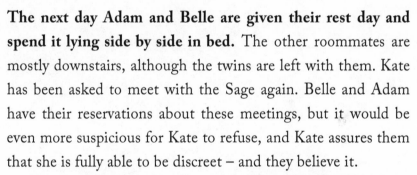

The next day Adam and Belle are given their rest day and spend it lying side by side in bed. The other roommates are mostly downstairs, although the twins are left with them. Kate has been asked to meet with the Sage again. Belle and Adam have their reservations about these meetings, but it would be even more suspicious for Kate to refuse, and Kate assures them that she is fully able to be discreet – and they believe it.

Fortunately, Peter and Paula have learned to play with each other in their wooden box crib, and Adam and Belle are able to focus on themselves with only the occasional break to check on the younger ones.

Adam notices that Belle seems more withdrawn than usual, and she has taken to stroking her tummy with her hands, while her eyes take on a far away look. He can guess what she's thinking about. Yet it worries him a little that she seems to be spending more and more of her time with herself and her own thoughts and less and less with him.

Eventually, once the twins have eaten a little mush that Adam has fed them, and fallen asleep in their crib, Adam returns to Belle where she is lying close to the wall.

"Belle, are you okay?" he asks, lying down beside her

"I don't know Adam. I don't know what we can do to get out of this horrible situation." She sighs. "I keep on growing, and the baby keeps on kicking, and I know it is telling me to get going, but I just don't know where we should go next."

She pauses.

"Well we know we have to find the keyholders, and we know now that means finding the Engineer from Ship 10 or visiting the pilot in Building 28," Adam says.

"I know we need to fulfill the Scavenger's Prophecy, but I don't see how we can if the Pilot has gone crazy and the last Engineer has disappeared. I feel more and more desperate but can't see a way out of this," she replies.

Adam gives her a hug, and tries to put a positive spin on their circumstance.

"We can do this, Belle, if we can find the Engineer. He'll help us start the Ship, and then we can get away before anyone Reveals us."

It is not the right thing to say. As soon as he has said the word Reveal, he feels her tense up. It is what she fears the most, and he has blundered straight into it.

"I think we have to find the Pilot, because she is the one who knows how to fly the Ship and without her we can't get it to take off anyhow," Belle counters. "We have to visit the Pilot and talk to her and see if she will help us."

"Yes, but that is too dangerous. A crazy woman might tell on us, or make a scene and get the Lawenforcers down on us. We can't just go creeping around Building 28, and our Lawenforcers have told us how horrible Sage Caring is. It's too dangerous," Adam insists.

"So tell me your plan."

He answers, "We find the Engineer who is lost. If the Ship can't be turned back on, no Pilot can fly it anyhow. So the Engineer has to come first. We have no reason to believe he is dead or crazy. We just have to work a little harder to get a lead on where he is."

"Nice idea, but no one seems to know where he is," Belle replies. "At least the Pilot may have things she can teach us, and she might even know where the Engineer is."

"You think a crazy woman is going to be our answer?" Adam retorts.

Putting into words both their fears.

How can a woman who has lost her mind help them escape? They slip into a troubled silence. Adam breaks it by first putting his arm around Belle and then whispering in her ear.

"You are my Pilot, and I am sure you can figure out this Ship," he says. "Let's do this first. Let's visit the Ship and see if you can make it work without the help of some old Failed."

He smiles at her, "You are the smartest and most capable person I know, so I am sure you can figure this out."

Belle looks at him and smiles. "My sweet little dreamer," she thinks to herself.

At the same time, visiting the Ship does have a certain attraction.

A positive distraction is perhaps exactly what they need right now.

"Okay," she says. "We will visit the Ship tonight."

Adam smiles and hugs her tightly.

...

Dark has fallen and their building is sleeping.

The roommates are all in their beds, and apart from some comments to close their day, each has succumbed to the air of melancholy in the room created by Adam and Belle. Even the little ones have settled down quickly, and Ann only had to tell them a couple of bedtime stories before they fell into the deep sleep of the innocent.

Ricky, Cathy, and John spent the day working hard cleaning the kitchens and storage rooms, which is always a particularly tiring task. By the time they come back to the sleeping room, they have no energy to talk, though Ricky did mention that Michael had been asking after the two of them. Belle says she will find him in the morning, and that seems enough for Ricky, who falls into a deep sleep as soon as his head meets the pillow.

Listening to their collective breathing, Belle is taken by just how much this group means to her. As she lies in bed, with Adam behind her, she wishes that things had not moved down this path. Being the oldest in the room, she feels an obligation to care for her younger roommates, but the baby that is kicking in her tummy has to come first. On that she is clear.

Turning to the wall, Belle takes a note from beneath her bed mattress and reads it once more. It has taken a number of iterations to get just right, and even now she can't really imagine what it will be like to read for the first time. She hopes that the others will see the love that she has tried to put into the words.

Dear Ricky, Cathy, Ann, John, Kate, Will, Peter and Paula,

You are my family. I love you each dearly. I know Adam does too.

I know that what I am writing here will be a shock and that it would have been better if I could explain everything in person. But I am worried that if I do, I won't have the strength to do what I now must. Which is to leave you and this building. Forever.

Adam and I have to go. We talked about this before when we went to the Far Side. Now it is even more necessary. I can't hide the baby that is coming. It is too big now. You know why it can't be found out. I don't need to explain that.

So we need to find a way to escape this place. Not just for Adam and me. But for all of us. So when you wake up we will not be here.

We need you to stay strong until we call for you. We are sure you will be safe here – safer than if you were with us. Try and cover for us. But don't lie to anyone if they see we are gone. Just say you don't know anything. That we left and you don't know why.

Then keep yourselves ready. I don't know how we will let you know when to come but we will. I promise.

I love you all.

Belle

As she re-reads the words she knows she is making promises she can't be sure she can keep. Even in her most optimistic frame of mind, she has been unable to come up with a way to bring the others with them.

She hates this.

Maybe this is what it is really like to be a parent. Having to tell stories to keep the family strong and motivated. Promising to protect and care for them even when you don't know how to care for yourself.

White lies.

"This is awful," she says to herself.

Deep inside her, however, her baby and it's primordial need for its mother's focus is driving her in this time frame. She doesn't even know it, but much as she loves them, the others can't compete with this internal voice that is driving her now.

She folds the letter up again.

She will leave it on the back of the door, so they will surely see it when they wake.

...

She waits until all of the others have settled into a slow pattern of breathing that suggests deep sleep. Then she reaches behind her and finds one of Adam's hands and gently squeezes it. He too has been waiting, and immediately squeezes her hand back.

Quietly they creep out of the sleeping room and down to the exit of Building 12. Looking through the door, it is surprisingly bright. A full moon night. A clear one at that. Everything bathed in a blood red translucency.

Like Adam's dream.

He thinks to himself that this must be a good omen. Perhaps Belle will make the Ship work and they will just float away tonight.

The one preparation they have made is to steal a fish oil lantern from the box outside Sage Certainty's room.

This idea itself generated perhaps the biggest debate of the day.

Adam was fiercely opposed, since the lanterns are perhaps the most precious objects in the building after Sage Certainty's swords. The precious fish oil that lights them is also treasured, hard won when every little bit of protein matters.

The lanterns are only used on the rarest of occasions when the Sage wants to hold a night ceremony or make a consequential announcement – in those cases a lantern-lit nighttime meeting only serves to emphasize the message in the minds of her Flock. Otherwise, when darkness comes everyone goes to bed.

"It's too risky," he told Belle. "The moonlight should be enough. Let's not try and steal a lantern, please."

"Adam, we won't be able to see in the dark of the Ship without one," she countered. "There is no point in going to the Ship if we can't go inside, so we have to take a lantern and enough oil too."

Belle wins the argument.

So their first stop as they creep through the quiet corridors of their building is Sage Certainty's room. Belle opens the box, and takes out a lantern and a small bottle of fish oil. She adds a steel and flint and slips them all into an old food bag that she is using as a small sack.

Ever so quietly, Adam closes the box behind her. Then they are at the door and looking out. Both knowing that if the lantern is missed, their lives are forfeit.

Another law broken. Their lives are over if anyone ever knows the abundance of laws they have broken over this last month or two.

Adam shivers, but in a way it makes no difference now. "Living on borrowed time," he thinks to himself.

Borrowed time with Belle is worth everything to him right now.

No sound comes from behind them, and moments later they are scurrying side by side across the Field to Ship 10.

···

Adam looks up at the gleaming silvery hull. He has lived within sight of this Ship, but never has he come so close. The laws do not permit it.

Now standing beneath it, he is overwhelmed by its enormity.

Here, under the Ship, it is clear that the vessel is less perfect than it appears from afar. When viewed from any of the buildings, the Ship stands like an enormous and solid building, and even though the drones no longer burnish its surface, still it reflects the light and shines and glows under the caress of sun and moon. The Ship itself is made of some special material impervious to the ravages of time. It still shines like polished silver, its mirror surface reflecting the sky, the buildings, and the Field.

However, once beneath it the reality of the Failing is driven home.

Inside the three legs, the Ship has dropped down parts of its innards and left them hanging to touch the ground. A narrow stair, some tubes dangling. The result of the great expulsion of the People. Unable to be drawn up by the Ship once the Intelligences deserted it.

As Adam gets closer he is first surprised and then delighted to see dark reflections of two ghostlike figures appearing on the side of the Ship just as they approach it. Their own reflections welcome them as they get to the closest leg, and turn around it and inside to stand under the Ship—now hidden from their building.

Looking into the clearing beneath the Ship, Adam can see that they are not the first to have come here. The area beneath is full of bits and pieces of metal and machinery abandoned by other visitors. Sent by Sages to gather items of use in the buildings.

Here on the ground are bits and pieces that have been abandoned as useless to these visiting parties. Broken equipment, flotsam and jetsam dragged out from the bowels of the Ship, and dropped down onto this area of Field below.

By now, any useful material has been fully integrated into the life of the buildings around the Field. Many a Lawenforcer's sword has been drawn and polished from pieces of metal salvaged from within the Ships.

Looking around, Adam feels a sense of deja vu. He has been here before.

Many years ago, as a little boy, he recalls creeping up the first few rungs of these steps that hang down in front of him—back in the days when going under the Ships was still permitted. He distantly remembers his elders bringing boxes and equipment down from the Ship above, but what it was is lost to him. He could not have been more than a toddler.

Adam leans his head back, tracking the steps that rise from the Field up to the Ship's base far above. He leans back even further and he can see a black rectangular shape. The source of this stairway. The hatch. This will be their access point.

Adam turns to Belle and says, "Do you want to go up first?"

She smiles. "Of course."

They begin their ascent. The going is quite easy for Adam. The stairs spiral around and around at a shallow gradient. While seemingly thin and fragile, the stairs are in fact quite solid, made from some light but ever so strong material. As they walk, it seems to dampen every sound. Only the rustling of their outer garments marks their passing.

About half way up, Adam becomes aware that this is not so easy for Belle. She is breathing deeply, and going slower. She hunches over and he reaches out to touch her back.

"Belle, are you okay?" he asks.

She pauses and turns towards him. "The baby is kicking and heavy," she responds. "It seems more awake today than ever. I can't tell if that is good or bad. Do you think it is good?"

Adam thinks. How can it be bad for the baby to be alive and

kicking? Isn't it always good for a mother to feel her baby and know it is active and lively?

"Belle, what are you concerned about?" he replies.

She is so positive. So optimistic. So pure. She hesitates to give words to her feelings, perched beneath the Ship on this staircase.

"Maybe the baby is trying to tell us to turn around and go back," she says hesitantly.

Adam laughs. "Silly, of course not. All three of us are just excited that we are finally going to escape from here."

His enthusiasm and positivity are just what Belle needs to hear. She smiles at him—a radiant smile of happiness that has been absent for a while.

"Thank you, Adam. That's right. We are leaving soon and all three of us are going to be just fine," Belle thinks to herself.

With that she turns back to the staircase and resumes the upward march.

...

Belle enters the Ship first. As Adam steps through the hatch, she takes his hand and guides him forward a few paces. It is dim in the Ship and their eyes are at first useless.

After a minute or two, Adam begins to see that it is not as dark as he had first thought on entering. Standing on the floor of the first hold, he can see that the light of the moon, reflecting off shiny metal walls, has created a world of dark black/purples and medium reds mixed with highlights of pink where the light meets a shiny surface.

A moment longer, and his eyes, now fully adjusted, allow him to look around from one side to the other of the hold and take stock.

They are in what appears to be a round room. A complete cross section of the Ship at this low level. Above, the Ship quickly curves outwards and each level will be larger and larger than this one, but here, the hold is already broad enough that the furthest walls are too dark to make out.

Around them are a few bits and pieces of equipment including some that are so large that the currently open hatch would have been too small for them to pass through.

Adam doesn't know the purpose of these items. They have never worked during his lifetime, but even if a Failed had stood beside him and named them, he would still have been none the wiser as to their purpose. Drones, tractors, reaches, pickers, all had their uses in a world managed and organized by the Intelligences. For Adam these are just remnants of the past. Shiny metal curios that have no value.

Despite these objects, the floor of the hold is remarkably bare.

Adam turns to Belle and says, "Did you expect the Ship to be like this?"

"I had no expectations, but this space is clearly not going to help us. This is what the Failed call the hold, and was filled by equipment that would be needed in their future homes. This is not where they controlled the Ship from. Remember that's at the top where the Pilot was – which is why Ship 9 is missing its top," she says.

"We need to go further into the Ship and find those places

if we are going to start it up," Belle continues.

She opens the sack and takes out the lantern.

"We need to find the doorway to the next level," she says. "It's too dark right now to be able to see where that would be, so it's time for us to light this lantern."

Filling it with a little of the precious fish oil, she kneels and works at the flint and steel to create a spark on her tinder. Quickly blowing softly on the lit tinder, she then passes the fragile flame to the wick of the lantern, which, primed by the fish oil, lights.

The small flame makes an enormous difference. Suddenly the hold comes to life. The remaining pieces of equipment cast long shadows onto the walls. Each movement that Belle or Adam makes, when combined with the flicker of the lantern flame, turns into enormous dancing shadows of their own.

Adam is exhilarated by this. His own shadow puppet world.

He turns around, delighting in the way his shadow leaps and changes in shape as he does so.

Holding out his arms he watches as his distant shadow self extends enormous arms to either side.

He makes his arms reach out to touch the shadow Belle. She giggles as he then makes his shadow playfully kiss her and hug her on the far wall.

Rotating a little more, he watches as his shadow envelops a black bundle leaning against an otherwise bare section of the wall.

It seems to him that the bundle moves.

"What's that?" he asks Belle.

"Who are you?" the bundle asks of him.

Chapter 29

Meetings in the Dark

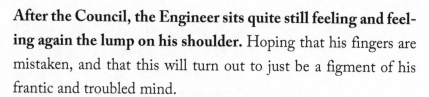

After the Council, the Engineer sits quite still feeling and feeling again the lump on his shoulder. Hoping that his fingers are mistaken, and that this will turn out to just be a figment of his frantic and troubled mind.

But try as he might, he cannot get the lump to go away. Indeed, the more he works it, the more it becomes real—not only in shape, but because it also begins to feel painful. Opening his other senses to the reality of its presence. A part of him.

His own little Mutation.

For any Failed or Pure, this would have been the cause of great fear. Once apparent, a Mutation begins an internal clock ticking. Counting down to the time when the Choice will be presented, and a decision will need to be made.

Given what the Engineer has heard this night at the Council, that ill-defined future moment has suddenly become imminent.

Soon the volunteers culling will occur. If he chooses not to step forward then, he knows that shortly thereafter he will be a part of the next phase in which he, and every other member of his building, will be inspected for Mutations just like this. Once found out, he will meet his end.

So what are his options?

He could run today. Before the beginning of the volunteering. The disadvantage is that he has not prepared for this. The advantages being that he can take more with him since others are also unprepared and he will avoid any Revealing between now and then. He can grab things if he goes before his is discovered. Later, the Lawenforcers will make sure the runners leave with nothing.

He summarizes again

Go now. Volunteer. Wait for forced Revealing, and then Stay or Go.

Four principal options. None of them attractive.

In the basement below the arena, his mind feels blocked and slow.

Four options and yet none of them calling out to him.

He thinks back to his youth, when he had been trained to consider just such options, and move quickly to decision and action. His task to make the final judgments in situations that the Intelligences fed him and used to assess his insight, speed, and intuition.

The Intelligences.

They would have known what he should do. They would have helped him make the right choice. When he was trained by them to operate his Ship.

Those had been great days. Days of courage and conviction.

He would have risen to the challenge then.

He would have needed to. The Ship would have required it of him.

The Ship.

...

Adam turns towards the hatch, planning to leave the Ship and run down the stairs.

Belle grabs his arm and holds him beside her.

"Who are you?" she shouts back.

"This is my Ship, you answer me," the bundle replies.

It is a man's voice, and hearing it Belle knows intuitively that she has nothing to fear. No one comes to the Ships these days, and when this voice had taken ownership for the Ship, she had heard the pride in it.

"We are from Building 12. I am Belle and this is Adam."

The bundle rises and becomes a black silhouette against the wall. It begins to walk toward them, and as it does so its shadow lengthens on the wall behind.

Belle can feel Adam pulling away from her as he watches the shadow grow, but she does not let him leave. Holds him tight.

"Stay with me Adam. I need you now," she whispers. She feels him settle.

Then the man is standing beside them.

He is taller than they are and bundled up in outdoor clothes. The flickering lantern in Belle's hand sends light across his face, making his eyes glitter.

"What are you doing here?" he asks.

"We have come to see the Ship and escape in it."

"Escape?" he asks. "What from?"

And just like that, he opens a floodgate and Belle finds their story pouring out of her.

...

It is still night. It is still dark. The three of them are sitting now. The Engineer told Belle to dowse the lantern long ago to save its precious fuel, and they have talked among themselves without being able to see each other clearly. Three dim figures sitting on the floor of the hold.

Belle shared everything. A problem shared, a problem halved. Or perhaps thirded?

Adam has mostly stayed quiet, but at certain points he has interjected comments into her narrative. Mostly points of emphasis about how strong, or wise, or clever Belle has been.

The man listened, his head nodding silently.

When Belle gets to the Prophecy, she can tell that the man takes special note. Leaning in a little. He breaks his silence and asks her to repeat it a second time.

Then Belle brings their story to a close. "Adam thinks that perhaps I can start this Ship and we can leave tonight. I think that is unlikely, but I wanted to come and see anyhow."

For a moment, the three of them sit in silence.

The man breaks the silence.

"You have found a keyholder, I am the Engineer."

Then louder in a voice that fills the hold, reclaiming the title he gave up long ago.

"I am the Engineer. This Ship is mine."

...

In the hours that follow, Belle and Adam move quickly through a series of emotional stages.

First, exhilaration. Believing that the Engineer will take them away this night. That he will just sit down at the Ship's controls, start it up, and fly it away.

They know no better.

Hugging, they celebrate their good fortune. Belle is ecstatic and Adam is so proud of her and so happy that his dream is turning out to be their long sought answer.

This stage is quickly ended.

"Do you know how to make this Ship work?" ask Belle

"Of course I do," the Engineer answers almost testily.

"Where will you fly us?" asks Adam

"I can't fly this Ship—only the Pilot can." He snaps back.

Then confusion.

"If you can't fly it, why are you a keyholder?" Adam asks.

"Hush, Adam," Belle answers. She is as confused as him, but not ready to voice it.

The Engineer has the lantern, and he is moving ahead now. Into the next level of the Ship. He clearly knows where he is going. Through a doorway in the hold. Up more stairs. Down a corridor, first narrow and then broadening. Through another room—this one smaller. Then into another space.

They don't know it, but the Engineer has reached his station.

By the flickering lantern they can see that this circular

room, smaller than any they have yet passed through, is filled by just one object.

A large control chair in the middle of the room.

The Engineer sits down in the chair, reclining back.

He becomes still, and Belle wonders what he is doing. What he is thinking.

"I needed to see this again. I needed to feel it," the Engineer says—the first words he has shared since he began his march towards this room.

Adam is not sure who he is talking to. He begins to frame a question, but the Engineer now turns to them and addresses them directly.

"This is the Ship's station. My station. From here I monitored all the Ships' systems. The Intelligences controlled the Ship, but I had to confirm each step until launch, at which time the Pilot and I worked in unison to confirm takeoff."

He pauses.

"We were taught manual takeoff sequences in our training, for scenarios in which the Intelligences were expecting humans to control the launch, but I can't remember them all. The Pilot would no doubt since takeoff was her prerogative. I do remember that the manual takeoff overrides still needed two of us—the Pilot to initiate, me to prime, and the Pilot to then confirm. I can't do anything here now by myself."

Then into despair.

Rushing into their minds like a black wave. Adam feels it flood in, overwhelming him. Belle drops to the floor beside him.

The Engineer goes on. "There is nothing I can do without the Pilot."

And just as quickly, they move out of despair.

Into hope.

The Pure are optimistic. For them, anything is possible. Everything starts with a positive thought. However far fetched.

"We know where she is. She is in Building 28," Belle declares in an excited voice.

"Let's visit the Pilot and do the manual takeoff," Adam adds.

They believe it as soon as he says it.

Chapter 30

Michael's Dream

Michael is sitting at a table
In the eating room of Building 12
He is alone among a crowd of People.

He does not understand why
But no one wants to sit with him
All the other tables are crowded.

Clatter of cutlery
Banging of plates
A cacophony of sound.

Noisily eating their food
Talking, sharing, socializing
He sitting alone at his table.

Meanwhile, there is a long line
Waiting to be served
Happy, noisy, excited to eat.

Old and young
Boys and girls
Failed and Pure.

He wants them to join his table
Maybe he should get up and join them?
He tries to but he can't.

He looks down at his legs
They are not working for him
He can't join the others.

His own body ignoring him
Refusing to work for him
Abandoning him.

"Give me a chance"
"Let me join the others"
"I don't want to be alone"

Michael holds up his knife
Maybe that will give him an answer?
The knife is bright and shiny.

He looks in the mirror formed by the blade
He sees his black eyes looking back at him
Then he understands.

He feels it with absolutely certainty
He is the reason why no one else wants to join
He is the reason why all the other People have moved
away.

They have left him
They have abandoned him
They know he is unlovable.

Chapter 31

They Have Abandoned Us

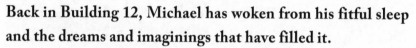

Back in Building 12, Michael has woken from his fitful sleep and the dreams and imaginings that have filled it.

In these nighttime hours he has feverishly thought enough for a lifetime, but there are still some questions he has. Some points of clarification needed.

Quietly, he has left his own room to seek out Belle and Adam. First creeping through the corridors quietly, and then increasingly noisily as urgency gets the better of him, he now stands outside their room.

He slowly opens the door and slips inside.

He can hear the noises of children sleeping. The littlest ones like the twins snuffling through snot filled noses. The older children breathing deeply in slow rhythms.

He stands and listens. His turbulent mind calms a little as he hears all these breathing patterns in the dark, and he takes a moment to also slow his own.

Then quietly he begins to walk across the room to the far corner where he knows Belle and Adam have their bed. Carefully stepping between the sleepers, making sure he does not wake any of them.

Arriving in the corner he reaches down to the blanket wrapped bundle in the bed.

"Belle," he says as he softly shakes the bundle to wake her. "I think you met my father." He believes it as soon as he says it.

"Belle, I need to talk about my father."

Then his arm is grasped from behind.

"What are you doing here?" comes an angry whisper. The voice is not Belle or Adam. Michael looks back and sees it is Ricky.

"I need to speak to Belle and Adam right now," he says.

"They have gone," Ricky replies. Turning, he shakes the bundle again, but the pile of clothes, tightly bound, can't wake up.

Belle and Adam have gone.

The room is coming awake. Children sitting up as they hear the voices of Ricky whispering and trying as best he can to keep things calm, and Michael, who in his desperation has forgotten the need for quiet and is now speaking with a voice full of passion and urgency.

"Where are Adam and Belle?" he demands. "Where are they?"

Michael has taken a long time getting to this moment, and now he wants to hear it. Wants validation that his father is still out there waiting for him. He needs to hear this, know this, feel this.

"I need to talk to them about something very important. I know all about their problem and the baby they are expecting, but I need to talk to them right now about something I need to sort out," he says, his eyes flicking from Ricky and then to each of the other older children as they sit up. Pleading for them to help him. Help him bring his unspoken dreams into reality.

But in the briefest of moments, those dreams are shattered. For after a short pause, Ricky breaks down and shares the secret he and the others have just been asked to keep. Hoping Michael can, in his greater maturity, take on this burden and tell the room what they should all do next.

"Belle and Adam aren't here—they have gone to find a way for us all to escape," comes his reply.

He holds out the letter that they read after Belle and Adam left. Each of them doing their best to pretend that they were unaware. Pretending to be asleep while listening to every muffled sound as Adam and Belle crept out into the night. Then taking the letter almost as soon as the two had left the room and reading it together in a huddled circle.

Over and over.

Now Michael reads it too.

"Why have they gone? What escape do they think they can make happen?" he asks.

"Belle says she will find a way for us to escape too," Kate says, her voice full of calm and belief. Confidently poised.

"They are going to send for us soon," John says. "See, she says so at the end."

"You have got to be kidding if you think they are going to come back for you," Michael says. "They have to escape quickly before the Sage finds out they are pregnant," he finishes.

No sooner has he ended, then the room erupts with the sound of crying as the children burst into tears.

"Look what you have done," Kate says to Michael, gathering

up Will and Cathy in her arms, hugging them closely. "You don't know Belle if you think she won't find a way to help us escape too," she continues.

Michael is about to tell her the reality of this world. "Stupid children," he thinks to himself.

But as he looks at Kate's face a voice from within him talks to him.

It says, "They have been abandoned. You know all about that don't you Michael? What are you going to do about it?"

And just like that, Michael is released. Able to move forward. To take on a new role. No longer the abandoned. Now the protector of the abandoned. Dawn comes and finds the room quiet and peaceful. Michael has calmed them down. He has stepped up.

Their new leader.

Chapter 32

For the Good of the People

It is morning.

In the center of the Field, deep in the heart of the Ship, Belle, Adam and the Engineer are working in the Engineer's station.

Meanwhile around the Field, outside every building, the Sages are about to make their first announcement.

They have prepared well for this moment.

For their Flocks it comes as a surprise. For their Lawenforcers, every step of their plan has been rehearsed and envisioned multiple times. So that Sage and Lawenforcers can work in unison in every building across the Field.

First step: The Rousing.

Rouse all of the People and bring them down onto the Field. Do it quickly, brook no opposition. Say little, be firm, they must come now as they are. Down to the Field, for a special Council of our Sages.

This has happened just after daybreak. The Lawenforcers have gone quickly from sleeping room to sleeping room. Waking, informing, directing.

Not as difficult as one might imagine. Ever since Building 27 burned, the Council of Sages has ensured that every member of each Flock is well versed in processes to get them safely out of their buildings in times of emergency. The Lawenforcers have just applied those processes in unison across all of the buildings at once.

So each member of each Flock is now out on the Field.

Second Step: The Assembly.

The Lawenforcers have pointed, prodded and organized until each Flock is drawn up in rows of forty across. As straight as possible, facing the center of the Field. No rhyme or reason for who stands next to whom.

Now every building has a block of People forty wide and twenty to thirty rows deep. All facing the center of the Field. Facing the two Ships that stand there. The Lawenforcers are in two columns to either side.

Third Step. The Silence.

This required careful design. The Sages had worked hard on this step. The first idea was to have their respective Lawenforcers call for silence. But more voices, added to the hubbub and murmurs of hundreds of People woken from their sleep and turned out onto the Field. How well would that work?

The Sages agreed that was not the answer. How could they

expect their Flocks to be silent when each among them would be asking what was happening? Why were they assembled like this? Why were they out under the rising sun, unprepared for it. People who had forgotten their goggles, left the outdoor clothes behind as they rose and followed the masses out of their buildings. Little ones crying.

Who could realistically expect silence in this context?

Sage Caring at this point had said he would be able to, but he was the exception and every other Sage had suggested they come up with another way.

So as each building door opened, and the first of the People filed out onto the Field, ushered by their Lawenforcers, their eyes were drawn to a wondrous sight.

In front of every one of their buildings is a low platform. All identical, save for Sage Gratitude's which also includes a large metal gong.

On each platform stands their Sage.

Sword held high overhead.

And in unison, twenty-seven Sages move into synchronized motion. Flowing, smooth, powerful, mesmerizing motion.

As each person sees their Sage on the platform ahead, they fall silent. Watching the greatest sword masters they know at work.

Twenty-seven shining silver swords arcing and rotating sending reflections of sunlight across their Flocks. A ritual display of Sworder skill.

Mesmerizing them into silence.

Fourth Step: The Readying

The Sages had gone through the calculations. How long would it take until the final building spat out its last person onto the Field? How long would they need to maintain their sword practice? So that once the final person joined their row, the twenty-seven Sages would stop in unison? And how to communicate that moment with precision?

None of them knew the answer precisely. Which meant that the sword show went on for a long time. Which also meant that it needed to maintain interest.

So by the end, the Sages were sights to dream about. Whirling vortices of highly trained flesh and bone and highly ground and sharpened flashing metal.

Rising to a crescendo that kept all eyes forward all mouths closed.

Then together, they came to a sudden stop.

Twenty-seven swords high in the air, facing directly upward. Sharp surface facing their Flocks.

Then just as suddenly, twenty-seven swords returned to their scabbards.

Fifth Step: The Announcement.

A handful of verses carefully crafted, precisely memorized, delivered in unison of volume, pace, and emphasis.

Twenty-seven Sages speaking as one.

"We have asked you to come together today

Representatives of our People, we join together

We are equal among ourselves and equal among our People

We know our burden, received not asked for

We come here to protect our charges
We know our task."
Then, less ceremonial, but just as orchestrated:
"We ask for sacrifices
We ask each to consider
Are you still needed?
Are you still wanted?"
On the last word, they pause together. Then go on.
"Our resources are too few
Our People are too many
Our Flocks are to reduce in number
Today we ask for volunteers."
Again, a pause for emphasis.
"Are you still needed?
Are you still wanted?
Are you the sacrifice?
Today we ask for volunteers."
Then silence.

Sixth Step: The Waiting.

Nothing more. Nothing else said.

Twenty-seven Sages now silent. Standing on their platforms. Still.

Waiting.

More than twenty-eight thousand People, all in silence, considering the words, their meaning, the decision that they imply.

Volunteer, step forward. Sacrifice.

And then what?

What would volunteering mean? What was the sacrifice that

their Sage was asking for? Was this the Choice? Go or Stay?

Or something else entirely? Something new.

The waiting continues.

Seventh Step: The Clarity

Suddenly, from the direction of Building 8, a gong sounds. Sage Gratitude has been counting down in his mind from a lofty number, and now he has got to zero and this moment.

The moment for clarity.

He sounds the gong on his platform.

Across the Field, the other Sages and Lawenforcers have been waiting for this moment.

At the sound of the gong, each Sage moves into motion. Sword sweeps from scabbard, whirls into motion, bringing thousands of eyes back into alignment.

Attention recaptured.

Then more.

"We ask for sacrifices

Step forward

For the good of each Flock

For the good of the People."

Then louder, chanting, synchronized, swords once more in beautiful motion.

"Are you still needed?

Are you still wanted?

Are you our volunteer?

Are you our sacrifice?"

On the final word, and propelled by the synchronicity and beauty, they step forward.

Those who feel unneeded, unwanted.

The sacrifices.

...

It is hours later that the Engineer brings Adam and Belle back into the hold, and across it to the open hatchway.

The sun is still hot on the Field as they creep down the stairs, and squat in the shadow behind the Ship's leg to wait for the safety of night.

The Field is deserted and quiet.

The three of them have no inkling of the horror that they have missed out on.

While they sat and talked deep in the bowels of the Ship, this Field has seen the first phase of the Flock reductions.

Volunteers called for, sacrifices taken.

Almost 10%. Almost three thousand heads rolling.

Now taken away.

Only the red damp Field marks the choice they took.

Failed, every one.

No Pure in these ranks.

These first ranks.

...

In the basement of Building 28, Sage Caring is back to do some more talking. As usual, he enters the basement alone and in need of someone to listen.

She is there as always.

He drops off her food in the corner by the door, and then goes to her side of the room. His lantern casting a little light and making shadows move around him as his walks towards her.

"Are you awake?"

She is always lying on the ground. Always conscious. Woken by his steps and the door opening. However, it has become a little courtesy that he asks her if she is awake to receive him. She will stay lying, and listen to him anyway, but he feels better when he pretends this is something mutual. He the guest, she the host. It helps him with his work.

This time, something different happens. As he prepares to squat in front of her, she sits up quickly with her back to the wall.

He is struck by this. He looks a little closer and the light of his lantern reflects off her eyes. They are fixed on him, open and staring. More importantly her face seems alive somehow. He finds it a little unnerving. He has not seen her like this before.

He pauses. Wondering. Still, he came here for a reason. To unburden himself as he always does. It really does not matter what mood she is in. So long as she is quiet and not in one of her screaming phases.

So he begins. "I want to tell you about my day. It's been a difficult one for me."

An understatement if ever there was one.

Over the next twenty or thirty minutes he tells her everything. Of the ceremony, the volunteers, and the sacrifice asked for and freely offered. The Failed who were ready to give of themselves.

Then he tells of his sword play. The enormous physical demand it took of him. As he worked his way through neck after neck. He dwells on his soreness and tells her of his pains and aches.

She does not respond—she never does.

Then he gets on to the core of why he came this time.

"I am worried about what is going to happen next," he says

He needs to share his apprehension about the next stage of the plan. It is his plan, but he fears its scope and the complexity of its implementation all the same. He plans to take a lot of heads, but is worried that something might backfire. Worried for his own skin.

As he talks about the plan, he feels a sense of a burden leaving him and a lightness beginning to fill him up in its stead. This is why he is here. Let her take his concerns from him.

She is a good listener.

He finishes by telling her his expectations. How many of his Flock he expects will be found with some flaw. Some reasons to be Revealed and Reckoned.

Then he shares the big issue he is grappling with. Whether or not he will be able to hide his own little mutation, behind his right knee.

It is good to share his fears with someone, especially some-one who carries no threat to his own circumstance.

For a moment he thinks she is about to respond, but no. Just the lantern flickering over her face.

He gets up, leaves the basement, and returns to his room.

She stays sitting for a long time.

Her mind now fully active. Calculating and recalculating.

Around the challenge he has described. The equation that he and the other Sages have determined to rebalance in the next phase of their work. Turning over his fears and looking at them from every side.

Her well trained Pilot mind is back.

It has a journey to plot, a course to map.

Unknowingly, the Sage has given her a purpose, and that was all she was looking for.

A new chance.

Chapter 33

Volunteer Aftermath

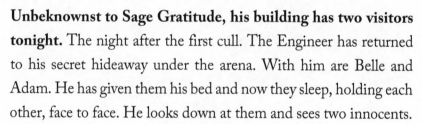

Unbeknownst to Sage Gratitude, his building has two visitors tonight. The night after the first cull. The Engineer has returned to his secret hideaway under the arena. With him are Belle and Adam. He has given them his bed and now they sleep, holding each other, face to face. He looks down at them and sees two innocents.

He sees their purity and knows it is good.

They have no inkling of what is about to happen around this Field. He is warmed inside by the knowledge that in their lack of understanding, in their freedom from anxiety and worry lies the secret that he himself wants to live. The simple way, focused on now and the certainty that all will be good. That all will work out for the better.

If only he could take that view so easily.

He has listened to each word that the Sages have uttered in their meetings and councils over the last few weeks, and he knows now that the end is coming fast.

One way or another, it is time for action.

His lump makes it impossible for him to rejoin the Flock. If the Revealings are scheduled for this evening or for next, it makes no difference in the long run. If he is there when they take place, he will be found out, then he is done for.

So from now until the end, he and these two Pure must go unseen.

He has a small supply of food that he keeps here in his secret place. But now, while the other two sleep, he creeps out into the sleeping silence of his building and steals more from the kitchens. Crams a sack with dried provisions and some leftovers—now cold but cooked root crops and some slabs of protein. He looks for dried fish but the barrel is empty. What he has will have to do.

He returns to his hideaway with his sack bulging. The two Pure still sleep. Only the Pure could sleep in the midst of such danger, oblivious to the risks of an open door and a surprise visitor. Still this hideaway has avoided discovery for years now, and no reason to think that will change this night.

He closes the door, puts down the new provisions, and then wakes them up.

He begins by telling them of this most recent meeting of the Sages. Of their intent to initiate a new round of culling. This time driven by the physical state of each member of their Flocks.

He does not need to elaborate. As quickly as he says it, Belle and Adam know the implications. Belle's hands go to her belly, but she is calm. The timing may have changed, but this is the end she has feared and imagined for so long, that his news does not carry any new fear with it.

"So be it," Belle thinks to herself, and squeezes Adam's hand tightly.

"What do you think we should do then?" she asks the Engineer.

He explains his plan, rudimentary as it is. He shares nothing of his own condition - of his growing mutation.

"Like we have planned, we must go directly to Building 28 and find the Pilot. I think we have an opportunity to go now and remain unseen as the People are all in shock from the first cull and the Sages and Lawenforcers are focused on their planning for the next stage," he tells them. "If we go now, I hope we can get to the Pilot before the buildings awake."

As he says the words, speaks the plan, it all seems so unlikely to him. A fantasy.

Ridiculous to think they can find her without being discovered, broach this reality with her—a madwomen. Rouse her from her craziness, convince her to help them, make her come to the Ship, and reactivate it.

Ridiculous.

But Belle and Adam don't think so. As the Engineer talks, they brighten. They are excited. They believe. He feels their positive vibrations. Crazy as it can only be, he finds himself becoming positive too.

"It just might work," he says to himself

He smiles.

These Pure are good for him.

He laughs out loud, and a moment later they laugh too.

...

In Building 12, in Adam and Belle's room, the little ones are sleeping.

However, Michael, Ricky, and Kate are huddled in the corner that once housed Adam and Belle. They are in deep discussion. Their voices low but intense.

First they have shared what they witnessed today. Each describing their experiences, their reactions, the implications.

Ricky recalls seeing one after another of their building members step forward to volunteer for the cull.

He shares his surprise that so many went forward willingly. So many Failed seeming to find this way out preferable to the struggle for food and well-being that Sage Certainty described in her opening remarks.

"Michael, can it be true that we need to reduce our numbers so much?" Kate asks, already assuming their new elder will know the answer.

"I don't know, but the Sages seemed to be sure that the carrying capacity has collapsed," he answers.

Kate shares an even more troubling insight. "I saw the strangest thing in the eyes of those who passed me to step forward," she says. "I swear I saw gratitude. They were grateful to be able to volunteer for an end that would be good for the rest of us."

Michael says nothing.

"These Failed are crazy," Ricky says.

They all agree, and the three of them discuss this point at some length. How can it be that giving up your life could be a good thing? In the end, they all come to the same conclusions:

Yes, the Failed who stepped forward did so of their own volition.

Yes, they did it for the good of the Flock.

Yes, they may have been exhausted with this life.

Yes, they might have been looking for an end.

But even then, the end did not justify the means. So many ends, all happening at the same time. They can't stand idly by and watch more ends. That they all agree. A shared consensus. But unsatisfactory all the same.

Michael brings the meeting to a close, telling them to go about the day and care for the little ones. He also asks the two older ones to collect extra food and bring it back to their room. But carefully.

...

Michael has thoughts about the volunteer cull that he has not shared with the others.

He has revisited the entire episode in his mind. From the very first moment they were all told to assemble, through the Sage's words, to the volunteering and the resulting slaughter. He too is appalled by what he saw. However, he is also appalled by what he felt.

He wanted to be one of them—one of their number.

As the first volunteers had begun to step forward, he almost did too. He could see the logic of the sacrifice. Let others live by giving up your own life. The ultimate sacrifice. The ultimate statement of unselfishness. The ultimate act of contrition.

He knows he is not worthy to be among the ones still living.

Why not exit the stage? A graceful act to help the larger community. Give up in an act of grace. Let those that go forward remember Michael as one who chose not to. Maybe then they will think fondly of him.

"Why not?" he thinks to himself. He knows the answer.

The Scavenger dream calls to him. He wants to believe it. That out there, on the Far Side, his own father lives waiting for him. Thinking fondly of him. Saving him through his own sacrifice long ago when he knew their Revealings were imminent. Leaving his son behind to live safely among the Flock.

That's the story he wants to believe right now. If that story is true, then he can't abandon hope.

"What to do?" he asks himself.

No answer comes. Let the shared room consensus be his for now.

...

In the basement, a spark has been ignited, which now has become an internal fire.

First, somewhere in the windmills of her mind, a little breath of air began to blow, made by Sage Caring's words that still linger on. Then the Pilot's disciplines of identification, evaluation, choice, and determination have kicked in. As taught her so long ago.

The Sage's comments and words have been shaped into her way of thinking. Disaggregated, atomized, scrutinized, and then reassembled into a new synthesis. One that a Pilot would use to plot a course.

She sees the hypocrisy in the Sage's words. His willingness to take other heads for no more than he has growing on his own body. But she does not spend much time on his condition. For the first time in a long time, she is interested in her own.

She has shed her clothing and stands in her basement naked. Revealed.

She has a focus. So no screaming now. Instead, she has work to do. Her hands are exploring her body in the dark. Creeping inch by inch. She starts at the top of her head, and lets her fingers feel every inch of her scalp under the lank blonde hair. She feels her eyelids, her nose and mouth, around her cheeks to her ears, and behind them, feeling only the blemish of the ancient hub. Everything else as it should be. Dirt and sores yes, but nothing untoward.

Then her neck, her shoulders. Lifting one arm and hand and letting her other hand feel it from shoulder to tip of fingers. Spending extra time in the hollow of her underarm. Seeking out some lump or lesion. Then the other.

Back to her torso. Examining her breasts. Her belly. The hard part, reaching around behind her to check her back. Then buttocks and hips. Forward to her pubic area. Down her thighs, her hamstrings, her knees, calves and shins, ankles and to her feet.

Searching for something unusual.

But she finds nothing. That gives her something to think about. It has been a long time since she thought there was anything good about her.

"Why don't I have anything wrong with me?" she asks herself.

It gives her something to think about. Why has she been left pure in body? Presumably because she has been in the dark away from the harmful radiation and rays of the sun.

"For what purpose?" she asks next. That takes more careful consideration. She sits down in the darkness, and as she ponders, her mind continues to click into action. Doing her Pilot's practice.

She is awakening.

...

Sage Gratitude has called a Council of Sages. They arrive quickly and file into the arena quietly. Too quietly.

Once the circle is complete, he begins straight away.

No formalities, no ceremony.

"We asked for volunteers, we carried out the sacrifices, we completed the first phase of this cull. Please make your reports," he says.

The Sages go one after the other. The reports are all essentially the same.

The volunteers that came forward were all older Failed. Many were among the most skilled – leaders in the various trades, worn down by the extra responsibility and willing to give up their burdens. They did not question the process. Went meekly to the sword.

For most of the buildings, a decile was completed. In some, it came close to a second decile—including Building 28, of course.

The Lawenforcers did their job efficiently. The bodies and heads were disposed of as planned.

Happy fish and well fertilized crops.

"How are your Flocks?" he asks next. "How are your Failed?"

Again around the circle. Again common answers. The remaining Failed have taken things well enough. It seems that most of them saw this coming, or at least see it as a necessary release for those who no longer want to stay, and who do not have the desire to go. A simple and quick exit.

"What of your Pure?"

Here the answers are more complex and unsatisfactory. The Sages are all Failed. As they seek to answer this question, the gap between them and Pure Flock members becomes apparent to Sage Gratitude. Few of the Sages give compelling answers.

Some report unease, some report distress, some report little acts of rebellion. None of them convinces him that they know how the Pure are actually feeling. Quite frankly, he does not know either.

Later, once he returns to his own quarters, Sage Gratitude goes through the plan in his mind. They have made a good first pass at reducing the Flock's size by almost three thousand. But not enough by far. This he was expecting. He smiles to himself. Sage Caring did a good job of outlining the more aggressive path. So good in fact that Sage Gratitude can shelter behind him and let him take the pain and emotion for what must come next. Since the next phase of culling will have to commence soon.

The Revealings will begin within the week. Let their Flocks sleep tonight, for tomorrow will come fast enough. Let the Sages and Lawenforcers gather their strength.

They will need it for the work ahead.

Chapter 34

The Pilot and the Engineer

It is the small hours. The Field is quiet. Out in the croplands, work continues, but in the buildings almost everyone is asleep.

In several of them, small groups of Lawenforcers are still preparing for the day ahead. A few Sages still sharpen their swords in the privacy of their rooms, or go through their practices, releasing their bodies from the tension and knotting of the first cull and preparing them for the rigors of the next. But for the most part, the Flock sleeps.

In Building 8, the Engineer, Belle and Adam are ready.

The Engineer has told them to take everything with them, assuming they will not return. So each of them is burdened. Mostly with food, but the Engineer also has a backpack full of equipment and manuals. Things that Adam and Belle have never seen before and cannot put a name or purpose to.

Most interesting of all, before leaving, they watched as the Engineer shed his usual clothing and unwrapped a bundle that he pulled out from under his bed.

In it is a light, silvery one-piece outfit which he now dons. It covers his body from his toes to the top of his head. Belle is amazed. It looks like nothing she has seen before.

Almost otherworldly.

Before she can say anything, he covers it up with his outer coat and once again appears as they all do. An unshapely lump.

The Engineer takes them through secret paths unknown to the others in his building, bringing them some hundred of so yards away on the Far Side of the Field. What the purpose of this passageway once was is now forgotten. But it serves to get them quickly and quietly outside and on their way.

Once in the open air, the night is still and cloudless. A faint light is coming from the departing moon, but it is still too early for the glow of the sun to be seen on the horizon.

The Engineer turns to them and makes sure they are ready. He nods to both of them, and then strides out in front.

They circle around the backs of the buildings and make quick progress until they are past the empty space of Building 27.

There it is, Building 28 standing alone.

Belle wonders at this. Can all their hopes now be dependent upon someone they have never met who supposedly lives under this lone building? It seems improbable even to her optimistic way of thinking.

However, it is the plan.

At the main entrance of Building 28, they take their first and biggest risk. This is not a building that the Engineer knows, and he is not prepared to try and find a back way in. So instead, he has decided on the direct approach.

They have rehearsed a story should they be stopped. They are here from Building 8 to collect some parts that Sage Gratitude says are needed for a repair to the fish tank pumps.

It is not a bad story for an Engineer to tell. He can pull this off if they are stopped. No Lawenforcer will know more about the fish tank equipment than this last Engineer.

Thankfully, the story is not needed.

They open the main door, walk in unnoticed, and turn straight to the main stairwell. Building 28 seems to be sleeping, as was their own, and before they can catch their breath, the Engineer has Belle and Adam on the staircase downwards.

They go quietly, and after three flights, they arrive at the bottom. In the basement.

It smells bad down here.

The Engineer is still in front. He stops now, and opening his sack, brings out the fish oil lantern that Belle and Adam had stolen. It takes a moment to strike a light, and then the lantern catches and casts its dim flickering light around the base of the stairwell.

A single large door stands before them.

Before entering, the Engineer turns and tells Belle and Adam to stay outside. He will go in alone. Perhaps one person is less likely to spook her, he says. They do as they are told and watch as he opens the door just wide enough to slip through, the lantern held before him.

As he goes, Belle and Adam are plunged into blackness. Adam lets out a gasp, and Belle reaches towards him, enveloping him in her embrace. Drawing him closer, until she, he, and baby between them are clenched into a firm oneness.

Adam folds into her, and feels the gentle kicking against his own abdomen.

He kisses her, and waits.

...

She has been sleeping, but not well.

So many questions, and no good answers. Her mind has awoken to the reality that she is sound in body. Not just because of the intense daily workouts of the last eighteen years. More to the point, her body is also free of mutations. Perhaps years out of the sun's light has left her free of skin damage, other than the albino white that has replaced her once golden brown.

Why?

The purpose she has been looking for subconsciously for so long is still evading her. Just out of reach. It can't be just to listen and ponder the decisions of the Sage. There must be something more there. She intuitively knows that she is made to play a part, but she can't put it into words.

So what is to be her purpose?

This is the question that is bothering her now as she examines it from every direction. Around and around. No sense can she make of it. Slumped against her favorite wall—the one that faces the door to the basement. So inwardly focused that she does not hear the door of her basement open, or see the dark figure with lantern held before it, until it is almost halfway across the room.

Then, with a rush she sees him.

And he sees her.

Suddenly, they are back together. As they were so many times in training.

Very different circumstances.

...

He knows what to say.

Secret words that all of them learned in training long ago. That confirmed their identity and initiated their sessions of training. Engineers, Pilots, they all had their codes, their unique identifiers. He shares his first, and then speaks hers.

She jumps to her feet. Standing straight at attention.

He repeats her code and the other elements of this sequence.

She knows now. This is no mistake. Those numbers, in that sequence, means so much. She doesn't need to think. It comes rushing back to her.

The first part is her identifier. The second the common command for help needed. A command that cuts through everything. Eighteen years of despair and madness washes away in a moment. Her training, so long unused, now surfaces with a rush. Pushing aside her madness, her disorganization.

"What do you want of me?" she asks him.

"It is time for us to try again," he says.

And turning, he goes back to the door.

...

Belle's first impression is of the stench, which is strong and unpleasant. It makes her feel sick to her stomach, although she has grown up in a world where cleanliness is almost an impossibility.

This is something all together different. This is the smell of someone who not only does not clean, but does not care. She lets the Engineer lead her across the room, Adam following, and in a few strides, she is beside him standing above a figure who sits on the ground.

"Sit down and tell me your story," comes a voice, at once soft and also commanding.

No crazy woman this. Her madness has gone much more quickly than it arrived. Driven out by a clarity of purpose. A mission. A new chance.

Belle does as she is asked, and Adam sits beside her too. The Engineer takes another pace and sits down beside the woman facing them both.

"Where to begin?" she asks herself.

"At the beginning," comes the answer.

So Belle starts there. Her beginning. She tells this woman, in the dark basement, about herself. Who she is, where she lives. Who else she lives with. All about Adam and her and what they did together. And where it has left them both.

She tells the other woman about the baby, and how precious it is, and how it has become her focus and purpose. As she does so, she pauses, expecting something, but she gets no response, so just keeps on going.

She talks about the options they have explored. Just as with Michael, she tells this woman about their trip to the Far Side, the Scavenger circle, and the Prophecy. Here, the Engineer interrupts her.

"Tell her exactly the words they told you. The exact words," he says.

So Belle does so, reciting them as she and Adam heard them.

"There is an escape, but we know not where to find it
Search for those who know the secrets of the past
They will know how to unlock it
The doorway through which you wish to pass
They are the keyholders, though no key do they bear
Go to them if you seek your escape
Go."

As she finishes, it is the Engineer that speaks first.

"Do you see what this means?" he asks.

"Not yet, but perhaps," says the Pilot. "Continue."

Belle tells the story of their return, of their trip out to the Ship, and of their meeting in the dark with the Engineer. As she does so, she can tell something has changed. Across from her, she sees two bright eyes focused on her. She can tell the Pilot is listening intently.

Belle explains how Adam and she want to restart the Ship and leave. Soon they will no longer be able to hide their baby from the inevitable Reckoning that will surely follow their Revealing.

Here, she for the first time, finds herself at a loss of how to proceed. With a rush, the worry and anxiety of the last few weeks overtakes her and she breaks into sobs. Adam leans into her, but it is the Pilot who speaks next.

"You are right to be fearful. I have been told the plan, and I know it for what it is. It is coming soon and it will be terrible—the carrying capacity of this place will no longer support us and our Sages will fix this...must fix this, now. Tell me why you think my Ship can be started."

"It is the Prophecy and we have seen it in our dreams," Belle says simply, and she feels Adam beside her nodding in agreement.

"You are the keyholders," she says. "You together can unlock this Ship and make it work again."

"Do you see this now?" the Engineer asks the Pilot. "The Ship is complete, but without two of us nothing is possible. We are two keys that need to turn together."

He pauses.

"I want this second chance to try and make this right."

"I want that too," she responds.

...

The Engineer has shown Belle and Adam across to the other side of the basement, and now he sits facing the Pilot. He is talking fast, and she is responding just as quickly. They talk back and forth. They are talking again about their aborted manual efforts to start Ship 10 after the Failing.

"Was there anything else we could have tried?" he whispers.

"Is there anything else we could have come up with?" she asks.

Almost twenty years of black despair have been blown away in a heartbeat in this meeting with two Pure and the Prophecy they are carrying. To both the Pilot and the Engineer, it had been impossible to imagine trying again. Without any self-belief, without any sense of optimism, without positive dreams to inspire, who would ever try anything as complex and critical and unlikely as a manual takeoff? Stripped of those most human of characteristics, they had sunk down to be less than human.

But now, these young people, these strange and troubling words, have appeared in their lives. The deep fog of despair that has clogged their minds and darkened their mindsets, is being blown away and replaced with a new bright light.

Ignited.

···

In all those years of training twenty years before, the Pilots had rarely interacted with the Engineers, and she had had no interest in them when their paths did cross. She, Pilot, had been in a class above all others. She had been aware of this Engineer of course. His purpose had been interwoven with hers in Ship 10. But she had not really paid any attention to him. Surprisingly perhaps, the Intelligences had not brought them together very often. Pilots working with Pilots, Engineers with Engineers had been the norm. The entire group coming together only rarely.

He, on the other hand, had always watched every move she made when they did come together. Watching her from afar whenever their training crossed paths. His own golden Pilot.

Now in this new time and place, she really notices him for the first time.

"What was your name?" she asks. "I don't remember."

"Andrew," he answers. "You are Dawn."

For hours it seems, the two sit and talk. Belle and Adam have left the basement and are sitting at the bottom of the stairwell. Inside they can hear the soft murmuring of the Engineer and the Pilot.

Adam has his arms around Belle. Bringing her close to him. He whispers, "Do you think they will find a way to get the Ship to work?"

Belle's answer comes without pause. "Yes they have to—they need their second chance even more than we need our new start."

She kisses him on the cheek. "Let's just wait. I am sure they will be out soon and then we will go to the Ship and get it working again." She looks into Adam's eyes and continues, "Once it is working we can figure out how to come back and take everyone with us."

They don't have long to wait.

The basement door opens and out of it comes the Engineer followed by the Pilot. He has taken off his outer garments and is again clothed only in his silvery suit. Behind him comes the Pilot also clothed in her old, but complete Pilot's costume.

"Why has she kept it, and how has it withstood the years of decay?" Belle wonders.

Regardless, as Belle and Adam watch, two similarly clad People stride out of the basement and into the stairwell.

In this moment, both Belle and Adam really believe with all their hearts that the Prophecy is coming true. Right here, right now.

They follow the others into the light.

Chapter 35

The Revealings Commence

A rumor has been circulating in the eating room where most of the People have come to hear the news. It is now twelve hours since the Lawenforcers locked the doors to Building 12. After the workers had returned from the fields, and before the next wave had left for the aquaculture and fish ponds, they had all been gathered in the largest space in Building 12.

It was crowded—perhaps a little less than would have been the case before the cull, but nonetheless, it was packed. There was a palpable sense of trepidation.

"What's going on?" Ann asked Ricky as she tried to reposition one of the twins onto her hip.

"Beats me," he replied "But I don't feel good about this."

The room companions were together in a tight cluster. John held the other of the twins while Kate was doing her best to keep the other little ones quiet.

"We don't know so let's not worry about it," Michael

interjects. He stands beside them. Since arriving in the night, and discovering that Belle and Adam had gone, he has been with them at all times.

In normal times, their absence might have been discovered. But the last few days had been chaotic. Michael suspects that Sage Certainty and her Lawenforcers are not yet clear on who has been culled and who is still among the Flock. In the blood and tears of the terrible massacre, the detailed record keeping has lost track. Afterward, the bodies were dumped and no one had the passion or desire to look closely at the heads as they were piled into one sorry heap.

Anyhow, Michael has been sleeping on Adam and Belle's bed ever since, and suffice to say, no one seems the wiser for their absence.

···

Now hundreds of People are packed into a large, but not really large enough space, all buzzing with rumors about what is going on. Fear just below the surface. The cull still fresh in everyone's mind.

"Why can't we go back to our rooms?"

"What's going on?"

"Is there work today?"

"Where are Betty, Bob and Leena?" as People notice the gaps in their familiar circles. Knowing the answer before they ask the question. Too terrible to contemplate, but formality demands they ask after those they have lived their lives with. So hard.

The Lawenforcers have not made things easier. They say they know nothing, and even those who can normally be relied upon to share a word or two are silent when questioned. Perhaps they really don't know what is happening.

What they do know is that they have to keep everyone in this room. The Sage has been absolutely clear about this.

"No one leaves, not for any reason," Sage Certainty has told them.

This they have assured. Doors guarded. No one entering or leaving. Which at first seems an inconvenience. As the hours go by it becomes a challenge, and then, a cause of enormous stress. The natural processes of the People's bodies carry on, but their practices are no longer possible with the bathrooms on the wrong side of the locked doors.

It begins with the little ones—the twins wetting themselves in the early hours. The crying begins almost immediately.

Later, many among the adults are also inconvenienced. Agreements are made, and an area to one end of the hall becomes a makeshift place that they begin to use.

It heightens their concern that even this most natural of processes is on hold today.

Then, just as the discomfort has reached a pitch that makes the Lawenforcers fear their ability to control the Flock, everything changes.

There is a sound of loud knocking at the door. The Lawenforcers swing it open, and there, framed in the center of the double doors, is Sage Certainty. She stands still with sword held in her right hand. Her left hand held up, palm facing the crowd. A signal for quiet.

As their eyes turn to the door, silence descends.

Sage Certainty waits. Letting the quietness deepen, and the

sense of apprehension build. Then she begins.

"I have asked that you be brought together today

My Flock, my People, we join together

I am equal among you

I know my burden, received not asked for

I come here to protect you my charges

I know my task."

Already the fear is there. On everyone's tongue. The taste like metal. Filling their mouths.

Not without design are these words chosen. Chosen by the Council of Sages to echo those spoken just a handful of days before. They had judged well that beginning this way will reach the subconscious minds of their Flocks just as planned. It is working.

"I have asked for sacrifices

I asked each of you to consider

Are you still needed?

Are you still wanted?"

Again, a pause.

"I think there are some among you that did not heed our laws

Who selfishly hid their conditions from our Flock

Let others step forward, when in truth it was your turn

Our laws make plain—a mutation should be revealed."

"My duty is clear

To protect you my Flock

I must demand a Revealing

And Reveal these hidden sins

Not volunteered when volunteers were asked for."

Now there is panic among the Flock. For some with sharper minds, and hidden mutations, have already divined what will happen next. Hurriedly, they step back, trying to flee. Others push forward hoping to make the door.

But too late. The Lawenforcers are quicker, and well prepared. Apparently, their lack of insight a ruse, now dropped on the words of their Sage.

Lines quickly form in front of Sage Certainty.

A hedge of steel rises as the Lawenforcers unsheathe their swords. A glittering display of sharp metal that repels even the most forceful of the would be escapees.

The Sage raises her voice, and now it is a command.

"Disrobe, and let us see your purity

Disrobe, and reveal your sin."

The Flock knows this tone. Those with nothing hidden do her bidding.

A mass of assorted coats and shirts and pants begins to fall to the floor.

•••

It has been going on for a while now. Not just in this building. But in every one around the Field. Sages and Lawenforcers at the door. The Flock mostly undressed, some still covered.

In every building the process is the same.

The Lawenforcers step forward, encouraging the closest, naked, to come to them. Then they quickly evaluate them. Looking at their skin from head to toe. Checking for lumps and bumps and distortions.

In most cases, the first to disrobe are indeed clear of mutations. Each time this is confirmed, another Lawenforcer steps forward and takes the person by the arm and leads them out of the room. Into the corridor where a pile of miscellaneous clothing is ready to cover them, and long tables with drink and food wait to reward them.

The work begins slowly, but as the Flocks begin to realize the routine, it picks up speed. Each Failed gets to the same insight quickly. If they have nothing to hide, it will be best to step forward as quickly as possible. So they do. Lawenforcers are ready in pairs, and the processing is quick.

Sage Certainty stands still in the threshold, her sword unsheathed. At first, she has no use for it.

Then, the first Revealing.

Unbeknownst to this Failed, a little mutation has been growing on her back—just out of reach of her knowledge. Buried between her shoulder blades. A disc of red, discolored skin and a center that is slightly raised. Not something that anyone would be aware of, dressed up in their clothing from morning to night.

She had quickly taken off her clothes, keen to leave this room, and make her way into the corridor beyond. Certain of her condition. Sure she had nothing to hide.

Unfortunately, she was mistaken.

As she stepped forward, those behind became quiet. Suddenly aware of her state as her last vestige of clothing dropped to the ground and her back was revealed for the Flock.

The red disc marking her out.

The hush in the ranks behind was sudden and unsettling. She sensed it, but it was too late. Noises behind, and she tries to turn, but now the Lawenforcers have her in their grip.

"Mutation!" cries the first Lawenforcer as he turns her and

sees her back.

"Where and what?" cries the other.

"Center back, red disc and bulge," says the first.

"Can it be other than Mutation?"

"No."

Her fate sealed, they march her to Sage Certainty in the doorway. She and everyone in the room knows what will come next. More ritual. But her choice. They watch and hear. As the Lawenforcers hold her firmly, the Sage steps towards her.

"We are the People, I am the Sage.

I protect each one, I protect the whole.

You have brought me to this Reckoning

I did not ask for it, I do not want it.

But I see this Mutation. I incur the Law"

And without hesitation, the sword comes down, and the head drops to the ground. The mouth open, eyes staring. As if to ask, "Where is my choice? You forgot my choice!"

It's true.

With blinding speed, the Flock is abuzz. There is to be no choice this day. Revealed is to be Reckoned. A new ritual. "Why can't they chose to Run?" "That is their right, why not this time?"

Unbeknownst to them, Sage Gratitude has decreed this change. Realizing that a large group running to the Far Side would only create future problems and a potential shift of power away from him and his Sages around the Field, he has decreed that there will be no running today.

The game has changed.

...

Now everything is chaos in the hall of Building 12. It is full of noise. Full of fear and panic. Still hundreds within, but no longer a Flock. More a seething mass of humanity. Everyone focused on themselves. No community left in this room. Individuals, intent on themselves.

At the back of the room, a desperate mob has formed. Those who know their condition. Those who can see where this process is leading them.

Some are still at the front, but now uncertain. The seed of doubt sowed in each mind. Could I, like her, not know my own condition? Could I too have a hidden mutation about to be unveiled to all?

Some turn to their neighbors, in fear and uncertainty.

"Please look at me? Am I clean?" one asks.

"Help me, I am good, I am free of sin?" inquires another.

And for many, the returning answer is affirmative, and in a heartbeat they are in front of the Lawenforcers, through the doorway, and into the corridor to be greeted by those that have gone before. Dressed again, and fed. Almost a Flock again. But the cohesion gone. A Flock of parts, not yet a whole.

For others, the answer is not what they want to hear. The neighbor in tears whispers to them. Points. Or just turns away in distress. More are taken and held, and their Revealing begins.

Sage Certainty is kept busy. Heads keep rolling.

As they do in every such room in this circle of buildings on this Field. The one remaining concentration of humanity on this cursed and troubled world is becoming smaller at a terrifying rate.

...

The mob in Building 12 has been restless,

Some have despaired—Failed to a fault. They have watched the process at the door, and finally, have made their own choice. Stepping forward. Revealing themselves. Choosing their own time of Reckoning.

These had heard the Sage's words and knew already. They had chosen not to volunteer before. Chosen to keep their secret. Had mulled on their futures for weeks and sometimes months gone past. Mentally, these Failed had already decided their choice would be to stay. Just hoped it would be later. Not now. But confronted by the need to make the choice now, they stepped forward.

Others were not so sanguine.

In the mob were the runners too. Those who would have chosen to go, and now, with their Revealing upon them, suddenly saw their sacred choice being taken from them.

How unfair.

At the back of the room, a miscellany of mutated Failed, and a solid body of Pure, huddling together. Not respecting this new process. Their minds as one. Set towards some other path.

In Building 12, the room has become lightly populated. The Lawenforcers are still here. Their Sage at the doorway still. Now tired, with her gown scarlet, as are her arms and legs. It has been heavy work for her—physically and mentally. But she knew it would be.

At the back of the room, perhaps two score Failed and all the Pure of the building. The former older and grizzled and mutinous in their shared mutation. The latter younger and united by their rejection of this moment. The youngest of course, crying out in their confusion, knowing only that this was a time to cry since the grim faces of their caretakers made nothing else possible.

At the very back of this mob in Building 12, Michael has a plan.

He has realized where this is all heading. Has confirmed with his hands that the window is too firmly secured. Now he is on his hands and knees with a metal serving fork picked up from the rack in which they are kept, hacking away at the cement wall.

He has quickly found that this is not such a difficult task. Years of neglect have dampened and weakened this cement and as his fork hacks away, it seems to become easier and easier to break away flakes, then chips, then blocks of cement.

The outside of this wall is seemingly even more deteriorated than the inside. Exposed to the harsh weather patterns and the intense radiation, this once solid cement has become a friable mass on the outside.

Others have seen what Michael is about, and have joined him. First Ricky, then Kate, and now others of the Pure. Those able to find a piece of cutlery or serving implement using those. Others tearing their nails as they attack with the wall with bare hands. Their optimism welling up. They will escape. As soon as this narrow slit becomes a new doorway to the outside.

Lacking this optimism, the Failed are still facing inwards. Some step forward and meet their fate. Others argue among themselves. Still unsure of which direction to go. Flee or fight, or lay down and stay.

Across the Field in Building 21 the mob becomes a fearsome sight as it boils and then erupts, rushing for the Lawenforcers, meeting steel with flesh, and eventually being cut down at the door.

In Building 19, the same, but to a different end. This time, the mob surges and is cut down. But the force of those behind pushes falling cut bodies into the Lawenforcers, trapping their swords to them. Unable to fight back, the Lawenforcers are crushed and then trampled underfoot. Still the Sage stands as a last defense. Sword in motion, resisting to the end. But Failed armed with stolen swords fight back, and unskilled as they are, soon they are hacking at their fallen Sage. Chopping and slashing in a fury that has stolen their humanity from them. Then as the Sage's life blood gushes to the floor, they gush out into the corridor beyond.

Around the Field, more the former than the latter. More buildings end this day with a clean Flock. In the building beyond, a mass of heads and bodies being cleared away, and a handful of bewildered Pure waiting for their Sage to come to them to help them make sense of this time.

Only in Building 12 has Michael broken out of the box. Applying creativity to a long planned, and seemingly ironclad plan created by the Council of Sages for this day.

The slit has become a hole, now big enough that some could squeeze through.

Michael has organized his team of hackers, and each side of the opening is quickly moving outwards, widening.

Now it is done. In a moment, Michael is through, onto the Field, followed by Ricky and their roommates and then the rest of the Building 12 Pure. As they go, the remaining Failed turn and see this new turn of events. The first hesitates, the next is through the opening. Like a ripple moving fast, this new choice passes through the mob and they turn as one and start to press back towards the hole and the promise of a chance to run. A choice after all.

As the mob turns, so the Lawenforcers take their chance, and swords out, they come forward. Driving cold steel into the fleeing backs of the remaining Flock members. Beneath how many coats and shirts were mutations sliced into two, bumps burst. Up and down the swords go, and quickly the remaining Failed are disposed of.

How many of Building 12 have made it out onto the Field? No one is counting. Maybe seven score, maybe more. Most of the Pure of the building are there. Running. Out in front, Michael is leading.

Towards the Far Side.

Chapter 36

Like Father Like Son

It has not been easy.

Even without the need for discretion, it is not easy to run with little ones to carry, and young ones who don't quite understand the need to move so fast.

When they stumble, they want to stay down and take a rest. But Michael is there to get them to their feet. Get them running again.

It is also not easy to keep the group together despite Michael's constant work and stream of orders. The faster ones want to surge forward, and the older, younger, and more pessimistic of the Failed just want to go slow. If Michael did not do something, their group would have become a long line strung out behind him.

It is not easy for him to explain why they can't stop—especially since they have no food or water to keep up their energy and their spirits.

What Michael has done is use terror to drive them along. He has created the impression that they are being chased. That the horror that lies behind them may soon catch them up. The Lawenforcers are hot on their tails.

This is what he says now as he sees some of the others dropping back

"We have to keep together. They will be coming now, picking off any stragglers," he warns.

The crowd of faces that is turned towards him is full of fear. They believe him.

Michael himself doubts that what he says is true. Runners are usually left to go alone to the Far Side. But this is different. This is a group of Pure, and a handful of Failed running together, and Michael has some uncertainty about what Sage Certainty will be telling her Lawenforcers to do. Hopefully, this just helps their cause—a reduction in the Flock.

But who knows.

So with all his heart and with all his voice, Michael shouts, "Stay together, keep going! We will be through the croplands before you know it, and then we can stop. But not yet. They will come fast, and we have to get to the Far Side before them."

He turns, and starts up again at a pace that will stretch, but not over stretch the slower ones. It is frustrating to slow his pace, but he knows it is the right thing to do.

It is hot and the sky is clear overhead.

Which they all know is a very bad thing. You don't go outside in the sun, and today is a sunny day. A very sunny day. Most probably a mutation day.

Michael can feel the sun beating down on him—he does

not have the right clothes on, and his head is exposed. He never expected to be in the croplands running for his life when he first went down to the gathering hall.

He is hot, sweating, and he can already feel the sunburn beginning on his ears, cheeks and forehead and on the back of his neck. Sweat is running in rivulets down his back and chest.

Still, he is lucky.

Most of the others have even less on, and some of them had already begun to undress at the command of their Sage before they became runners. A few are just in t-shirts and leggings. Much more of their skin exposed to the hot sun's rays.

The first thing Michael had done, when they left the Field and entered the croplands, was to call a halt and make a few adjustments. He had moved the little ones from Ann and Cathy's shoulders to those of two of the Failed men who were running with them. Then he had tried to reallocate some clothing to make sure the naked had some covering, and everyone else could at least feel reasonably protected.

For his own part, he had given away everything he was wearing except for his coat, pants and shoes. His t-shirt, and underwear were now worn by others. Fortunately, the other Pure had been quick to give up an item or two each. Not much help where the younger ones were concerned, although he could see that one of the Failed women was crammed into what must have been Cathy or Ann's second layer. Tight and uncomfortable but at least some protection from the rays that sought to burn and corrupt.

For him giving up his other clothing had turned out to be a blessing in disguise that had helped him keep going, keeping him a little cooler in this blazing sun.

Michael has risen to this new challenge of leadership. But he is also feeling the burden that comes with it. He was attentive to Belle and Adam's story, and he is doing his best to retrace their steps. However, for what he has in mind, no deviation will be acceptable. As he looks for each reference point that they mentioned, he is full of inner fear and doubt. Is he on the right track, or is he taking this group into a new and unmapped place? The latter will be disastrous.

Michael must keep on the right path.

Michael is going to find the Scavenger group and his father.

He is sure of it.

It is what is driving him forward.

...

At the Scavenger camp, daytime practice has begun.

Men and women. Novice and master.

Swords many years in the making and roughly beaten rods of metal or shaped staves of wood. It makes no matter.

This group of Scavengers are lined up in front of their leader James. A small group showing great intensity of focus. Each slice of their practice the only now for any of them. This moment is everything. In unison they move, led by one in front, but none are behind. They move together.

Intensely accurate, like a many part machine locked in timeless precision. Yet perfection never quite reached.

They practice their swordplay with the single mindedness of those who gave up life a long time ago, and now practice together in their acceptance of their purgatory. Their place of waiting.

Waiting for the end.

Becoming closer to perfection in their waiting.

And just as predictably, as the sun moves through its cycle, so do the other Scavenger camps. Each working through their practice. Each led by a volunteer master who passes on each long practiced and perfected movement.

Clusters of sword masters preparing for their end.

Which is approaching them quickly now.

...

Up ahead, Michael can see the buildings that Belle described to him. Squinting, he can make out some glints of light in front of one.

Twinkling, sparkling, glittering.

He turns to Ricky, who has been keeping step with him at the front.

"There they are. The Scavenger group we are seeking. I think I can see them," Michael says. "I want you to stay here as a group. I will go forward and make contact."

Michael turns without waiting for a reply, intending to go alone, but Ricky is having none of it. Instead he keeps walking forward too, just a step behind Michael.

Michael in his concentration and purpose does not notice.

His focus is now absolute.

On the meeting ahead.

...

Practice is coming to an end.

The final movements. Complex and advanced so that few in the group have mastered them. James turns and turns again, sword accomplishing motions so fluid and flowing that it seems more like a ribbon of quicksilver than a bar of polished metal. He comes to the end, and his group finishes with him as one.

Now is the time for quiet individual contemplation, and James turns to find a place to sit. As he turns, he hears a shout.

"Hello...hello," a voice cries

The Scavenger circle turns as one and looks towards the direction that the shout has come from. They can see a few hundred yards out a group of People are coming their way.

"Prepare!" James shouts, and as one they bring their weapons to the ready.

Scavenger raids from other groups are not infrequent, but this seems different. This group is coming from the edge of the croplands and not from the Far Side.

James steps forward, and says to his circle, "I want you to stay here as a group. I will go forward and make contact."

And with that he turns and marches towards the fast approaching group.

His Scavengers follow him.

No one is going to wait behind this time.

...

So they meet.

Similar height. Pale skin. Black almond eyes. Jet-black hair.

One older and dressed in rags but with a strength and suppleness that has come of years of practice out here in the Far Side. The other, younger, but softer, also in rags. They each look at the other, sizing up. It is Michael that speaks first.

"I knew I would find you, father."

It is enough to turn James dumb. Behind each there is a splash of sound as their respective groups break into voice. James just stares, and then smiles.

"I have been waiting for you," he says.

Chapter 37

The People's Dream

The People are dreaming
The same dream.
Apart and together
In so many heads.

They are dreaming about what went wrong
How they did something they should not have.
How they stumbled and fell
How they gave up, and gave in.

How they stayed when they should have left
Or left when they should have stayed.
How their bodies made them do it
Or how they let their minds win.

So many false feelings
So many wrong emotions

So many bad decisions
So many chances lost.

Which led them each
Down the wrong path
To the same outcome.
The wrong outcome.

Common shame and guilt
In their collective dream.
They want to go back
To that moment.

If only they could
Relive that choice
Take the other turn
Walk the other path.

Go left not right
Up not down
Say yes not no
Or no not yes.

Change the outcome
This time through.
All dreaming the same dream
Getting to the same ending.

"Please!" they dream
"Please!" they ask
"Please!" they beg.

"Let me go back
Let me do it again
Let me get it right."

"Give me a second chance."

Chapter 38

Less Haste, More Speed

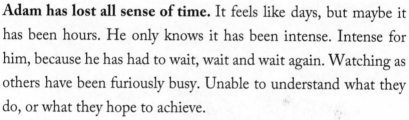

Adam has lost all sense of time. It feels like days, but maybe it has been hours. He only knows it has been intense. Intense for him, because he has had to wait, wait and wait again. Watching as others have been furiously busy. Unable to understand what they do, or what they hope to achieve.

He can see them together. Two parts of a whole. The Pilot, Dawn, giving the Engineer, Andrew precise but impenetrable commands. The Engineer responding in kind.

"Review manual sequence step 15. Engage the manual override on system five," she says.

"System five non responding, but no errors reported. Unable to verify if step 15 will function on engagement," he responds.

"Return to step 4 and iterate the stage lock," he says.

"Will do."

And so it goes on.

They have worked like this across the Ship. First in his room, then in hers. Adam holding the light for them. Intent on matters he can't comprehend.

Belle too has lost the plot for now. But unlike Adam, she had taken a torch and gone exploring by herself. Oblivious to Adam's request for her to stay with him.

Adam wishes she were watching this with him. This well coordinated effort by two supremely well trained professionals. Commanding the Ship. Manually putting it through its sequences. One step at a time.

Marching towards a whole that he imagines is their escape. Though each step seems so confusing and insufficient.

At the beginning, he had expected it to be short and sweet. Do one thing, do another, and then they would be on their way. Instead this iterative, connected but confusing barking out of numbers and confirmations and feedback. The Pilot and the Engineer are working together as one. But it is a one that Adam can't begin to comprehend.

Fortunately, they know exactly what they are doing.

...

Long ago this Ship was well designed. By Intelligences that, in their massively parallel artificial Intelligence, had imagined all possible futures and had then engineered in scenarios for each. Including even this one. A future in which these so fragile, but important humans would need to take control of the Ship without support. Without guidance.

Deep within the Ship rested power that could be unlocked without the help of the Intelligences. Power reserves intended for that 0.0000001% future in which somehow their charges needed to move forward without guidance.

No Harm would come from unconsidered options.

So a complex process designed to lead to a manageable outcome. A dumbed down, most basic of Ships, controlled by their charges.

But still a living Ship.

This was the process that Dawn and Andrew were working. Guided still by the Intelligences through the intense training laid down years before, grooved into their subconscious minds. Now unlocked and brought forward by the commands and responses they each gave each other.

Andrew's mind revealing another layer of process as Dawn asked for another step. Her mind lighting up with another pattern each time he responded and countered with his own words.

Two well trained People with minds unlocking in unison.

As this plan—the Intelligences' backup of all backup plans—is put into effect.

They are one.

One together, and one with their Ship.

Human and machine.

As it was meant to be.

...

Belle is back.

"What's happening, Adam?" she asks as she squats down beside him in the Pilot room where he watches the Pilot and Engineer. The four of them squeezed into such a small space.

"I don't know," he whispers. "They are still doing things to the Ship. They are up to step 36, but I don't know if that's good or bad."

The dialog between Pilot and Engineer now so abstract to him that he has given up any hope of comprehension. His only clues being the rise and fall of their tone. Sometimes he hears a little more excitement in their voices, he believes. It has been a while since they iterated backwards to an earlier step. Now they seem to be only moving forward. The numbers rising one at a time as each step is completed.

"They seem to be making progress, but I don't know how far they have come, or how much more they need to do," he tells Belle.

"Let's ask them. Let's find out when we will take off," Belle says, moving forward.

Adam pulls her back. "Don't disturb them, Belle," he says quietly. "I don't know what they are doing, but I feel we should not break their concentration. Watch with me."

Belle hesitates, her intuition to get things moving through the force of her will. Tell them what they need to do. Get this escape started. But like Adam she also knows she is out of her depth here.

She sits down beside him. Smiles to herself as Adam puts his arm around her.

She takes his other hand and puts it on her belly, which is round and protruding and which has been more active than ever since they got this Ship process underway.

"Baby is awake," she whispers in Adam's ear. "Baby is excited we are leaving."

Adam can hear the happiness in her voice, but he can hear the desperation too. His Belle is an open book to him, and he knows that everything she is right now is focused on one thought. Escape.

Adam lets her hold his hand to her center and straight away he feels it. The patter of tiny feet on the other side of this thin wall. This thin wall of Belle that separates the three of them.

"I think it's going to be alright," he whispers to his love.

"I know it will be," she replies.

...

Another age, and then—

"Final step confirmed, all systems confirmed," the Pilot says.

"Confirmed," the Engineer responds

And then they shout and stand and in their emotion they come together. Hugging tightly into one. A hug that is intense to the point of being painful. Dawn crushing Andrew, and him crushing her just as tightly back.

"Confirmed," he says again.

She puts her head back, opens her mouth and begins a triumphant cry, but he stops it just as soon as it begins with his lips on hers. Her cry in his mouth. Filling him with her joy. Tears come. Mingling.

Besides them, Belle and Adam are up on their feet. Sharing in the moment. Infectious euphoria fills the room.

Four of them celebrating together.

...

The Pilot has grown in stature now. Dawn is fully in control.

"We have confirmed the viability of a manual launch," she tells them.

Belle and Adam want to ask questions, but the powerful, forceful figure that speaks to them allows for no interruption.

"We will move directly to launch sequence," the Pilot continues. "Engineer, take the passengers to their capsules and go to your station. I will engage manual sequence in 30 minutes, and once the Ship systems engage, we can begin launch countdown."

"Confirmed," he responds.

He takes Belle and Adam firmly by the arms and marches them out of the Pilot bay and into the corridor beyond.

They are moving fast. Any thought of care in the dark left behind. The Pilot and Engineer are back, and they know every inch of this Ship.

"We need to get you into a capsule quickly," the Engineer says. "That's the safest place for you, even if the full systems are not active. They will protect you from the acceleration and I will come back and get you once we have taken off."

Then they are there. Lines of gleaming capsules, now empty of their charges long expelled onto the Field, open and awaiting.

The Engineer stops at the first, and turns to Adam. "Step in and lie down," he says.

Adam looks at Belle, and she can see the fear in his face.

"Don't worry Adam, we will get the ship to take off and then we can come back and get all of the others," she says, and stepping forward, she climbs into the capsule and lies down.

The Engineer leans over her. "Just lie still, and whatever you do, don't try and get out of the capsule," he instructs her. "It is the safest place for you during the launch, so just be patient and whatever happens around you, don't leave here."

Then he moves on to the next and Adam climbs in and lies down. Belle sees him in her peripheral vision as he looks at her on his way into his capsule. Her lover.

She lies back, and looks up. The cover of the capsule pivots from above her head where it is hinged to the base, extending upwards above her. It is a soft white color and even in the dark it seems to glimmer. Perhaps from the light of the Engineer's lantern or perhaps from some inner glow from the capsule material itself.

Now the Engineer is standing between their two capsules.

He can see them lying side by side. Untidy in their rags. Two innocent and unprepared children looking up at him.

He stands tall, and finds it in him to say a few more words.

"Trust us. We are going to do this together," he assures them.

And then turning away, he hurries to his own place. His Engineer's chair.

...

As he arrives, he can tell Dawn has initiated the first steps. In his Engineer's chamber, the running lights have lit softly. He wonders for a moment what other Ship's systems have come awake? Have the capsules closed?

He has to hurry now.

He sits down, and as he does so, her voice comes to him from deep within his station. A backup speaker placed ions ago for a scenario where his Intelligence might lose connection to the implant behind his ear. A scenario just like this one.

"Engineer, confirm your status," she says.

"Passengers encapsulated, Engineer in position," he responds.

"I have engaged final countdown, manual sequence," she continues.

He feels a wave of emotion but his training kicks in and he moves into action. His eyes flickering over the virtual controls that have flicked into his line of sight as he settled into position. His skin ragged and torn, but still functional, it appears.

His hands engage the glowing lights, and he begins his work.

They zig-zag down the countdown together. A single working organism.

It is getting close.

Exhilaration building.

Beneath him, the Pure lie in their optimism and wonder. Fear washed away by this unbelievable reality.

His own optimism rising.

And as his conscious mind engages with Dawn in their final steps together, his unconscious mind releases.

Levels above him, Dawn is fully focused on her task, but deep in her mind too, chemicals release and memory banks are opened. She too released from her long held belief.

Together they release from the subconscious belief of failure.

Failed no more.

...

"Confirming final countdown sequence" the Pilot says, and deep below her, the Engineer hears it in the speaker behind his head.

"Ship 10 confirms readiness for launch," he says.

"Ship 10 confirmed," she responds.

"Launch sequence commencing."

She begins to count the seconds. "5, 4, 3, 2, 1…"

She presses the big red button.

…

As she does so, deep within the Ship something wakes. A fifth mind flickers into consciousness.

In the tiniest fraction of a second, sensors awake, and across the Field, readings are taken. In that same moment, calculations are made, equations weighed. And conclusions reached.

This mind, mightiest of all, awake now, assesses the context, evaluates the circumstances, engages the laws, and concludes.

Harm.

And in that same briefest of moments a decision is made, and the sequence is broken.

No Harm.

…

She presses the big red button.

Nothing.

Another Failing

Final Failing?

Chapter 39

Sworders in Action

Back on the Field there is fear and doubt.

Those survivors of forced Revealings have been settled down into an uneasy state by their respective Sages. Each building's front door is manned by Lawenforcers. The Flocks are full of confusion and shock. Their minds a jumble of chaotic thoughts and feelings. While each person struggles internally with their thoughts and feelings, the armed conflict is over for now.

In five of the buildings, this is not the case. Instead, ranks have been drawn up and hostilities have commenced. Mobs of unruly People shouting and jostling and arguing about what to do and how to do it.

In these buildings the People are armed and ready. They are going to war. With their own. Failed, Pure, Sage, Lawenforcer, just names. Titles put on People by People. Now each will be revealed for what they are.

Flesh and blood.

So similar and so consistent in its reaction to sharp, cold steel.

The god of chaos is unleashed in these five buildings now.

...

Sage Gratitude has planned well. He knew that the Council's plan was not perfect. Expected that a few buildings would erupt and perhaps Sages would be lost under a mass of trampling feet and clawing hands wielding their knives and even a captured sword or several. The People coming for their Lawenforcers and the Sages who command them.

So he has levied a toll of every building. A tenth of their Lawenforcers have been sent to him, while the Flocks grumble and fear in their locked in isolation. Each Sage adjusting to this change in plan as their Lawenforcer force becomes depleted in favor of their Voice's new strategy.

This reserve, at the command of Sage Gratitude has waited until his own building's process is nearing its end. Then quickly, building by building, Sage Gratitude has led them. A tall and imposing figure, his leadership and inherent air of command have given order whereever he has passed. Stopping at each main entrance to ask and receive the code word that tells that all is well in this particular building. Then repeated to the next. And so on.

At Building 12, they are told of the hole in the wall and the escape, but it is too late. Michael and his group of Pure and Failed have fled the Field. Sage Gratitude pauses, considers the options, and decides it is best to assess the full picture by visiting all the buildings before making a decision regarding the next phase of this work.

At Building 19, as well as four other buildings no looked for answer comes—no code shared. Instead, his questions are answered with shouts and cries of insurrection. Threats and curses.

The doors are barred, and locked from within. Sage Gratitude knows the inevitable. These buildings are lost. Sages and Lawenforcers most probably no more in these five locations.

Within each, the mob has won, at least for now.

Chaos reigns.

He posts Lawenforcers at each front door, and moves on. Until the circumnavigation is completed and he has a clear assessment.

Twenty-two buildings in which the process is complete. Five where work is still to be done. One where an escape has been successful but which is now back under his control.

Those lucky few are now on the Far Side. No longer of his concern.

Or so he thinks.

• • •

Sage Gratitude moves on to the next step of his plan. He dispatches Sage Caring with the reserve of Lawenforcers to see if he can resolve the conflict in the five renegade buildings.

Sage Caring jumps to the task. He splits the reserve into five, and sends them to each of the renegade buildings. Some of the Lawenforcers he has told to guard the front doors, but more he has told to gather materials. Flammables. Dragging them to the five buildings until each has stacked to either side piles of wood and debris and burnable trash.

"Light the fires," Sage Caring shouts.

Three words from him, and flames spring up across the Field. Under the hot sun, quickly moving through the piles to lick at the sides of each of these five buildings. Flames that feed on the dry material turning them into five raging infernos in minutes.

As the fires grow in scale, dark black clouds of smoke rise. In the crackling heat, first one, then another building bursts into flame.

Fire plunging into the darkness of five buildings.

Top down, Bottom up, sideways in.

Fire, and smoke penetrating into rooms where the People cower.

And within each of the five buildings, the same movement begins. Down, forward, and then to the front door. Until within these burning buildings, a mob of People pushes against their respective exit doors.

Shouting and crying and pleading with those at the front to open the doors and let them escape.

And just as consistently, the result.

Five front doors burst open, and the respective mobs emerge. Chaotic and in crisis. Smoke in lungs and eyes. Fear in hearts and minds. Rage and anger forgotten as the fire and smoke comes and they flee. Into the sun and the bright light of the Field.

Where drawn up, in five phalanxes they find the Sage's troops.

The sun gleams down on sharp, cold steel.

And as the People stumble forward, in their crisis and fear, so the swords begin to swing and whirl and heads begin to fall.

...

Across the Field, Sage Gratitude looks on as he sees Sage Caring taking actions he would never have been able to order. Doing the unthinkable, setting fire to the renegade buildings. Sage Gratitude knows of course, the secret of Building 27. Knows Sage Caring's history and propensity for dramatic and unacceptable action. Sage Gratitude knows he could never do what Sage Caring has just done, yet he also knows what needed to happen. His great skill has always been to get others to do his dirty work, even though they usually don't know they have been manipulated to that end. Sage Gratitude is very good at this type of politics.

He watches the Flock shrink, inside suffering along with his People, on the surface calm and seemingly unaffected. He has long mastered this demeanor that makes him their leader. A figure of calm, in command, when all around him is in chaos.

...

This is not a fair fight. Tired, frightened People mostly unarmed, fleeing from fire and being cut down on the Field by sharp swords in the hands of expert swordmasters—Sages and Lawenforcers alike.

Not fair at all.

Heads are rolling fast, but in one respect the balance is not all in favor of the Sage's forces.

There are simply more People erupting from these burning buildings than there are People to oppose them.

As the pressure from behind builds, as the buildings burst into flame and the panic of those within reaches desperation level, so too does the pace at which the People erupt onto the Field.

Even the fastest of the swords can't keep up with this pace of work.

First in front of one building, and then at another, and soon at all five, there is a growing chaotic mob of People pushing outwards, and a thin line of Lawenforcers moving backwards under this expanding mass.

Thin lines that are themselves becoming thinner and thinner as the circumferences of the semi-circles they have to defend become ever larger.

Pushed back, the Lawenforcers also find themselves being increasingly turned from attacker to attacked. For here and there, they are confronted by others wielding weapons and the easy work of beheading is replaced by the much harder work of armed combat.

Here a Lawenforcer falls with split skull and in falling gives up another sword to a member of the mob, who wields it against the next Lawenforcer in line.

Another falls, this time pulled down by a host of People at once. Some with knives but more tearing and beating with their hands and feet in their panic.

Across the Field, the Lawenforcers are shrinking in number. Sage Gratitude sees this and moves on to the next step.

"It's time for reserves from the other buildings," he shouts in his loudest voice. Across his forces, the sound of their Voice gives direction to each member, and Sage or Lawenforcer, they prepare for the next stage of work.

This was a step he had hoped he would not need to take. But on his command, messengers go out to the other buildings, and each Sage is asked to release a portion of their Lawenforcer squads to join the fight with Sage Caring at the five renegade buildings.

Not his preferred plan, because it weakens the guardians of the other score or more Flocks and creates a risk of additional insurrection around the Field.

A dangerous step to take indeed.

Still, the balance is with Sage Gratitude's forces. Well trained, well armed, well prepared. They take more heads than they lose by an order of magnitude. The battle, while chaotic, still favors the Sages and the pile of bodies in front of each of the five burning buildings is growing fast, mostly fueled by those fleeing the fires behind.

"Sages, to work," he cries, and this time it is not only the Lawenforcers whose swords are at work. Now much more potent swords spring into action, and for a while, four of the five semi-circular mobs contract a little as ferocious Sages join the fight. Helping Sage Caring complete the task he was set but which he has been unable to complete.

It seems that the tide is turning again.

Chapter 40

Carrying Capacity Redux

Failed again.

"How can this be? How can this happen again?"

They are both thinking it.

Pilot and Engineer. Dawn and Andrew.

Both slumped down in their respective chairs.

Both staring dumbly ahead at red buttons that serve no purpose.

Other than to stand as witness to their complete and utter failure.

"I have failed, you have failed, we have failed," the refrain in their troubled minds

No second chances.

Not worthy of naming.

Just call me Failed.

...

Somewhere in between them, levels below the Pilot, levels above the Engineer, lie the Pure.

They are unaware of what has just transpired. They can't know the absolute depression of Failure. Even if they did know the state they were in, they would not know how to feel as the two Failed feel at this precise moment in time.

For the Pure are perfect in mind. Optimistic in outlook. Uneducated, uninformed, unknowing. For them anything is possible. Everything starts with a positive thought. However far fetched.

Adam and Belle lie just a few feet apart on their backs staring up at the lids of their capsules.

Believing that it's going to be alright.

That they are about to escape this hard and merciless world.

For themselves, and for their baby.

"We will have our second chance."

...

Out on the Field, the world is at war.

The sun looks down, the Earth looks up, and both see the heads dropping.

For Earth is merciless and indifferent to how the People treat themselves when it comes to its terrible work.

But Earth does not control this stage.

...

The battle has raged back and forth.

Eventually Sage Gratitude is able to take a deep breath and relax a little. The Lawenforcers report to him that they have been successful in keeping the mobs separate – making sure they can't converge and pool their forces. Divided, the Sages have been able to conquer and the battle seems won. Sage Gratitude is about to give his mental thanks for his Sages and their Lawenforcers and their merciless work. Then, from between the buildings across the Field arrives another force.

Bearing shining swords too.

Michael, his father, and the Scavengers have arrived on the Field of battle. It has taken a while for Michael to explain why their help is needed, but once the Scavengers have heard what has been happening back at the Field it has not taken much to rouse them. Scavengers all have suffered at the hands of the Sages and Lawenforcers. Made to run. Now they are happy to run back to settle old scores. Michael and James at the front. Ricky just behind Michael – no Sworder he, but a long wooden stave in his hands picked up as they crossed the croplands. The rest of their group, Cathy and Ann and the smaller children including the twins way to the back among a group of more mutated Scavengers who can't wield their swords as well as they once could do. Kate has left with a group that has made its way over towards Building 12. Despite Michael's command that she stay with the others. She has her own mission it seems.

Two cohorts of terrifyingly perfect Sworders meet on this dusty Field, and as they battle more cuts, more thrusts, more slices.

Their work is deadly, and the impact horrifying.

20,020

20,015

In one part of the Field, the Scavengers are being pushed back by Sages and Lawenforcers, Sage Certainty at their head. She is leading by example. Until, confronted by three swords at once, she takes a cut and another and falls wounded and unable to fight on. In that moment, as a sword rises to make the final cut, there is a high-pitched cry and a small figure throws itself across the Sage's body.

"Leave her, she deserves to live," cries Kate.

In any other part of the Field, two heads would roll next, but here, surrounded by members of Building 12's Flock, the cry is quickly taken up, and the swords move around the Sage and her protector to find other heads to take. Kate standing over the Sage's fallen body until the battle moves away.

20,010

20,005

In front of Building 28, the battle goes against the Lawenforcers who have already dispatched most of their Failed opposition, but find themselves no match for this new and well trained force of Scavenger Sworders. Here are James and Michael side by side. Fighting together now, although truth be told, it is James that is master in this field, with Michael protected by James' whirling blade, even if he does not realize it. James is not going to let his just found son leave him beneath a Lawenforcer's blade.

Sage Gratitude from his place behind the front lines can see things are moving against him and his Lawenforcers. He considers for a moment whether he should take his sword, and his intimating size and strength and join the fight. Perhaps he can make this day a success after all. Bring the momentum back to his side. But again, a good politician knows when to fold his cards. Sage Gratitude turns and walks back towards his building. Time for his own backup plan.

Behind the thin line of Building 28 Lawenforcers, Sage Caring has stayed protected, using his powerful voice to lead them from behind. Out of the way and out of danger. Now a wedge of Scavengers comes towards him, cutting through his Lawenforcers. Ricky among them hitting to left and right with his wooden stave. He is working hard, using all of his youthful strength. But his wooden stave cannot last forever against sharp metal, and eventually, a Lawenforcer sword cuts cleanly through the stave, leaving Ricky with only a short club length piece in his hand. He tries to use it, but the Lawenforcer's longer reach prevails, and, luckily for Ricky, it is the flat of the blade that delivers a glancing blow to the side of his head. Ricky falls senseless to the ground. The fight quickly moving around and beyond him.

Sage Caring turns to flee, but it is too late. A Failed on the ground, cut and bleeding, grabs the bottom of his robe and holds on just long enough for the Scavengers to reach him too. In a moment they surround him. Blood stained swords raised around him. In a last ditch attempt to save his life Sage Caring throws himself at their feet. He begs for their mercy. Hands held up in prayer.

"Spare me. I am a good man. I care about my Flock and for the wellbeing of each of you!" he cries. "Spare me!"

Today there is no mercy. Another human head falls and…

20,000

…

Then, everything stops.

No more Harm.

Forces too great to imagine rise up and brush away the warring humans, rolling them and wrapping them in gentle waves of buffering safety. Unnatural forces pulling them apart, protecting them from each other, and from themselves.

No more Harm.

Coddling them like the fragile precious shells that they are. And then, with a thunder that blasts away any traces of human anger, or fear, or passion or love—

The Ship rises.

Leaving faces raised up in awe below it.

As it departs the Field.

Chapter 41

Second Chance - Countdown

The war is over.

The Ship has returned from its brief launch and circumnavigation. Back in the center of the Field, the Intelligences, freed of the paradox of what to do when they could only Harm some by rescuing others, now resume their work.

Almost twenty years before two Ships of 20,000 capacity each had been well balanced, but in a flash one became incapacitated. 40,000 into 20,000 would not go. The Intelligences, no longer able to build another Ship, could see no way to compress 40,000 People into one Ship. Every option they developed, every choice they contemplated led to Harm. Nothing would compute. No remaining satisfactory solutions left to them.

So the inevitable outcome.

The Intelligences closed down and waited until the People solved the equation. Brought their own numbers into line with one Ship's carrying capacity. Then, in that moment, when the equation balanced again, then the Intelligences came back to fulfill their mission. Protect their fragile human charges. Ensure no more Harm.

20,000, the magic number that allowed the balancing of their math.

Their one remaining great Ship's carrying capacity again in balance.

Balanced by human ingenuity - or human fallibility.

Allowing them to come again and take their rightful place.

Now the Ship is ready again.

Fully prepared.

Failed or Pure.

Sage, Lawenforcer, Scavenger.

It makes no difference now.

The Intelligences have taken charge and those titles are brushed aside.

A couple of decades of human categorization.

Swept aside by the simple distinction that has once again taken force.

Intelligence or human.

One or the other.

Final countdown has begun.

Dawn is at her station. Andrew at his.

Both there only for backup.

Launch Intelligence firmly in control.

Between them just less than 20,000.

After a few too badly wounded have slipped away,

Are safely stored away in their capsules.

Adam and Belle in theirs.

The Intelligences look over all.

Caring for each and every one.

But just a little bit more for Belle's capsule.

That soon will contain two.

It's time.

For humankind's.

Second chance.

Chapter 42

Epilogue - Earth's Dream

Earth is tired.

Earth feels stretched
Stretched too thin
Stretched to the limit.

Too many People.

Asking too much for too long
These demanding, needy and disruptive People
Where have they come from?

Earth remembers millions of years of peace and balance
The cycles
But always with balance.

Never stretched like this.

But these People
Appeared, multiplied
Everywhere.

Their demands too high
Demanded too much
Earth failing.

• • •

Now, like a blessing.

In a terrible roar
With a mighty rush they go
Earth knows not where.

But it feels it
Knows it
They are gone.

With that realization
Earth awakes from its nightmare
Stretches.

Knows the task ahead
Ten thousand years
Ten million.

It matters not
Earth is sufficient
Time to get started.

Chance will be a fine thing.

The End

Author's Note

This book is a work of fiction. Names, characters, places and incidents are either the products of the author's imagination or are used fictitiously. Any resemblance to actual persons, living or dead, or actual events is purely coincidental.

Really.

I would like to thank everyone who made this work possible. My family for being supportive and especially to Alison who, when first I awoke and told her my dream, said I absolutely had to write it down. James Zhang for encouraging me to be creative too, and for all the team at Concept Art House and especially for Ken Chou, my brilliant illustrator and cover artist.

To Julie Tibbott, my editor who was able to bridge from developmental, to copy, to line editing, and in so doing made everything much less burdensome and more integrated. To my readers, Tallulah Le Merle who gave me comprehensive edits, and Monique Aguerre, Belle Jenkinson, and Evelyn Lenz who also read the book in draft and gave me positive and constructive feedback. Robin Vuchnich who worked on the interior and cover layout did a very professional job and we all love the results of her work.

Finally, I would like to thank Jeff Bezos and Amazon.com. Without your inventiveness and the global publisher platform you have created, first time novelists like me would still be banging on the doors of the traditional publisher monopsony. The reader can decide whether the access you provide is a good or bad thing in the specific case of *"Second Chance"*

Last, but not least, to you the reader. You took the risk of spending your time and money on this book, and you, apparently, reached the end and are reading this final paragraph. If you did, then my heartfelt thanks go to you. Thank you so very much for being here. Let me know how I can make the next one even more to your liking.

Matthew Le Merle
Tiburon, California
January, 2019.

Made in the USA
San Bernardino, CA
19 March 2019